IMPROPER
Christmas
Nights

AMANDA McCABE
BARBARA MONAJEM
LAURI ROBINSON
JOANNE ROCK

MILLS & BOON

Published in Great Britain 2014
by Mills & Boon, an imprint of Harlequin (UK) Limited,
Eton House, 18-24 Paradise Road, Richmond, Surrey, TW9 1SR

IMPROPER CHRISTMAS NIGHTS © 2014 Harlequin Books S.A.

A Very Tudor Christmas © 2013 Amanda McCabe
Under a Christmas Spell © 2013 Barbara Monajem
Under a New Year's Enchantment © 2014 Barbara Monajem
Snowbound with the Sheriff © 2013 Lauri Robinson
Summoned for Seduction © 2010 Joanne Rock

ISBN: 978-0-263-25038-1

009-1014

Harlequin (UK) Limited's policy is to use papers that are natural, renewable and recyclable products and made from wood grown in sustainable forests. The logging and manufacturing processes conform to the legal environmental regulations of the country of origin.

Printed and bound by
CPI Group (UK) Ltd, Croydon, CR0 4YY

A Very Tudor Christmas

AMANDA MCCABE

Amanda McCabe wrote her first romance at the age of sixteen—a vast epic, starring all her friends as the characters, written secretly during algebra class.

She's never since used algebra, but her books have been nominated for many awards, including a RITA® Award, an *RT Book Reviews* Reviewers' Choice Award, a Booksellers Best Award, a National Readers' Choice Award and a Holt Medallion. She lives in Oklahoma with a menagerie of two cats, a pug and a bossy miniature poodle, and loves dance classes, collecting cheesy travel souvenirs and watching the Food Network—even though she doesn't cook.

Visit her at www.ammandamccabe.com and www.risky regencies.com.

Chapter One

England, 1569

"Hush, Bea! They will hear you. We'll never be able to hear what's happening if they find us here," Margaret Clifford whispered fiercely as she and her cousin squeezed into the tiny closet right above her parents' great hall at Clifford Manor. Beatrice was her best friend, but she *was* three years younger than Meg's eighteen, and inclined to be giggly. It had been that way ever since Bea's parents, Meg's mother's sister and her husband, died and Bea came to live with them as a toddler.

Beatrice clapped her hand over her mouth and huddled closer to Meg as they knelt on the floor. "I won't say a word, Meg, I vow it."

"I never should have let you come with me," Meg murmured. She had tried to slip out of their shared chamber without Bea seeing her, but she hadn't been quick enough. Beatrice had begged and cried so very much that Meg knew she had to drag her along. Time was short, and she had to discover what her parents were talking about with Lord and Lady Erroll.

Meg drew her velvet skirts close under her and she lowered her knees to the rough plank floor and tried to peer through the tiny knothole to the hall below. Bea clutched at her sleeve, fairly vibrating with excitement, and Meg had to shush her again. She could barely hear as it was. And it was vital that she hear.

God's truth, but it was so maddening that her parents refused to talk to her! They treated her as if she was the veriest child, younger even than Beatrice. She was not a child at all now. She was more than old enough for...

For marrying.

Was that why the Errolls had come to Clifford Manor now? Meg curled her fists against the wood floor, feeling her heart pounding. *Please, let it be true!*

Yet it all seemed too, too glorious to ever be true. Ever since she had seen Robert Erroll at the Christmas festivities a few months ago, ever since they'd danced, touched, looked into each other's eyes, she had not been able to think about anything else at all. Even when she walked in the garden with Bea, or when her mother shouted at her for snarling the embroidery silks, she could only see Robert Erroll's sky-blue eyes. Could only remember how it had felt when their fingers twined together.

Remember—and wonder when she might see him again.

Until today. Today when she'd been walking along the lane, and glimpsed a horse galloping toward her....

"'Or call it winter, which, being full of care, makes summer's welcome thrice more wish'd, more rare...'" Meg hummed the Christmas song as she swung her basket. *Go fetch some eggs from Mistress Brown, Margaret,* her mother had snapped, shooing Meg's little twin brothers out from underfoot. *You are of no use to me with your daydreaming today. Beatrice can finish the mending.*

The Cliffords were an old family, at Clifford Manor for centuries, but not rich enough to hire people do all their mending for them. Or fetch their eggs.

It was a chilly day, a cold wind snapping at her cloak as smoke curled from Clifford Manor's old chimneys behind her, but Meg didn't care. She had a few moments to be alone away from the chaos of her home. Not even Beatrice was with her today to interrupt her thoughts. The farther she walked, the quieter the countryside grew, until she could imagine she was dancing again.

Until she spun around the corner of the lane, humming louder, and saw the great black horse swooping down on her.

Meg screamed and ducked toward the hedgerows, snagging her cloak. She almost fell into the mud, and the panic fell over her like a cold cloud as her hood drooped down in front of her eye.

The horse thundered by, mere inches from her foot. As she struggled to push herself right, she heard the great beast whirl around and a man's shout.

Meg shoved her hood back and glanced back over her shoulder to see a man leaping down from his saddle. His clothes were fine velvet and leather, cut close to a handsome body and far too fine for the local gentry.

"Are you hurt?" he shouted, and reached up to sweep off his plumed hat as he ran toward her.

The panic was brushed away in a warm rush of joy as she saw it was *him*. Robert Erroll. Back again at last.

"I—I am quite fine, Master Erroll," she called, hurrying toward him. "You do seem in a great hurry."

"Mistress Clifford!" he said, a wide, bright grin breaking across his face. He was so very handsome, with his dark hair ruffled by the wind around his face. "I'm on my way to your own house. My parents are to call on your family, but their new coach is too slow for me. I'm most happy I came on ahead now, if it means I can see you."

Meg laughed as she tilted her head to look up at him— he was so wondrously tall. And he laughed with her, too, his face even more beautiful in mirth, if that was possible.

"Pretty Mistress Margaret," he said. "I have thought of you often since our New Year's dance."

Meg felt a burst of raw, pure joy that he remembered, as she did. "Have you indeed, Master Erroll?" she answered pertly. A country miss she might be, but surely she knew better than to seem too eager. Especially with a man like this, a handsome, strong court gentleman. "Most extraordinary of you."

His laugh rang out even louder, sweeter. "Do you mean to say you have not thought of me at all?"

"Life is busy here, you know. Not so busy as at the queen's court, perhaps, but we have little time for idle thoughts." Meg turned and slowly strolled along down the lane, wondering wildly all the time if he watched her, if he would follow.

And follow he did. She heard the fall of his booted feet on the dirt, and he quickly caught up to her as they reached a low stone wall. He caught her arm in his gloved hand.

Meg swung around to him, startled and excited and scared all at once.

"Court is full of color and scandal and events of all kinds, assuredly," he said. "But you would rival any lady there with your beauty and sweetness, Mistress Margaret. I've never seen eyes like yours…."

The tips of his fingers trailed over her cheek, the merest featherlight touch, but it made Meg shiver as she stared up at him. Oh, how she wanted to believe him! How she wanted his sweet words to be true. And indeed he looked at her as if she had always dreamed a handsome suitor might, with a solemn wonder writ on the chiseled planes of his face.

But she also knew that her eyes were the plainest of browns. And she knew, too, that what she was doing here with him was not something a proper young lady should do. That if her parents saw her they would be angry, and part of her wanted to run away from these feelings.

The bigger part of her, the part she feared meant she was not entirely proper, made her stay.

"I—I fear you seek to flatter me, sirrah," she said, trying to laugh.

"No flattery. If you could see the women at court…" He gently traced a strand of her brown hair that had escaped her hood. "There are none like you."

His hands slid down her arms, his touch light, teasing. Until suddenly his arms were around her waist, tugging her closer to him. She went with him, unresisting. She was overcome with curiosity, with that heady, overpowering emotion he always evoked when he came near her. It made her feel dizzy with it, with his nearness, and she clutched at his shoulders to hold herself up.

How wonderful it was to feel like that, Meg thought giddily. Like too much spiced wine, or lying in warm grass on a summer's day. He made her senses whirl and spin, just from the feel of him under her hands, hard and warm and alive.

It frightened her, but it was also so very exciting.

As she looked up into his blue eyes, she felt as if she was caught in a dream. Yet everything was so much more immediate, so much brighter and clearer than anything else she had ever known. Then, wonder of wonders, his eyes grew darker. His head bent toward hers and he kissed her.

The touch of his lips was so soft at first, like the brush of warm velvet, sweeping over her mouth teasingly. When she swayed closer, her hands clutching at his shoulders, that kiss deepened.

"Beautiful Meg," he whispered hoarsely before claiming her mouth again. Hotter, more urgent, rougher.

Something hidden deep in Meg's heart responded to that urgency, growing and filling her until she feared she would burst with the splendor of it all. Her lips parted on a moan, and she felt his tongue slide shockingly against hers. His hands twined in her hair, sending the pins scattering to the ground as he used the dark strands to hold her with him. She moaned and opened her mouth willingly to his passionate kiss. His touch, the taste of him, made her feel wonderfully as if she was flying.

In his arms she felt free at long last. She felt truly alive, and she wanted that so very much, even if it was only for a moment and then she had to go back to her dull life. Surely a moment couldn't hurt her?

Or maybe a moment could end everything she had ever known. She didn't care. She only wanted *him*.

She wrapped her arms around his shoulders to keep from falling to the ground. His hands fell free from her hair to unfasten the ties of her cloak and let it fall from her shoulders. The cold wind brushed over her, making her shiver, but then there was only the heat of his body all around hers.

His open mouth slid from hers to kiss her neck, the soft curve of her shoulder above the neckline of her plain gown. His teeth nipped lightly at her skin, making her gasp and shiver all over again. Her head fell back as she hoped he would kiss her even more, even further, letting the delicious feelings wash over her.

"Beautiful Meg," he whispered roughly. He caught the hem of her skirt in his fist and dragged it up until she felt the cool wind rush over the bare skin just above her stocking, just as she had hoped he would. He caressed her through the thin knit of her stocking, his fingertip dipping behind the ribbon of her garter.

It was shocking—and wonderful. No one had ever touched her thus, and she wanted yet more and more. His hand slid higher, enticing, teasing, and when she moaned he gave a hoarse laugh.

"Passionate Meg," he said.

"Passionate for you," she answered, holding him tighter.

Everything vanished until there was only him and her and that kiss, that touch. Only that one perfect instant she wanted to go on forever and ever.

But it was a forever that was shattered all too quickly.

At first Meg was sure the rumbling sound was her heart, pounding inside her with such joy she knew it would burst. She held even tighter to him, for he was the only thing that could keep her from shaking apart. But he tore his mouth from hers and stumbled back, letting the cold wind rush over her again. Her skirts fell around her in disarray.

Then she heard it, closer with every second. A carriage rolling on the lane, not her heart at all.

"Quickly!" Robert said. "We can hide behind the wall."

Before Meg's whirling mind could make sense of what

was happening, he wrapped his strong, warm hands around her waist and lifted her over the stone wall. He caught up her fallen cloak and leaped after her, drawing her down with him until they crouched on the chilly ground, their backs to the rough stone.

Meg could hardly breathe. He was still so close to her, the heat of his hard, strong body wrapping all around her, but it felt as if he had gone from her entirely. He turned away from her to peer over the wall as the crash and rumble of the coach came closer.

A cold hollowness crept through her, and she wrapped her arms tightly around herself. She still could not fathom being torn from such pleasure. What had happened?

Had she kissed him all wrong?

She turned to peek over the wall. The coach was almost upon them, a glossy brown-and-gold vehicle splashed with mud and frost and drawn by a team of splendid matching bays. Ordinarily, Meg would have been fascinated to see it; only the queen and her highest nobles had such things for traveling. But now she was all too aware of Robert Erroll next to her, watching the coach with narrowed eyes.

Meg glimpsed a woman's pale face at the window as it bounced past, the feathers on her velvet hat waving. The hair pinned beneath it was the same shining black as Robert's.

Then they were gone, as suddenly as they came. Robert slumped down beside her, and Meg suddenly realized something.

"That was your parents," she said. And he had hid her from them.

"Aye," he answered. He lifted her up from their hiding place, still seeming so distant. "Come, let me see you home,

Mistress Margaret…." And that, aside from pleasantries on the cold weather, was all he said to her on the walk back to Clifford Manor….

His parents. And he had not wanted them to see him with her. The more Meg remembered the scene that afternoon the more sure she was.

"Meg!" Beatrice hissed, tugging at Meg's sleeve again. Her cousin's touch pulled Meg back to the present moment, to their hiding place above her parents' great hall. "What is happening now?"

Meg shook away the memory of Robert's wondrous kiss, and his terrible distance after. She peered back through the knothole to see her parents with the two elder Errolls next to the blazing fire.

Robert had not appeared at supper, hours after he'd left her at the kitchen door with a bow and a quick kiss to her hand. Only his parents had been there, his portly, bearded father swathed in a velvet and fur doublet, and his beautiful, black-haired, chilly-eyed mother. Meg's own mother had seemed quite startled they were there, though she had scrambled together a creditable feast and made sure Meg and Beatrice were well-dressed.

The conversation had only been of court news and the weather, naught about their son. And Meg dared not ask. She and Bea were sent away soon after the meal.

"Hush, or I won't be able to hear a thing," Meg whispered, peering closer.

Her father was pouring wine into everyone's goblets. "We are honored by your visit, of course, Lord Erroll," he said. "We get little enough word of court here."

It was Lady Erroll who answered. "It is most unfortunate for you, Master Clifford. Everything happens at court, does it not?"

"But we must look in on our estates from time to time," Lord Erroll said. "We are on our way there now. Knowing we were going there, the queen herself asked us to deliver a message to you."

The queen? Meg heard Bea gasp, and she grabbed her cousin's hand to quiet her. It was all far too much excitement for one day in their tiny corner of the world.

"Her Grace?" Meg's mother cried. "The queen has a message for *us?*"

"Aye," Lady Erroll said, seeming quite as doubtful as Meg's mother. "She has heard you have a pretty, amiable daughter, as indeed you do, as we have seen her ourselves tonight, and we understand our son met your family at a New Year's banquet. Queen Elizabeth wishes for her to come to court, to see if she might suit as a new maid-of-honor."

"Meg!" Beatrice whispered, almost crushing Meg's sleeve with her enthusiasm. "Did you hear that? You could serve the queen."

Meg had indeed heard it—she just couldn't quite believe it. Her, go to court? She couldn't even wrap her thoughts around it. It was true that once her grandmother had served one of old King Henry's queens, and her father sometimes went to court to present Queen Elizabeth with a New Year's gift, but there had never been talk of *her* doing such a thing.

And—and if she was truthful to herself—she had to admit that wasn't why she had hoped the Errolls had come to Clifford. She'd dared hope they came to propose a betrothal.

Her throat felt thick, but she refused to cry in front of Bea. She should not cry, not over silly dreams.

But the way his kiss had felt….

Meg shushed Beatrice again and twisted her head so she could see her parents' faces. They looked at each other in that quiet way they always had together, as if they could communicate with their gaze alone. It was always maddening to try and decipher what they thought.

"Our Meg is young yet," her father said. "And she has little training for a court life. This news is a surprise, and a great honor. We must think about it."

Lady Erroll shrugged. "As you think best, of course, Master Clifford. But court is truly the best place to secure a family's fortune. Our own daughter is but sixteen and has been a maid-of-honor for a year now. And our son…" Her languid voice suddenly turned proud. "Our son has a great career ahead of him. Her Grace is sending him as part of a delegation to Paris. He will be gone for at least a year, and when he returns we have hopes of a very great marriage for him with one of the Howard girls."

"If he can cease to be such a care-for-nothing," Lord Erroll grumbled into his wine. "Running about London with those young bravos…."

Lady Erroll shot him a scowl. "Robert is young and handsome. Why should he not enjoy himself now? He has a brilliant future ahead of him. The right marriage will surely…"

Meg could hear no more. She broke away from Bea and scrambled out of the closet. Lifting the heavy hem of her skirt, she ran as fast as she could along the corridors and down the stairs.

"Mistress Margaret!" a maidservant called as she dashed past. "Wait! I have…"

But Meg could not stop. She feared her tears would blind

her, and worse, people would see them. Her hood tumbled from her head and her hair fell free, but she scarcely noticed.

On the staircase landing, she paused to catch her breath. She stared out the small window there as she gasped for breath past her stays. The night sky was clear, the stars glittering sharply with the cold, and the moon gleamed on the rutted driveway beneath. Everything was perfectly still, as if frozen.

Suddenly there was one spark of movement, just beyond the line of trees that led to the gates. Meg went up on tiptoe, trying to see what it was.

For just an instant, a stray beam of moonlight caught on a figure on horseback. A face, pale in the night, peered up at the house from beneath the plumes of a fashionable cap.

Meg's heart pounded again, and she felt the spark of excitement, of distant hope, break over her cold disappointment. Robert Erroll—it had to be. Had she not seen that very hat tumble from his head only that afternoon?

She ran down the stairs and through the doors into the cold night. But there was no one there, no horse, no plumes, only the brush of the wind through the bare trees.

"Hello?" she called. "Are you out there?" Nothing. And her hopes plummeted yet again.

"Meg!" Beatrice cried, and Meg spun around to see her cousin running out of the house after her. "Why did you leave like that?"

Beatrice's golden hair shimmered in the night, and her blue eyes looked big and shocked in her pretty child's face. Meg suddenly felt ashamed of her wild behavior, her silly hopes that a man like Robert Erroll, a man going to France on a mission for the queen and with a future marriage to a Howard, could have had serious intentions toward *her.* It had all been a foolish dream. Lady Erroll was right: they all had to look to their own futures.

But, oh! It had been such a sweet dream while it lasted.

Meg walked slowly back to Bea, her feet feeling as heavy and slow as an old woman's. She took her cousin's arm and smiled at her, glad of the covering darkness.

"I just needed some fresh air," Meg said as they turned toward the house. "It was very stuffy in that closet."

"But isn't it exciting, Meg?" Beatrice said, bouncing on her toes. "You might go to court, to see the queen herself! You will dance and sing, and have such pretty clothes...."

Meg had to laugh at Bea's bubbling enthusiasm. She knew she should feel it herself, and perhaps she would soon enough. If she could let go of her silly dream of being Lady Erroll.

"It's surely not certain I will go yet," Meg said.

"Oh, you will! And maybe one day, when I'm older, I shall join you there. Wouldn't that be so merry, Meg?"

"Aye," Meg answered quietly. Before they went back through the doors, she glanced back one more time. But the garden was still empty. Surely he had never been there at all. "Merry indeed."

Robert drew in his horse once he was sure he was hidden by the trees and looked back to the moonlit house. Margaret still stood poised on the doorstep, staring out at the driveway, and for an instant he was sure she saw him there. The wind toyed with the dark satin fall of her brown hair and caught at her skirts. She rubbed at her arms as if she was cold, but she didn't turn away.

And he had to fight himself with every ounce of strength

he possessed not to wheel his horse around and gallop back to her.

"God's blood," he muttered as his fists tightened on the reins. He knew it was a bad idea for him to come to Clifford Manor, but he couldn't help himself. He had to see her again, and he'd been so sure that once he did he would realize that whatever strange enchantment she'd cast over him when they'd danced was just that—an illusion.

How could it be otherwise? The queen's court was crowded with beautiful women, witty, sophisticated women it was all too easy to laugh with and tease. To lure to his bed.

And Margaret Clifford was so young, so wide-eyed, so free of courtly guile. When his sister had teasingly suggested he dance with the "country mouse," he'd thought it might be amusing for a few minutes.

Never could he have anticipated how it would all feel. Her trembling hand in his, the dark eyes looking up at him, her smile, her lithe grace. Her laughter, so open and real, unlike the practiced trill of those court ladies. Enchantment indeed.

And when they'd walked around the hall together after their dance, she'd asked him what he did at the court and he found himself telling her things he had hardly dared even think of. Of dreams and ambitions his parents and friends thought him too indolent to pursue.

Yet Margaret had listened, asked him solemn questions—believed him. Robert had never known such a feeling.

And that was why he could not go back to her now, no matter how much he longed to. If he went back now, begged her to be his, presented his suit to her parents, he would know he wasn't worthy of her. He had to prove himself in order to win her. To give her the life her pure heart and true beauty deserved. His family had a fine name but no fortune now. They thought he should marry an heiress to help them, but he was sure he had the keys to their salvation within himself.

He had to, if he wanted to marry where he chose.

This voyage to France was the first step. He would show the queen, his family, Margaret, that he could do so much more than dance and preen around court. He would make his fortune, then come back for her when they could be truly together.

The note he had given the maidservant to deliver to Meg would surely tell her what he could not say face-to-face. He could only pray now that she would wait for him, would write to him that she felt the same.

"Wait for me, fair Margaret," he whispered, and spurred his horse into a gallop, leaving Clifford Manor behind.

"Nay, we mustn't!" the maidservant said with a giggle. She backed away from the footman until her hips rested at the stone edge of the well in the kitchen garden, hoping he could see her bosom in the moonlight, prettily displayed above the edge of her smock. He *had* to follow her now!

And he did. He seized her around the waist, dragging her close to him as she giggled even louder. He growled as he buried his face in her bosom, his beard tickling.

As he tossed her apron aside, the contents of her pockets—a bundle of herbs, a handkerchief and a folded note—tumbled unseen into the well....

Chapter Two

London, December 1571

"Can you believe it, Meg? We are to be goddesses!"

Meg smiled at Bea as her cousin took her arm and pulled her through the doors of Cecil House in Covent Garden. They were part of a flock of young ladies and gentlemen of the court recruited to perform in a masque celebrating the upcoming wedding of William Cecil, Lord Burghley's, daughter Anne to the handsome Earl of Oxford. Lord Burghley was the queen's chief secretary and closest adviser, and the earl the most eligible of noble bachelors. It was the wedding of the year, an essential event in the Christmas festivities, and to perform in the masque was a great honor, a chance to be seen in front of the whole crowd.

But Meg would just as soon *not* be seen. After nearly three years of being at court for part of every year, she had found the chiefest joy there to be in observing all that went on. The people surrounding Queen Elizabeth were like a swirl of brilliantly colored glass, dazzling, gorgeous, enticing, but liable to cut if touched.

"I am just here to chaperone you, Beatrice," she said. She held onto Bea's hand as the other masquerade actors crowded into the entrance hall around them. Bea was always liable to dash off when she became too excited. And, being somewhat new to court and eager to see and do everything, Bea was *always* excited.

Like now. Bea held tightly to Meg's hand as she stared around her with bright eyes, taking in the rich tapestries covering the linenfold-paneled walls, the thick carpets underfoot, the blazing fire in the grate that all chased away the icy day outside the grand edifice of Cecil House.

Beatrice bounced on her toes. Meg smiled at her, and wondered if she herself had ever been half so excited by life, half so eager to rush out and grab onto its glittering promise with both hands. Perhaps when she first came to court, first saw the queen and all the bejeweled splendor around her?

Nay, Meg remembered sadly. When she first came to court, she'd been too cast down by the loss of a handsome man who was never hers to begin with. Who had only been a silly girl's dream.

A man who never came back from France, but proved himself so valuable to the queen that she sent him on to Venice and thence to the wilds of Muscovy, where he formed alliances and gained royal honors. Lady Erroll was always boasting of her illustrious son.

But Meg was glad he didn't come back. He would only remind her of how silly she'd once been. Now she was too busy, too responsible, too *old* to have such fancies. As she'd said to Bea, she was only here to play chaperone now.

Beatrice would surely make the glittering marriage Meg could not.

"Nonsense, Meg!" Beatrice cried, at last turning her attention from the grand house and swinging around to smile at Meg. "You are no elderly spinster to spend your days clucking at wild young folk. You are much too pretty for that."

"Not even a fraction as pretty as you, Bea," Meg said fondly, tucking back a strand of her cousin's golden hair that had fallen from her velvet cap. "That is why I must keep an eye on you."

"Nonsense, I say! I am perfectly sensible, dearest cuz. I know better than to listen to *their* blandishments." Bea tossed her pretty head disdainfully toward the young swains who watched her. "I will take nothing less than marriage, and a grand one, too. Just like Anne Cecil."

Meg thought of Anne Cecil, the reason they were all there on this cold day, to rehearse festivities for her grand nuptials. Her match was outwardly a splendid one indeed—the handsome young Earl of Oxford. But Mistress Anne was barely fifteen, sheltered and carefully educated by her protective and powerful parents, and the earl was known as a fiery-tempered troublemaker. Mistress Anne would be a countess, true, but would she find happiness?

That was what Meg wanted for sweet Beatrice. Happiness.

"Just be sure you choose a good man, Bea," she admonished. "A kind one who will know what a great treasure he has in you."

"We must find such a man for you first, Meg," Bea answered. "You are surely not too old to marry."

Meg laughed. "It's true I have no need of a walking stick

just yet. But I have met no man at court whose company I could bear for more than an hour altogether."

Bea's eyes widened. "Is it because of Master Ambrose? It was so sad…"

Meg shook her head. When, more than a year ago, her parents proposed a match between Meg and the son of the Ambrose family, she had tentatively agreed. Why not? Her dreams of grand romance were gone, and Master Ambrose seemed nice enough. When their barely month-old betrothal was ended by his sudden passing from a fever, she had felt only sadness for his poor family.

And realization that she probably was not meant to be married.

"I have recovered from all that," Meg assured her cousin. "I am entirely attentive to finding a good match for you."

Before Bea could answer, Mildred Cecil, Lady Burghley, wife of the chief secretary, appeared at the top of the stairs. All conversation and laughter immediately quieted, for the tall, long-nosed, stern-eyed Lady Burghley was formidable indeed. She gathered the fur edges of her black velvet robe closer around her as she studied the courtiers gathered in her hall.

Her daughter Anne hovered behind her, a small, pale-faced girl whose light brown hair and tawny silk gown blended her into the paneled walls.

"Thank you all for coming here today," Lady Burghley said. "The wedding is only days away and there is much work to be done. If you will follow me…"

Lady Burghley swept down the stairs, Anne hurrying behind her, as servants in the green-and-gold Cecil livery leaped to open the doors to the great hall. Meg and Beatrice were swept along by the crowd into the cavernous space.

There was scarcely time to take in the painted beams of the ceiling high overhead, the glowing tapestries of red, blue and green, or the glittering plate piled on the tiered and carved buffets pushed back against the walls. They were hurried to the far end of the long room to where a stage had been built for the wedding masques.

Servants were still putting the finishing touches on the painted scenery, and seamstresses were huddled over yards of carnation silk and gold satin for the costumes.

"This is the Grove of Diana," Lady Burghley said with an impatient wave at the still-unfinished painted trees. "Over there shall be the Bower of Flora, and there the House of Night. We shall need nine Knights of Apollo, nine Hours of Night, nine…"

Suddenly the doors to the hall opened again, and Lady Burghley frowned at the group who dared to arrive late. Everyone else craned their necks and went up on tiptoe to try and see. The ladies broke into giggles, hastily muffled.

Bea was no different. "Look, Meg!" she whispered excitedly. "'Tis Peter Ellingham."

Meg bit back a smile. Peter, Lord Ellingham, was a very handsome young man, as golden as Bea and as eager about life. He had been paying much attention to Bea of late, asking her to dance with him at banquets, playing lute duets with her and games of primero, all under Meg's careful watch. They laughed and gamboled together like pretty puppies.

Bea pretended not to take him seriously, but Meg wondered. Perhaps Bea, like Anne Cecil, would be a young bride, but only if Lord Ellingham proved himself worthy.

Meg turned to study the newcomers. Lord Ellingham was indeed there, clad in peacock blue and green, grinning at

Bea. With him were his usual friends, young men as good-natured and lighthearted as himself, likely to make fine Knights of Apollo.

Meg suddenly glimpsed a darker movement at the edge of the crowd, and she turned to study it closer.

Suddenly the crowded, stuffy room turned freezing cold and she couldn't move. Her hands shook, and she clenched them in the folds of her skirt. She couldn't tear her gaze from the man who stood at the edges of Lord Ellingham's merry group. For it was the one man she had thought—hoped—never to see again.

It was Robert Erroll.

Like her, he had grown older in the three years since she'd seen him, but the time sat well on him. His face, framed by a neatly trimmed fashionable goatee, was leaner, even more chiseled, browned and slightly weathered by the sun and snow of his travels. His black hair was longer, swept back from his brow and touching the high black collar of his purple velvet doublet. His hand was curled around a jeweled dagger at his belt, and he watched the enthusiasms of Peter Ellingham and his friends with a small, wry smile on his sensual lips.

Then his gaze swept over the room—and came to land on her. His eyes, those oh-so-blue eyes she remembered so well, widened a bit as he saw her there. Despite the crowd around her, she felt horribly exposed with nowhere to hide. His smile flashed broader for just an instant. But then a veil quickly fell over his eyes, his smile, leaving nothing but a mask of fashionable boredom. He gave her a small bow.

"Attention, please!" Lady Burghley called. "We have no time to lose."

Meg was so very cold, her head spinning so she feared she would faint. "Excuse me for a moment, Bea," she gasped.

"What..." Beatrice said, obviously bewildered. She tried to catch Meg's hand, but Meg managed to slip away. She pushed her way through the crowd, seeking an escape route.

With the new arrivals, the hall was even more crowded and confused than before, and Lady Burghley was striving to regain control. In the confusion, Meg was able to slip past the shifting tide of people and through the still-open doors into the empty entrance hall.

She ran down a long corridor, not knowing where she was going. The rise and fall of all the voices blending together faded behind her as she hurried along the darkened passageway. A few servants passed her but paid her no attention, for they were on their own urgent errands. Everyone was focused on the wedding preparations, and surely Lord Burghley himself was at the queen's side at Whitehall, getting ready for the Christmas season festivities.

Why did Robert have to come back now, after all this time? She'd been able to put her youthful folly, her romantic dreams, behind her, and now here he was. Making her feel just as young and giddy as ever, just from one look from his beautiful blue eyes.

He would just have to go away again. Soon. And in the meantime she would have to seek to avoid him. That shouldn't be so hard, should it?

Meg turned down another corridor and then another, until suddenly she found herself confusingly in the entrance hall once again. Bewildered, she tripped over the edge of a Turkish carpet and fell forward. With a startled cry, she shot her hands out to catch herself....

And found herself with a fistful of warm, soft velvet instead.

Strong, hard-muscled arms came around her and held her steady. It was Robert Erroll—she knew it even without looking up at his too-handsome face. She could smell the clean, cool scent of his soap, and her traitorous body still knew his touch. She made herself go very still, and not panic and run again like a ninny.

"You must have an urgent appointment somewhere, Mistress Clifford," he said quietly, his voice deep and smooth, like spiced wine on a cold Christmas night. "Is it still Mistress Clifford, or have you a new name?"

"I— Yes," she murmured, staring hard at the gold buttons of his doublet. "And I hear you are *Sir* Robert now, for all your good deeds to the queen."

"I am not sure how good they are," he said with a hint of laughter. "But I am indeed Sir Robert now. It's been too long since we met."

Since they'd met—and he'd kissed her and trifled with her girlish affections when she was too silly to know better. If anyone did such a thing to Bea now, she would beat them over the head with their own bodkin! It was infuriating how men thought they could play with girls' tender hearts like that and then run away, completely unaffected.

"Not quite long enough," she said. She tried to slide out of his arms, but his hold on her just tightened, drawing her closer.

"Did you never think of me at all after we parted?" he asked, the laughter vanishing into a strangely serious tone.

"I have been much too busy here at court to ponder such trifles," Meg said, hoping she sounded cold and distant.

Dismissive. "There are so very many people about. Surely you have been busy, as well."

Busy kissing women from Paris to Muscovy, she was sure.

"I have seen a great deal, 'tis true," he said, still holding onto her. "But I never met anyone else like you—Meg."

"True. I am not most women," she said, trying once more to tear herself out of his arms. "I have forgotten all about you."

"Meg, you can't mean that," he said, and for an instant he sounded truly hurt. But Meg knew better now than to listen to any man.

"Don't call me Meg," she said. "I am Mistress Clifford."

"You've always been Meg to me, in my memory. What has happened to you?"

"What do you mean?" Meg realized she wouldn't be able to break free of his arms, so she went very still and stared at the high embroidered collar of his doublet, at the hard line of his jaw. And suddenly, she wanted to cry, because she just wanted him to go on holding her. Wanted to feel again the way he'd once made her feel. So alive and free.

But she knew that could never be again.

"You look like the Meg I remember," he said. His hand slid down her arm, rubbing her soft satin sleeve over her skin until his bare fingers touched hers. "You're even more beautiful now. But your eyes are so cold."

In a burst of anger, Meg cried, "You mean I'm not the foolish girl I once was? The one so easily lured in by pretty words and kisses? I've learned my lesson well since last we met."

He raised their entwined hands to study her pale, ringless fingers as if he had never seen them before. As if they fascinated him.

"Do you still take what you want with no thought to anyone else?" Meg whispered.

Robert's eyes met hers, and for an instant she saw a bright flash of something like anger or pain in those ocean-blue depths. Then they went ice cold again. "You know nothing of what I've done in my life. If only you had…"

"If only I had what?" she said, bewildered.

"You drive me mad," he growled, and suddenly his arms came close around her again. He pulled her body hard against his, drawing her up on her toes, and his mouth swooped down to cover hers.

He wasn't harsh, but he was deliciously insistent, his mouth opening hungrily over hers, his tongue tracing the seam of her lips as he sought entrance. She opened for him, meeting him eagerly as a raw, hot hunger swept over her and she couldn't resist it.

She hadn't realized until his mouth claimed hers again how much their long-ago first kiss lived in her memory, how much she had longed to feel that way again. That sensation of the real, everyday world, where she had to be the sensible, practical Meg, flew away and she felt herself falling down into pure emotion. It was terrible, delirious—and all too wonderful.

Robert's hand slid down her back as their kiss deepened, pulling her body closer into his. He caressed the curve of her lower back through her satin bodice. When she moaned against his lips, his hands slid under her hips and lifted her high against him.

As she held onto him, her head fell back and his lips slid down her arched neck. The tip of his tongue tasted the hollow at the base of her throat, where her pulse beat out a frantic rhythm. How she wanted him, even after all this time!

She knew she should berate herself for it, but it was an emotion so dark and primitive it seemed she could not banish it.

His hand cupped her breast through the stiffened satin, stroking it until she moaned again.

"Meg—it's been so long…."

"I know," she gasped. She threaded her fingers through his black-satin hair and drew his mouth back against her skin. He hungrily kissed the soft skin of her neck, his breath warm. She could only hear the mingling of their harsh, uneven breath, the pounding of her heart in her ears.

One of his hands slid lower, grabbing the slippery fabric of her skirts and drawing them up. The cold air swept over her bare skin like a whisper. A chilling touch of reality.

Meg suddenly heard a burst of laughter beyond the closed doors of the great hall, and the noise reminded her where they were. At Cecil House, with half the court just a room away. She tore her lips away from his, struggling to breathe. Her emotions tumbled over each other inside of her, lust, confusion, joy, anger. It was surely madness.

"Please," she gasped. "Please do not do this to me again."

"Do what, Meg?" he said hoarsely, his breath warm on her skin. "All I ever wanted was…"

"Meg?"

Meg spun around at the sudden sound of Bea's voice. Her cousin stood at the edge of the room, staring at Meg with startled eyes.

Meg felt Robert ease away from her, into the shadows under the staircase, and she hurried toward Beatrice. She swiped her hands over her damp eyes and tried to smile. "Am I needed for the masque now?"

"Y—yes," Beatrice murmured, still peering past Meg

into the shadows. "You are to be an Hour of Night, I think. Who was that with you?"

"No one at all," Meg said, firmly steering Beatrice back into the crowded great hall. "An old friend of my parents', who has been abroad for some time. He was offering his greetings."

"Truly? He seemed rather young to be friends with my uncle." Beatrice tried to glance over Meg's shoulder, but Meg pushed her into the great hall and slammed the door behind them.

"Perhaps so," Meg said. "But never mind that. Tell me about our roles in the masque...."

Margaret. Meg. It was really her, at last, after all these years. But she was not entirely the Meg he remembered.

Robert raked his fingers through his hair, pacing up the Cecils' corridor and back again, the sound of his bootheels on the polished wood floor the only noise to break the silence.

From beyond the closed doors of the great hall, he heard the sunburst of youthful laughter, cut off by a stern word from Lady Burghley. He knew he should be in there, keeping an eye on his kinsman Peter Ellingham, but he had to regain his calm senses first. All he could see, all he could think about, was Meg's cool, fathomless dark eyes, looking at him as if she had never seen him before.

She had never replied to his letter, left at Clifford Manor before he went on his travels to make his fortune, and he'd always known there was a chance she wouldn't wait for him. In truth, they barely knew each other. A dance, a walk, a kiss. But in those few meetings had been a—a knowing. A realization, such as he'd never had with anyone else. She was the main reason he was driven to make his fortune thus.

Everywhere he went, Paris, Rome, Venice, the frozen wasteland of Muscovy, he remembered her. She was why he did what he did, so he could be worthy of her pure spirit. But the Meg in his memory, with her quick laugh, her bright enthusiasm for everything around her, seemed vanished.

In her place was a cool, still statue, a court lady with coiffed hair and the armor of her embroidered gown. It gave him such a chill to think of his dream of Meg Clifford, so long cherished, was vanished.

And yet—yet for just a moment, after that fiery kiss, he looked into her dark eyes and saw the glimmer of his Meg. Like the gleam of a diamond under ice, precious and beautiful. Far away, but not completely beyond reach.

If he could just crack that ice.

The front doors of Cecil House suddenly banged open, letting in a blast of icy wind and the loud clatter of a group of young men. It was the bridegroom, the golden-haired Earl of Oxford, surrounded by his posturing cronies. Their swords clanked, their furred cloaks swirled, and their laughter echoed mockingly off the luxurious walls of the bride's dignified house.

Robert couldn't help but feel sorry for young, quiet Anne Cecil, despite the luster of the title she would soon acquire. He was only glad Meg had not ended up married to such a one as Oxford and his friends. That she was still available—if she would only listen to him.

"Erroll!" Oxford called. "Come to celebrate my nuptials, have you? Every man should be wed, or so my guardian says. I vow you will be next...."

Chapter Three

Meg was lost.

She held tight to the reins of her horse and tried to peer through the snow, falling so heavily around her now that the whiteness disoriented her. She cursed herself for leaving the hunting party, but when she turned away from them down another path the day was cold and gray but clear. The snow had come on suddenly, too fast for her to turn around, and she couldn't even hear the echo of their laughter in the muffling silence.

Aye, she was foolish indeed to run away. But when Robert joined the party, the day had turned all closed-in and confusing. She didn't want to see him, to hear his voice, watch his smile, and remember his kisses—remember what a fool she had once been over him.

What a fool she could *still* be, if she let herself.

She would have left the party and gone back inside the palace, hidden her ridiculous feelings away in her own chamber, if she hadn't already been mounted on her horse. Luckily Bea was too preoccupied with Peter Ellingham to see Meg's blushes, and Robert seemed intent on making the too-solemn bride-to-be Anne Cecil laugh. He was very good at that—making ladies forget themselves.

And now Meg was lost, a long way from the palace.

"This way!" she heard someone shout through the snow. "Meg, can you hear me?"

The voice was hoarse, tinged with worry, but Meg knew it was Robert. She recognized his voice all too well, and her heart pounded at the sound of it.

"I—I am here," she called back. "I fear I am lost."

"Just stay where you are! I will find you."

Meg took a deep breath and forced herself to stay still. Running away had got her into this trouble in the first place. At last Robert appeared out of the whiteness, a figure all in black, his short cloak swirling around him, his cap tugged low over his brow so she couldn't see his expression. He reached out a gloved hand to seize her bridle.

"I noticed you were missing and feared you had become lost in the snow," he said. "I saw a hunting lodge not far from here. It looked empty, but we can shelter there until the snow ceases."

He had come looking for her? The thought made her shiver even more than the snow. Meg nodded quickly. She didn't *want* to be alone with him in an empty house, forced to face their past with no distractions around them, but she knew she couldn't stay where she was. The cold was seeping through her fur-trimmed riding clothes and into her very skin.

She swiped away the damp snow from in front of her eyes and nodded.

He led her slowly back down the path and over an icy bridge to where a small, square, dark brick house loomed out of the snow. It was indeed a hunting lodge, far enough from the city to be quiet, but near enough to be an easy travel to court. The windows were dark and no smoke curled out of the chimneys. But a wreath of holly hung on the door, a small sign of the festive season.

"Holly," she said whimsically as Robert helped her down from her saddle. "My nursemaid used to say fairies would hide under the prickly leaves to get away from the winter's cold."

"That's an old tale indeed." His hands lingered at her waist, warm through her woolen doublet. She swayed toward him helplessly, but he stepped away.

She shook away a pang of regret at losing his touch.

"Why don't you go inside while I settle the horses?" he said quietly. She could read nothing from his voice, his eyes that watched her so closely. His gloved hands clenched into fists.

She nodded and hurried inside. It was a small house, she saw as she made her way through a narrow corridor into a sitting room. Plain and functional, with carved beams criss-crossing the low ceiling and a dark wood floor covered by a luxurious green carpet. A few chairs and stools were scattered about, and painted cloths hung on the white-plastered walls to keep out the draft. A swag of greenery hung over the large fireplace.

Surely a court family lived here, Meg though as she swept off her damp cloak and hung it on a peg. She would have to thank them later for sheltering her.

Her and Robert.

She shivered as she remembered that she was not alone there. That he would be in that cozy room with her at any moment. Part of her knew she should run from him, even into the snowstorm, because she knew all too well his effect on her. But she stayed where she was.

"You are cold," he said behind her, startling her. She spun around to find him stepping through the doorway, ducking his head under the low lintel. She thought again how very kind the years had been to him, carving his youthful beauty into something truly extraordinary.

"No, I'm fine," she said, but he swept off his fur-lined short cloak and laid it gently around her shoulders. Its fine, soft folds smelled of him, of lemony French cologne and clean, cold air, and it still held the warmth of his skin.

"I'll build us a fire," he said. He took her arm in a gentle clasp and led her to a cushioned cross-backed chair near the fireplace.

"You know how to build a fire?" she said, bemused.

Robert laughed as he knelt down by the grate and reached for the wood piled up beside it. "I am not completely useless, Meg. I have learned many useful skills in my travels."

"Nay. Not completely useless, I suppose," Meg murmured. She sat back, wrapped snugly in his cloak, and watched as he shed his close-fitting doublet and set about building a fire. She wondered where he *had* been and what he had done in the time they were apart.

The long, lean muscles of his strong back and shoulders shifted beneath his thin linen shirt, and she remembered too well how his bare skin had felt under her touch. She swallowed hard and tried to turn away, but she feared she could not.

Soon he had a fire blazing in the grate, crackling and snapping, driving away the cold. He found a jug of wine and some bread, and they shared the repast in silence for several long moments. Gradually the warmth and the wine worked their subtle magic, and Meg found herself relaxing back into her chair. Robert leaned back against her legs, his body hard and strong through her skirts. It almost felt like what might have been.

"Tell me what else your old nursemaid said about Christmas," he said, as if he sensed that they should not yet talk about personal matters. Of what had once driven them apart. This was too sweet a moment.

Meg slipped down to sit beside him on the carpet, near to the fire. She stared into the cheerful red-gold flames, sipping at her wine as she remembered the old tales her nurse would tell by the nursery fire.

Meg stared into the fire and remembered Christmases when she was young, the feasting and music, the games she and Bea would play trying to divine their future husbands. But she couldn't tell Robert of those silly, girlish games.

"There was a song we would sing," she said, "about the holly and how no matter what comes it stays green and true." As love never did. Softly she began to sing the old words.

"The holly and the ivy, when they are both full grown, of all the trees that are in the wood, the holly bears the crown..."

"The ivy... The ivy..." she faltered, and whatever she was going to say was lost when he leaned closer and brushed his lips softly over hers. She felt their breath mingle, the damp heat of his skin, his lips. It was more intoxicating than any wine could be.

"Meg..." he whispered.

She didn't want him to let her go. For that moment, surrounded by the snow and the fire, the past dropped away, and she was just that young girl again, longing for this touch. She knew she should not be with him, that she had to keep being the sensible, staid Meg she had become at court. But she was so tired of being that girl.

Before she could think, she wrapped her arms around him and pressed her lips harder to his. She felt his hands close around her waist, and he shifted their bodies so they lay next to each other on the soft carpet.

"My sweet Meg," he said hoarsely, and his tongue traced the curve of her lower lip, light and teasing, before she parted her lips to him and he slid inside to taste her.

And she soared up and up, free, even if it was only for the moment.

Through the haze of her dream, she felt his touch slide around her hips, pulling her closer against him, their bodies so close even a snowflake couldn't come between them. She arched against him and felt his erection, the proof that he desired her, too, through the layers of their winter clothes.

He groaned deeply, and their kiss slid down into a wild, frantic need. Her fingers plucked at the lacings of his shirt until she could touch the bare, smooth, warm skin of his chest. She felt his breath catch under her touch.

Sensations raced through her, like lightning over her skin, and she remembered that only he had ever been able to make her feel alive like this. She dug her fingers into his hard shoulders and held him with her as their kiss deepened. She wanted more and more, wanted to forget....

But he drew away from her. "Meg. My pretty Meg," he said roughly. He pressed his forehead against hers, holding her as their ragged breath mingled. "It can't be this way. Not now. Not yet."

Meg was deeply confused, cold where she had been warm, dizzy and lost. He was leaving her again? "What do you mean?"

He just shook his head, and gently set her away from him. "It must be right. After all I have done…"

Meg shivered, feeling abandoned all over again. She gathered her disordered clothes around her with shaking hands, unable to look at him, to say anything at all. She just wanted to escape.

"It has stopped snowing," he said. "We should go back and find the others."

Only then did Meg notice that the gray sky was clear outside the small window. Why, then, did she feel colder than ever?

Chapter Four

The bride looked beautiful, Beatrice thought as she stood beside Meg and watched Anne Cecil, now the Countess of Oxford, proceed into her parents' great hall on her new husband's arm. Her gown, white satin embroidered with gold-and-silver thread twined in a pattern of vines and flowers, gleamed in the light of thousands of wax candles. Her hair fell down her back in a tumble of artful brown curls, bound around her brow with a wreath of pearl flowers. She looked as every bride should, Beatrice thought—like a fairy princess.

Yet she didn't even glance up to acknowledge the cheers of the crowd gathered for her wedding banquet, or the flower petals they showered over her. She gazed at the floor as she walked behind her parents, holding on to her new husband's arm, almost as if she was marching to the gallows.

The Earl of Oxford, however, just as splendid as his bride in a doublet of white and gold with a pearl-edged cap on his pretty head, waved and bowed. He didn't look at his bride with her bent head.

It would not be thus when *she* married, Beatrice vowed as she tossed her last handful of petals. Her husband would look only at her. He would not care if they married at West-minster Abbey before hundreds of courtiers and the queen herself, as Anne Cecil just had, or if there were satin and pearls or roasted peacock on gold plate. He would not care if she wed him barefoot in her shift, for he would want only her. She was determined on that.

As the newlyweds made their bows to Queen Elizabeth, who had attended the wedding herself and now sat on a dais to watch the feast, Beatrice leaned forward to see if she could catch a glimpse of Peter Ellingham. As she had suspected—and hoped—he watched her, too. He was so handsome, so witty and full of fun, and such a fine dancer. She did so enjoy his company, his pretty compliments, and his sweet notes and bouquets.

But she was not yet ready to march down the wedding aisle herself. She was no Anne Cecil to be forced to wed so young. If Peter Ellingham would but wait a while...

He grinned and waved at her, and Beatrice covered her giggle behind her hand.

Meg tugged at her arm. "Beatrice, please! What if Her Grace saw you?"

"The queen is too busy talking to the happy couple to notice me," Beatrice whispered back. "Besides, we aren't at the Abbey now—we needn't be solemn. We can have a little fun before the masque."

The edge of Meg's lips quirked in a quickly hidden smile. "Well—just a bit of fun, mayhap. You deserve it after all your good work on the masque."

"And so do you, Meg! You have been working so hard of late. You must promise me that you will be merry tonight, too." Beatrice clutched tight to her cousin's hand. Meg was always so serious, so responsible. She always took such good care of Bea at court. Meg deserved so much more than one evening of dancing. She deserved— She deserved…

She deserved a fine prince of her own. A man who saw her great beauty and would marry her in her shift if need be, just as Bea dreamed of.

Beatrice scanned the gathered crowd, the swirling, bright kaleidoscope of brilliant silks and velvets, emeralds and pearls. Everyone watched Queen Elizabeth, the peacock-center of it all in her blue-and-purple gown, her high-piled red-gold hair twined with sapphires and amethysts. Everyone but one man.

And he was looking at Meg.

Beatrice studied him carefully. It was Sir Robert Erroll, the current star of the court who had newly arrived from Muscovy. A tall, handsome, mysterious man who all the ladies giggled about. Unlike the brilliance around him, he wore dark colors, tawny and black, his dark hair waving away from a face even Bea, who was choosy about male looks, had to admit was quite perfect. His eyes, a glowing blue even from across the crowded room, were focused on Meg.

And Meg, Bea was fascinated to see, pointedly looked anywhere *except* him.

Most interesting indeed.

The bridal couple took their seats just below the queen on the dais, signaling the start of the dancing. Musicians, hidden high on a balcony above the revelers' heads, struck the first notes of a pavane as servants moved through the crowd offering spiced wine and trays of delicacies.

Beatrice saw Peter Ellingham making his way toward her, an eager smile on his face.

"I suppose you will want to dance with the handsome young Lord Ellingham now, Bea," Meg said.

Indeed she did. Peter was an excellent dancer, and one of the few men who could keep up with her in a galliard or volta. But Bea had a new mission in mind now for the evening. She hurriedly scanned the crowd looking for Robert Erroll. He was still watching Meg, a small frown creasing his brow. Meg, though, still would not look at him.

Bea tried to give him an encouraging smile, nodding toward her cousin. Maybe she could get him to ask Meg to dance. His frown turned puzzled.

And Peter was nearly upon her.

"Indeed I do want to dance," Bea said quickly. "But only if you will, too, Meg."

Meg laughed. "You know I don't often care to dance, Bea. I enjoy watching others more graceful than me. You go dance, and I will have some of Lord Burghley's excellent wine."

Meg took up one of the offered silver goblets, and Bea tried to see if Sir Robert had gotten her little hint. He had vanished into the crowd.

Peter reached her side, bowing over her hand in an elaborate, courtly salute that made her giggle. "May I have the honor of this dance, fairest lady?"

"Go, enjoy yourselves," Meg said. "Just remember we must change into our costumes soon, Beatrice."

"I remember." Beatrice let Peter lead her into the forming dance. As she took his hand and waited to begin, she whispered, "Do you happen to know Sir Robert Erroll, Peter? I thought I saw you with him at rehearsal."

"Never say I have lost you to him already, fairest one!"

Beatrice laughed. "Of course not! He is so old. He must be all of twenty-six. But I did see him watching my cousin."

"Your cousin? Was he?" Peter's eyes lit with a spark of interest. He was always up for a fine lark—that was one of the reasons she liked him. Perhaps he would even help her with a bit of matchmaking in a good cause. "As it happens, I do know him a bit. His mother is a kinswoman to mine. But I have only talked to him a few times since he returned to England."

"He is very handsome," Beatrice said. "But he seems quite lonely."

"Lonely? Nay, he is always surrounded by people in his lodgings."

Beatrice remembered the way Robert Erroll had looked at Meg, with such passion and longing. She shook her head. "What your kinsman needs, Peter, is a good, strong-hearted wife...."

Meg carefully slid through the crowded hall to find a spot near one of the tapestry-hung walls. All around her was music, the patter of dancing, leaping feet, the rustle of rich silks and satins, the scent of wine and expensive perfumes. All the desperate energy made her head spin.

She took a goblet of spiced wine from a footman and sipped at it as she scanned the dancers for a glimpse of Beatrice's golden hair. Her cousin was skipping and twirling with Peter Ellingham, the two of them whispering and laughing together. Bea seemed very well-occupied at the moment.

And Robert Erroll was nowhere in sight. At least for the time being, she could take a deep breath. She had been able to avoid him ever since their kiss in the abandoned hunting lodge. She had almost—almost—been able to forget it herself.

Meg closed her eyes as she took a deep gulp of the wine. Why, *why* did he have to return now, when she had nearly forgotten how foolish she once was? And why did he have to be even more handsome than before? She didn't need the terrible distraction of him in her life.

"Will you dance with me?" she suddenly heard someone say behind her, his voice low and intimate.

Startled, Meg whirled around to face him. Some of the wine sloshed from the goblet onto her silk sleeve.

"God's teeth," she whispered. "How could you startle me so? This is my best gown."

"Forgive me, my lady." He reached for her hand, his long, sun-roughened fingers closing around her wrist as his other hand took away her goblet and handed it to a passing servant. He took out his own handkerchief and gently blotted at the small stain. "I must speak with you, Meg."

"Really?" Meg murmured, trying to look anywhere but at him. Trying not to feel anything at all when he touched her. She wasn't succeeding. "Surely we said all we needed to three years ago. It was the merest flirtation, quickly over."

His hand tightened over hers. Startled by the suddenness of the movement, her gaze flew to his face.

His blue eyes were dark as he stared down at her intently. "It was not meant to be. Surely you knew that?"

Meg was confused. Her memories seemed so clear from those few precious days they'd had together. He had kissed her and then left for France; surely that made it a mere flirtation, the likes of which she saw every day at court. But her feelings from then were so much more mixed-up, like the swirl of spices in her wine. "I know no such thing. You were a worldly gentleman of the court, and I was a young girl who knew little but her own home. A fine amusement. When you hid me from your parents..."

"Because I knew I had to prove myself to you, to everyone. Only then could I present myself to you properly and honorably. I told you all of that. I thought, hoped, you were waiting."

Meg's confusion grew, and she shook her head. Was he speaking some foreign language she did not know? For she could barely comprehend his words. It was like a romantic epic poem of the old chivalric days or some such. "How could I have known such a thing? Did you think me a mind reader?"

Robert scowled. "It was in the letter I gave your maidservant. I dared not go to your house to find you."

"I never received such a letter! When you left without a word of farewell, I knew I was only a trifle to you."

"Meg, I never..."

"Meg, we must away to dress for the masque!" Beatrice suddenly cried, cutting off Robert's bemused words. Dizzy with confusion now, Meg pulled her hand away from Robert and spun around to face her cousin. Peter Ellingham stood just behind her, watching them.

Beatrice's bright eyes flashed between Meg and Robert. "You must be the famous Sir Robert Erroll! No one can speak of anything but your exotic travels of late. I'm sorry to whisk away my cousin, but I will return her after the masque."

"And I must show you something very important, Robert," Lord Ellingham added. He and Beatrice gave each other strange, secret little smiles, quickly gone.

Beatrice seized Meg's arm and drew her away, chattering all the while about the masque. Meg glanced back, desperately seeking one more glimpse, one more word, from Robert. What had he meant? What *letter*?

But he was gone, vanished into the crowd with Peter Ellingham. And Bea, surprisingly strong for such a sprite, kept dragging her away.

They made their way out of the crowded hall through a doorway hidden behind one of the tapestries. Beatrice led Meg up a narrow staircase and down a long corridor, chatting all the time. Occasionally she would pause to peer out a window, her words slowing but never halting.

As they turned down yet another corridor, Meg had a sudden suspicion. There were no other people in that part of the house, but she couldn't get even a word in between Bea's laughter.

At last they reached a closed door at the darkened end of the corridor. "Here we are!" Bea cried. "We must change quickly."

"Beatrice, what are you…"

Beatrice pushed open the door and shoved Meg inside, cutting off her words. Before Meg could even spin around and demand to know what was happening, the door slammed shut. She heard the sound of a bolt clanking into place and Bea's light footsteps running away. Only the echo of a giggle was left behind, and Meg was alone in a dim, windowless chamber seemingly lit only by one candle.

Fear and anger tangled up in her mind. "Beatrice!" she cried, banging her fists on the door. "What is the meaning of this? Come back at once!"

"She won't be able to hear you," a voice came from the darkness. "I fear we are alone."

Her heart pounding, Meg whirled around to see Robert standing in the single circle of candlelight, his arms folded across his chest as he smiled at her.

She was quite trapped with him. Alone.

Chapter Five

"What is the meaning of this?" Meg cried. She was trying to stay calm and coolheaded, to not show him her emotions at being near him again. Leaving herself open to him had only wounded her last time. But her voice came out sharper than she'd intended, and she couldn't seem to stop shaking.

She pressed her back to the locked door and stared at him in the flickering shadows. The candlelight carved his face into stark, elegant angles and cast his eyes into mystery.

"I think you will have to ask your cousin that, fairest Meg," he answered, far too composed for her liking. There was even a hint of amusement lurking in his voice. "And my kinsman Lord Ellingham. He was the one who led me here."

Beatrice and Ellingham, conspiring together in this prank? Meg almost laughed. It was so silly, if it wasn't also so infuriating! What could Bea possibly be thinking? "Why would they do such a thing? Bea is mischievous, 'tis true, but not cruel."

Meg closed her eyes. Nay, Beatrice was not cruel. So whatever her intent was in this prank, it was because she thought she was being kind. Had Meg somehow showed her feelings for Robert to her cousin? She had always been so careful not to speak of him to anyone.

Yet here they were, together, alone, with nothing but the hurts of the past lurking between them like a gray ghost. Meg studied his face, so close yet so far. He was not the beautiful, laughing young man she remembered, and had cherished so secretly in her memories. He was harsher, darker, with secrets of his own in his eyes. He drew her to him even stronger than before, in a way she had never known before.

"It's been so very long, Meg," he said roughly. "I thought about it, wondered how it would be when we met again at last."

He had thought about her, as she had him? Against her will, Meg found herself intrigued, curious. "Is—is this how you imagined it?"

He laughed, the rich, deep sound all-enveloping in the small room. "Not in the least. But you are more beautiful than ever, Margaret. And I know your tender heart is still in there."

Suddenly, in one lithe, swift movement, he was across the room and at her side.

With a rough groan, he dragged her against him and covered her lips with his. As his tongue slid into her mouth, she met him eagerly, longing for the emotions only he could make her feel.

No matter how they had come to this strange, unreal moment, no matter what would come after, she knew she needed him. It had been coming for such a very long time, and now it was upon them.

His fine velvet doublet had been unfastened, and she

pushed it off his shoulders. It fell to the floor and she slid her hands under his thin linen shirt to touch the warmth of his bare skin. She wanted more and more of him.

"Meg," he whispered. "Are you sure?"

But she didn't want him to talk. She didn't want anything to yet intrude on this dream.

She nodded, and in answer he kissed her again, roughly, nothing held back. Her head fell back as his tongue plunged deep into her mouth. She met him with her own bound-up passion, her arms holding on to him tightly as she dug her nails into his back through his shirt.

He picked her up off her feet and whirled her around until they tumbled together dizzily to the floor. She was vaguely aware that Beatrice and Lord Ellingham must have left them provisioned, for they didn't land on a cold, bare wooden floor. There were soft blankets piled there, and her foot pushed over a jug of wine with a metallic clatter. But then Robert was over her, above her, and he was all she knew.

He tore his shirt off over his head and tossed it away before he leaned back into her. He kissed her throat, the soft skin swelling above the pearl trim of her bodice.

"How have you become even more beautiful?" he whispered.

Meg longed to believe him, to believe this moment was real. But she couldn't hear his words just then. She wanted nothing to mar her dreams.

"Shh," she said. Her hand slid along his strong, muscled back, and skimmed over his hard backside before she traced the band of his breeches and tugged their laces free. Maiden she might have been but few others at court were, and she had listened to their chatter about the bedchamber. And she had imagined just such a moment with Robert for too long.

His manhood sprang free from the fabric confines, hard as iron. She traced her fingertips lightly over its hot length, and he groaned deeply. Bolder, she touched him closer, up and down, fascinated by it. By him.

"If you don't stop, fairest Meg," he said hoarsely, "I fear this will be over before it begins."

Meg laughed, and suddenly everything was wonderfully real. He pulled out of her arms and stood to hastily divest himself of the rest of his clothes. Soon he stood before her splendidly naked, his bare skin turned golden by the candlelight.

"I—I feel rather overdressed now, I fear," she said.

Robert laughed. "Let me help you with that, then."

He drew her up beside him and unlaced her fine bodice, her satin skirts and farthingale. As the garments fell away, she suddenly felt shy, unsure. She shivered, half-drawing away from him.

But then his lips touched the bare curve of her shoulder, and the cold uncertainty turned to the fire of need. She trembled as he traced the tip of his tongue over her skin, as he drew the jeweled pins from her hair and let the length of it tumble free. His breath caught, grew rough, and she knew he was as enraptured by the moment as she was.

She lay back in the blankets and stared up at him in the flickering light. He studied her, too, and she could only hope he enjoyed what he saw as she did with him. He was so glorious, like an ancient god, and for that night he was hers as she had dreamed of for so long.

She held out her arms to him and he came to her, kissing her lips, her neck, her shoulder, the softness of her bare breast, until she could bear it no longer.

She wrapped her legs around his lean hips and pulled him against her. His skin was satin-smooth, hot, damp. She traced her eager touch over his back, his strong shoulders. She pressed her lips to the pulse at the base of his throat, tasting the salty-sweetness of him. She craved him like she never had anything else, needed him.

"Meg," he whispered. He buried his face in the curve of her shoulder, holding his body taut above hers. "Have you dreamed of this as I have?"

"Yes," she gasped, but then she could say no more. She could hardly breathe as his mouth, open and hot, slid over her skin. He swept aside her tumbled hair to kiss the shell of her ear.

She felt the rush of his breath, the light bite of the edge of his teeth on her soft earlobe, and it made her shudder with a lightning-rush of heat. She arched up into him.

"Do you like that, my Meg?" he said.

"I feel as if I'm falling," she gasped as the room seemed to whirl around her.

"I'll be here to catch you." His fingertip slid between her parted legs, tracing her seam before he slid deep into her wet core. And Meg let herself fall free into the pleasure.

"Please, Robert," she begged, wanting so much more.

His breath was ragged as she spread her legs farther and pressed himself between them. His hips drew back and slid forward, and she felt the stretch and burn as he slid inside her. She gasped at the new sensation, the fullness of him joined with her at last.

He plunged past her maidenhead and he went very still.

"I don't want to hurt you," he said, his arms rigid as they braced against her.

"It's better now," she whispered. Afraid he might leave her, she tightened her legs around his hips to hold him with her.

And it *was* better. The burning ache faded as her body grew accustomed to his, leaving only an enticing glimmer of sparkling pleasure. Leaving only him and her together.

He drew back one slow inch at a time, almost sliding out of her before he flexed his lean hips and drove deep again.

"Oh!" Meg gasped as he moved again and again, faster, deeper. That twinkling heat of pleasure grew and grew, expanding low inside her until every part of her ignited to fiery life. She instinctively learned his rhythm and met him as they moved together, faster, more frantic.

Behind her closed eyes there were sparks of gold and silver, shining, burning. She heard a strange humming in her ears, growing louder in a rising chorus. She cried his name aloud, wanting more and more. More of *him*.

Then all thought, all sense, flew apart as those sparks exploded. She felt as if she was soaring free into the sun.

Above her, Robert shouted out her name, his back arching, his head thrown back in abandoned pleasure. He fell to the blankets beside her, their arms and legs entangled.

Meg slowly sank back down to earth from the stars. She had never felt so tired and light—so confused and giddy. She was with Robert now, in a way she never could have imagined. She didn't know what would happen tomorrow, or even in the next hour.

But right at that very moment, she knew she was where she should be.

Chapter Six

"Surely they will be missing us by now," Meg murmured as she stretched luxuriously and curled back into Robert's arms. Their little prison chamber was chilly with no fire, but his lean, muscled body was warm wrapped around hers. She couldn't quite care that someone missed them, not with him so close to her.

She couldn't quite care if she ever got out of that room at all.

Robert's fingers toyed lazily with her loosened fall of hair, wrapping the strands over his throat and his naked chest. "I doubt it. Peter snatched away my costume for the masque, which I was carrying when he and his ruffian friends shoved me in here. I'm sure he and your cousin have found replacements for you in your part."

Meg laughed. Surely one Knight of Apollo or Hour of the Night looked the same as another behind the gilded masks. "Then we must have another hour at least before they release us and explain their behavior."

"Are you sorry not to have your moment of glory before the queen?"

"Moment of glory?" Meg propped herself up on her arm to gaze down at his face in the dying candlelight. How handsome he was, her knight, gilded golden in the light, his hair tousled and his eyes lazy and smiling. She could never have dreamed they would end up in such a place. "I would rather stay here forever than face another moment in such a crowd. I've had my fill of such 'glory' over the last few years."

Robert reached up to trace his fingertips over her cheek. "Do you not like your court life, Meg?"

"I like it well enough sometimes. The people can be amusing, and I enjoy the plays and the music," Meg answered, thinking back to how she had lived since she last saw him. "But for all the time—nay. It grows wearisome then. There is no place to rest or think."

"I want to hear about everything you have done," he said, drawing her back down against his shoulder. "The people you have met, everything you've thought and dreamed of…"

Meg laughed. "My life has been dull indeed compared to yours. I want to know all about your travels. Such strange lands you have seen."

Robert grinned down at her lazily as his fingers traced a light pattern over her bare shoulder. "'Tis true I've seen much. Golden palaces in France, streets made of water in Venice. Snow as deep as a man's head in Muscovy. I have enough tales to bore you for many evenings to come, Meg. When we are old and gray by our own fire."

Many evenings to come? Did he, could he, mean that? Meg scarcely dared hope. "I want to know…" She suddenly remembered something he had said, a few vital, fleeting words before they were parted in the great hall. She sat up straight, drawing the edges of the blanket around her shoulders as she stared down at him. "What was that about a letter, Robert?"

He sat up beside her, bracing his forearms on his knees. His face looked solemn. "The letter I sent you three years ago, the night my parents came to Clifford Manor. I have cursed myself a hundred times since then for being such a coward as not to tell you those words myself. But I feared if I saw you again, I would never be able to leave you. And I had to prove myself to you first. Prove I was worthy of you. My family had no money, you see, and I had to make our fortune."

"Worthy of *me?*" Meg whispered, bewildered, hopeful, scared. "I never got such a letter. I've spent so long trying to forget your kiss. Trying to tell myself I could not be worthy of *you.*"

Robert's hands suddenly clenched into fists, his jaw growing tight. "Then I am a double-damned fool, Meg, for what I did. All this time we would have known, planned..."

"Nay!" Meg reached up to press her fingertips to his lips, stopping his words. A surge of pure, warm, summertime joy flooded through her, washing away the misery and loneliness. "Surely it is enough that we know all now. And, with thanks to our interfering cousins, we have had this night."

Robert took her hand in his, holding it as tenderly as if it was the most fragile, precious jewel. "Is this one night all you want, Meg?"

"It is more than I ever thought to have," she said. "I know the truth now, and I can be free. So can you."

"I never want to be free of *you.* Not for a single night again for the rest of my life." His fingers tightened on hers, and his eyes closed as if he struggled with his words, with the flood of emotions rushing over them both. Just as she did. All she could do was hold on and let it carry her away.

Meg was sure all of it was a wonderful dream, too perfect to be real. Yet their touch, the warmth of his body close to hers, it *felt* so very real. So true. Just as she had imagined it in her most secret fantasies.

"I can make a home for us now, Meg," he said. "The queen is to give me an estate of my own. A place only for us, where we can belong together. Where I can spend years making up for my foolishness three years ago. If you will only let me try."

"Let you?" Meg felt the tears she had held back for three long years fall free, warm and healing as they dropped on their joined hands. Like a benediction for their future. "Oh, Robert. All that matters is now, you and me. Everything that we can do together." She gave a choked laugh. "All the evenings you will bore me and our children with tales of your travels."

"Then, Mistress Margaret Clifford," he said solemnly, with a catch of tears in his own voice. "Will you do me the honor of giving me your hand in marriage?"

Meg looked up into his brilliant blue eyes. She had prayed for just such a moment when they'd first met, but she knew that only now could it have been so very right. So perfect. They'd had to be ready for each other, and now they were. It was perfect.

"Yes, Robert Erroll," she answered. "I will marry you. At last."

Robert laughed and swept her into his arms. "Then I can tell you one more secret."

"No more secrets, I beg you!" Meg cried, holding on to him very tightly.

"Oh, you will like this one, my love," he said with a wicked grin. He reached down into the folds of his doublet and pulled out a shining brass key. "I have had the key to this room all along...."

* * * * *

Under a Christmas Spell

BARBARA MONAJEM

Barbara Monajem grew up on the west coast of Canada in a land of mountains, cedar trees and rain. When not gazing dreamily at the mountains or climbing the next-door neighbour's forbidden cedar tree, she spent her time curled in an armchair with a book, waiting for the rain to stop so she could go back outdoors to play. Little did she know that the rain was tempting her to another sort of fun—a lifelong addiction to an alternative to real life. Apart from a short period of competition with a childhood friend who read impossibly fast and who won the most-books-per-week competition hands down, all this reading was pure pleasure. It inspired Barbara to write her first fantasy about apple tree gnomes when she was eight years old.

At the age of twelve, Barbara and her parents and sisters spent a year in Oxford, England. Since most of her childhood reading was Brit lit, it's not surprising she felt entirely at home. She spent that year exploring Oxford by bus and on foot, spending her pocket money at Blackwell's Bookshop and playing twosy-ball against the school wall. She had the unimaginable thrill of grubbing around in an archaeological dig, unearthing shards of pottery while secretly hoping for bones instead. She got to explore Stonehenge and walk on Hadrian's Wall, but she still regrets not being allowed to spend the night in the haunted tower at Warwick Castle. Still, that year in England firmly grounded her in a love of history. When her mother introduced her to the books of Georgette Heyer, her desire to write Regency romances was born, although she didn't admit it to herself for years.

After returning to Canada and surviving her school years (which included a best-forgotten foray into teen melodrama), she studied English literature at the University of British Columbia. Marriage, children and a move to Montreal ensued. Through the long and cold-but-beautiful winters, stories simmered inside her. Several years later, after moving to Georgia, USA, she completed and published a fantasy novel. After that came a romance that is still under her bed and a few mysteries that kept turning paranormal, no matter how much she tried to remain at least somewhat realistic. Frequent visits to New Orleans may have had something to do with this. She succumbed to the dark and lovely moods of the French Quarter and wrote several paranormal romances.

And then, all of a sudden, she caved in and wrote a Regency romance and immediately became hooked. Now she divides her writing time between paranormal and historical worlds, although an urge to combine them has already raised its pesky little head.

Barbara loves to hear from her readers. She can be contacted through her website.

The office of a warehouse near the Thames, London, December 1815

"The war is over," Lord Valiant Oakenhurst said. "I'm not involved in the game anymore."

"You're not doing much else," said the Master of the British Incubi, at ease behind his massive desk. "Unless you're planning to return to the family fold."

Valiant gave a tiny internal shudder. Not only did he find the estate of his pompous father, the Marquis of Staves, completely unbearable, but he wasn't wanted there. Inevitably he caused trouble. Far better to cause it in places where his unusual abilities were appreciated. In some ways, wartime had suited him very well, but now he wanted…

He wasn't going to get what—or rather, whom—he wanted, and it was irrelevant to this discussion. He glared, wondering why the annoying fellow still wore a mask. Secret identities shouldn't matter anymore. "You know I can't return to the bloody fold."

"Precisely, so you may as well make yourself useful. Sit down, Lord Valiant. Your restlessness irritates me. This won't take long."

Valiant shrugged and took the proffered chair.

"We wish you to awaken the sensuality of a Miss Southern, but there cannot be a genuine liaison except in the lady's imagination," the master said. "Her virginity must remain intact. In fact, you must not even attempt to kiss her."

Valiant narrowed his eyes. "Or else what?" He'd had enough of being judged as if he was still the fifteen-year-old who'd been removed from Eton for deflowering a respectable virgin.

The master didn't answer his question, merely saying mildly, "It's only for a fortnight. "You will send her erotic dreams and cast admiring, even smouldering glances at her, to get her, er, juices flowing, so to speak."

Valiant huffed. "For what purpose, if she is to remain a virgin? I don't relish playing the tease."

The master gave an amused snort. "You've lied, cheated and murdered for your country, and yet you object to a little sensual teasing?"

"The war is over," Valiant repeated. "I'm tired of playing those games." He was stuck with his magical abilities—or at least they seemed magical when he tried to explain how they worked. Plenty of men and women were competent seducers, but few could plant images in the sleeping minds of their targets, rendering them helpless with desire. No wonder incubi and succubi had been seen as demons for centuries, but that was unfair. Val had no wish to harm anyone. He'd been forced to use his abilities in unpleasant ways during the war, but in peacetime, he shouldn't—and wouldn't.

"War is never truly over," the master said heavily. "England will always need gifted individuals to protect her." He straightened and steepled his fingers together. "However, that is neither here nor there. Miss Southern is an intelligent woman of excellent breeding, with a moderate fortune, but she refuses to marry where she does not feel affection. We hope that the awakening of her sensual side will make her more amenable to, er, falling madly in love."

This made no sense at all, but the master never orchestrated anything without good reason. "Why do you care whether she marries?"

"I don't, but someone I value does. You're not the only person with obligations."

How typical of the master to combine a reminder that one was beholden with a cheap show of sentiment. "How very affecting." Valiant sneered. "What if the stubborn Miss Southern falls in love with me? You may end up owing your valued someone far more than you do now. I warn you, my obligations don't extend to marriage."

"Then you'll have to tread carefully, won't you? Although come to think of it, marriage may be just what you need—but not to Miss Southern." He passed a folded sheet of paper across the desk. "Here are your instructions. You are to attend a Christmas house party where Miss Southern will also be a guest."

Valiant opened the paper. "At the estate of Viscount Westerly." He gave another internal shudder. He could well imagine it—idiotic traditions that must be adhered to no matter how antiquated. It would be just like being back in the family fold.

He shook his head. "Lord Westerly detests me. He won't want me at his party."

"I trust you'll find your way around such a trifle as that," the master said.

The private parlour of an inn on Grub Street, London, also in December

"My dearest Lucille," said the Mistress of the British Succubi. "How kind of you to visit me."

"*Oui*, I am extremely kind." Lucille Beaulieu rolled her eyes. "To come here, I had to postpone some very boring plans. Life is moving at the pace of a stubborn donkey. I hope you mean to give me something interesting to do."

The mistress's eyes twinkled through the slits of her mask. She was almost pleasant to deal with now that the war was over. The mistress had been extraordinarily kind to her, helping her establish herself in English society, and Lucille made a point of paying her debts.

Except one, which she could never repay. Thoughts of it—fears, as well—still kept her awake at night. She had finally begun to feel safe, but one persistent enemy was all it took.

A maid entered with a tea tray. When the girl had gone, the mistress poured Lucille a dish of steaming hot bohea. "You are to arouse a certain nobleman's interest in sensuality," she said.

Lucille made a tiny moue. "I do that merely by being myself." At twenty-eight years old, she found herself almost yearning for the approach of age and the loss of sensual appeal. Not that she would be entirely useless after that, for she would never lose the seemingly magical ability to send erotic dreams. But such dreams were a gift, bestowing harmless pleasure on the recipient, whilst seduction often led to irreparable harm.

"Yes, my dear, but this man is a difficult case. He is a peer lately returned from the war."

"A soldier?" Lucille barely managed to keep the dismay from her voice. Soldiers had taken her parents away to prison and the guillotine when she was only four years old. As a rational adult who had spent years in the proximity of armies, she should be accustomed to soldiers, but…no.

"Not any longer, for he has sold out," the mistress said. "He is thirty-one years old—an appropriate age to marry, but he refuses to do so."

The tea did not taste quite so delicious anymore. "Surely you don't expect me to wed him." Lucille had already been married five times. Some of the marriages had been legal and some not, but all of the husbands had been disposed of—although not by Lucille—when they had ceased to be useful to the powers that be. She hadn't loved any of them, but nor had she wished them dead.

"No, for we should be obliged to kill him, should we not?" The mistress laughed.

Lucille didn't. She had joined the British Succubi as an angry young woman. At first she had been quite blood-thirsty, using her skills of seduction to do whatever was needed…but seeing one's husbands done away with—not to mention many others one encountered during the war— had changed that. She wished there were ways to use her talents to help others rather than to harm them.

The mistress patted Lucille's hand. "Merely a jest. Those days are past. You are free to marry whomever you choose."

Since the only man Lucille would consider marrying despised her, this was unlikely.

"Marriage might be just the thing to relieve your boredom, but probably not with Lord Westerly." The mistress stirred sugar into her tea. "To return to the matter at hand, he is an upright and intelligent man. He was one of Wellington's aides-de-camp and a brilliant code- breaker, but the unpleasantness of war affected him so badly that he has well nigh become a hermit."

The unpleasantness had taken its toll on Lucille, too, but in an opposite way—a constant need to be with people, to be up and doing.

"He shows no interest in women. He will not even take a mistress," her hostess said. "And no, he doesn't prefer men, nor was he wounded and incapacitated. His is an emotional problem that must be resolved, and you, my dear, can arouse even the most difficult cases. Think of it as a way to use your talents in a peaceful cause."

It would be a challenge. It might occupy her mind for a while. Maybe it would help her to forget. But she could never be forgiven, and that was what mattered most.

"The peerage is far too full of substandard fools," the mistress said. "For the future of England, one cannot let even one intelligent nobleman refuse to marry and carry on his lineage." She passed Lucille a scented envelope. "Here are the particulars. It has come to our attention that Lord Westerly's aunt is planning a fortnight of Christmas festivities at his Hampshire estate. You will doubtless find a way to attend."

An English country Christmas! During her childhood, Lucille had spent several years with an English family. Holly and mistletoe, plum pudding and roast goose… She sat back in her chair and sipped her tea. Perhaps some aspects of this mission would be fun.

Hampshire, a few weeks later

Shortly before dusk on the twenty-third of December, Lord Valiant Oakenhurst rode into a copse a short distance from Westerly House. He hadn't done what he was about to do in ages, and the last time he'd been lucky not to kill himself in the process.

This time he was slightly better prepared. He wouldn't ruin good clothes in the process, because this was England, not wartime France, so he didn't need perfect cover. Today he had purposely chosen a threadbare shirt and a too large coat he wouldn't have given to a groom. He took out two cravats and set them conveniently ready for use.

Then he removed a loaded pistol from his saddlebag, took very, *very* careful aim, and shot himself in the arm.

Hell! It was only a scratch, but it hurt as badly as last time. His horse, formerly a cavalry mount, must have forgotten its training, for it took exception to the sudden noise, snorting and sidling, and almost unseated Valiant against a tree. Cursing, he got it under control, barely preventing the cravats from slipping to the ground. He shed his ruined coat, wound the cloths about his arm and tied them as tight as he could with his free hand and his teeth. He was still bleeding, but it would have to do.

He wheeled his horse and set out for Westerly House.

As dusk fell, a coach-and-pair carrying Lucille Beaulieu and her new friend, Theodora Southern, turned through the gates of Westerly House and slogged slowly up the drive.

It had been all too easy to arrange. One look at the guest list the mistress had supplied her, and she'd known whom to choose. She and Theodora moved in different circles, but occasionally they had attended the same ball in London. A carriage breakdown before the gates of the vicarage where Theodora lived with her parents and a fault in the axle that would take more than a week to fix—an obvious ploy to anyone in the game—was all it took. The Southerns wouldn't have dreamed of turning a stranded gentlewoman away, and Theodora was far too polite to admit that she didn't remember meeting Lucille. She had succumbed readily, allowing acquaintance to become friendship, and had even seemed pleased when Lucille suggested accompanying her to the house party. The ease of it, which would have been a relief during the war, now made Lucille rather sick.

She tried to concentrate on the positive aspects of this journey. Every country house had its traditions. Perhaps the ladies would accompany the gentlemen into a wood to fetch the Yule log. They might assist in delivering gifts of food to the tenants on Lord Westerly's estate. She longed for the comfort of traditions. Of family life, which she had never truly known. Since the age of four, when the soldiers had taken her parents away forever, she had always been the outsider—fostered by families in France, then Spain, and lastly England, allowed in on sufferance, never truly belonging.

She followed Theodora's gaze out the carriage window. Westerly House had not yet come into view, but up a small rise stood the tumbledown walls of an abbey.

"Those are the famously romantic ruins?" Lucille asked. So bleak and desolate, resembling her life. She liked Theodora—such a calm, composed woman, sure of her worth but not the least high in the instep, and with a lively sense of humour. So…well-balanced. In other words, what Lucille was not and didn't know how to be.

Theodora's pause and her tiny shake of the head showed that her thoughts had been elsewhere. "Yes, aren't they beautiful? Just like in a Gothic novel." A tall man came into view, striding up the rise toward the ruins, and she uttered a soft, "Oh."

Lucille's heart sank. She'd wondered, judging by tiny nuances in Theodora's speech, if she had a *tendre* for Lord Westerly. Theodora had told her that she'd decided long ago to marry for love or not at all. Perhaps this was the reason why. "Is that Lord Westerly?" Lucille asked.

"I can't tell for sure from behind," Theodora said after another pause. That was almost certainly a lie. "I haven't seen him for several years. He's the right height and build, though."

Evidently he dwelt firmly in Theodora's memory and heart. She didn't think Theodora had any hope of marrying Lord Westerly—if he had wanted her, he could have asked her long ago, for they had known one another since childhood—and yet Lucille's own heart squeezed at the thought of seducing her new friend's secret love. It was a betrayal, and Lucille wanted no more of those.

She didn't think this would be a happy Christmas for Theodora. His lordship's aunt had invited a number of eligible young ladies in the hope that he would take a fancy to one of them, and Theodora's role was to help out as a sort of secondary hostess.

"He's a fine figure of a man," murmured Lucille.

"He was a soldier," Theodora said. "Maybe that keeps a man in good trim."

Perhaps I can arouse him without seducing him, Lucille

thought. That would not be so despicable. "Perhaps I shall flirt with him," she said tentatively. "It will make this aunt of his angry, *non*?"

"You are a strange person, Lucille," Theodora said frankly, but she was smiling. "First you invite yourself to someone's party, and then you make plans to annoy them."

Lucille chuckled. "I am truly bad, *n'est-ce pas*? But I am no danger to these young things from whom he will choose. I don't wish to marry again, merely to amuse myself. Will there be many handsome men, do you think?"

"Unfortunately not," Theodora said. "I am acquainted with everyone on the guest list. Lady Westerly—" that was his lordship's aunt "— has made a point of ensuring that all the male guests are either married, inept or dead bores."

This wasn't the best of news, but if Lucille flirted with the other men, as well, her concentration on Lord Westerly would not be obvious. If she sent him sensual dreams, too, it might suffice. There would be good food and drink, and festivities to keep her mind off things she preferred not to think about. And best of all, nothing to remind her of the game.

It was only a mile or so, but by the time Lord Valiant reached Westerly House, he didn't have to feign feeling a trifle under the weather. Strange how the lack of any real danger robbed one of the usual grim control.

He urged his horse up the drive to where a gentleman and two ladies hovered outside a coach while footmen unloaded trunks and bandboxes. It seemed an ideal moment for a dramatic arrival until he glimpsed a familiar pair of wide violet eyes. He blinked, so astonished and overwhelmed by memory that he swayed in the saddle.

He stared. It was truly Lucie. Damn and blast the master. What was she doing here? A surge of rage sent him into wartime mode. This wasn't what it seemed.

Back into the game.

As he slid off the horse, people hurried around the coach. "Highwaymen," he croaked, grasping his injured arm and stumbling to one knee, sensing without seeing the contempt in Lucie's gaze. "Winged me."

"Heavens, how dreadful!" The other lady rushed forward—an ordinary-looking Englishwoman, not a conniving succubus. "Lord Westerly, send a man for the doctor," she ordered. "James, Charles, help this poor man into the house."

"Lord Valiant Oakenhurst?" said Lord Westerly as two footmen set down the trunk they carried and hurried around to help. "What the deuce are you doing in Hampshire?"

"Getting shot," Valiant mumbled. "It's only a scratch." He squeezed his eyes shut as if in agonizing pain—actually, the throbbing in his arm was nothing compared to seeing Lucie again—and reopened them. "I could ask the same of you."

"I live here," Lord Westerly said.

"The devil you say." Val infused surprise tinged with distaste into his voice, slung his good arm across the shoulders of one of the footmen, and made the most of staggering into the house.

What in the name of God and all the saints was Val doing here?

Lucille watched aghast as one footman helped her former lover into the house, while the other ran to the stables to send a groom for the doctor. She'd always wondered about his background, which could have been anything judging by the many roles he had played. Now she knew, and a cold trickle of fear invaded her gut. Oakenhurst was the family name of the Marquis of Staves. Val was not only a spy and assassin, but a man of power and influence in England.

Whereas she was a traitor to both France, the country of her birth, and England, which had given her sanctuary, and Valiant Oakenhurst was the only one who knew. What an unusual name Valiant was, but appropriate. She'd known him by several names, but during their intimacy he'd been simply Val.

But why would a man of high birth use a desperate ploy to gain entrance to Westerly House? The last time he'd shot himself in the arm, he had nearly bled to death. Lucille knew because she had been the one to save his life.

She'd caught that flicker of rage in his eyes. He still hated her, even though the war was over and France had gone down to bitter defeat. He had followed her for months after the betrayal and had had her watched during Napoleon's first exile. She had lived in daily expectation of violent death. After Waterloo, she'd hoped it was all over. Lately, she had almost begun to believe she was safe.

Evidently not. None of it should matter anymore, but he would never understand, brutal, uncomplicated Englishman that he was. He had surely come here because of her, but how had he known she would be here? And what did he intend to do?

A ghastly question yawned chasm-like before her. Was she prepared to take his life to save her own?

Valiant hadn't killed anyone for several months. With the war over and done he shouldn't have to, but he knew a brief, furious urge to return to London and murder the master. He didn't want to deal with Lucie.

Except to bed her. He didn't think he would ever stop wanting that. An incubus should have a certain amount of natural resistance, but when it came to Lucie he was as susceptible as any other man. More so, because he'd fallen hopelessly, idiotically, in love with her, and then been devastated when she'd ruined his mission by warning a French spy, thus aiding the man's escape.

Compared to that pain, the hole in Val's arm was a mere twinge, and yet he had protected Lucie from the death she'd deserved at the risk of his own life. Did the master know about any of this? Had Val been sent here as some kind of test?

He lay back on the pillows, fuming. He didn't give a damn about the master's reasons. His life was his own now, but if he'd known Lucie would be here, he would have sought a less hazardous method of getting into the house party. He had already refused to let the doctor bleed him. His gunshot wound was a mere scratch—he'd done the job much better this time—but he couldn't afford to handicap himself further. The mission had suddenly begun to matter.

By a stroke of good luck, Miss Southern, the capable lady who had ordered even Lord Westerly about, had designated herself mistress of the sickroom. This surprised him; he'd expected a manservant at best or a slattern at worst, since everyone knew about his reputation with women. He lay back on the pillows, hoping he looked harmless, and tried to mask the throbbing in his arm with erotic thoughts.

Theodora Southern wasn't the sort of woman who appealed to him. She was pretty enough, but matter-of-fact and entirely without guile. Maybe she didn't find men sexually attractive. He could probably change that temporarily, but it seemed as pointless now as it had in the office of the Master of the British Incubi. Rebellion simmered within him. He'd had enough of being manipulated...but for the moment, until he knew what was going on, he might as well do as he'd been told.

"You're a stubborn man, Lord Valiant," said Miss Southern after bidding the doctor farewell. "You'll get a good sleep and feel much better in the morning, if only you will take this draught the doctor left for you."

He gazed at her from under his lashes, smouldering as best he could. "I'm sure you're right, Miss Southern," he drawled, "but I prefer to remain in possession of...all...my powers."

Had he made her blush? He couldn't tell in the candle-light.

"As you wish." She set the glass on the table by the bed. "I shall leave it here for you with some small beer to wash it down with if it tastes vile, as I'm sure it will. I must go to dinner now, but a servant will be here soon with some gruel. Unless you mean to refuse that, as well?"

He grinned at her, the same grin that had slain many hearts. "No, I prefer to remain at least partly in the good graces of my nurse."

"It has nothing to do with my good graces," she said crisply, "but rather your well-being."

"How gratifying," he purred, "to know you have my well-being at heart."

"Of course," she said, and would have left in a hurry, but he put up a hand.

"Tell me," he said. "I know Lord Westerly from our Eton days, and I recognized Lady Westerly, his aunt, but who is the other lady who was outdoors when I arrived?"

"Madame Beaulieu is a friend of mine from London. Her carriage broke down near my parents' house, so rather than stay with them she opted to come here with me."

So that was how Lucie had managed it—a standard ploy, but she must have known he would find out and recognize it as such.

He let Miss Southern escape. He'd certainly had *some* effect on her. Once her firm footsteps died away, he got out of bed and crossed to his valise. He put his spare pistol under the covers and a knife beneath his pillow, although he doubted he could bring himself to use them. He climbed back into bed to wait.

He dozed until a servant girl arrived with the gruel. "Is everyone else at dinner?" he asked. "No other invalids but me?"

"Yes, my lord. No, my lord," the girl said, blushing as she curtsied and left. He drank the gruel and allowed himself to sleep, reasonably sure Lucie would stay out of the way for at least a few hours.

She didn't come to him in the flesh, but she invaded his dreams.

Lucille tried to concentrate on arousing Lord Westerly's interest, but her tentative efforts at flirtation met with indifference. She didn't know what to make of him. He was barely polite and more withdrawn than anyone she had ever known. She should persist—she had always persisted until her missions succeeded—but she couldn't stop thinking about Val. "How is your patient?" she asked when Theodora hurried into the drawing room just before dinner, looking as if she had dressed all by guess.

"Reasonably well, but stubbornly refusing to taking a sleeping draught," Theodora said. "Lord Westerly, he says you were friends at school."

His lordship's nostrils twitched. "We knew one another at Eton."

Ah, so they hadn't been friends—had perhaps disliked one another. That might explain Val's desperate measures, although if he wanted to kill Lucille, he could have done it easily in London or in France or Spain during the war. Why here, and why now?

Lucille seethed with impatience all through dinner, followed by tea and whist. She found out the location of Lord Valiant's bedchamber by asking Theodora if she meant to check on him before retiring.

"I suppose I must," Theodora said. "I wish I needn't."

"But why?" Lucille said. "He is a good-looking man, *n'est-ce pas*?"

"Yes, but…he makes me uncomfortable. He has a rakish air about him. Not that I haven't encountered plenty of rakes—one can't avoid them in London—but Lord Valiant is different. I am thankful there is no mistletoe in the house, for he is precisely the sort of man who would try to trap one under it."

"No mistletoe? I hadn't noticed. Is there none hereabouts, or does Lord Westerly disapprove of Christmas kisses?"

Theodora reddened. If it hadn't already been obvious that she had a *tendre* for the man, it was now. "No, there is plenty of mistletoe, but Lord Westerly ordered it taken down. His aunt is upset, because she wanted him to have the opportunity to kiss all the young women she has invited without compromising any of them. Perhaps she will be relieved at his decision now that Lord Valiant is here. I don't think Lord Westerly likes him."

His lordship came up behind them. "No, I don't," he said, curt and tight as ever. "He is completely amoral where women are concerned. I'll come with you."

He is not truly amoral, Lucille thought, wishing she could defend Val aloud. She shouldn't want to defend a man who probably intended to kill her, but she had always been a fool where Val was concerned. Amorality was common amongst incubi—another of the reasons they were sometimes seen as demons and made excellent spies—but Val had his own code of honour, even if it was not quite the same as other men's. Succubi made good spies, too, but that was an empty way of life, far worse for a woman than for a man. Lucille couldn't bear it anymore.

She bade Theodora and Lord Westerly good-night and watched from her bedchamber doorway as they entered a room far down the corridor. Soon they emerged and retired to their respective chambers.

Lucille loaded one of her pistols, secreted a knife in her shawl, and set off down the corridor. When she reached Val's door, she hesitated, tempted to storm right in. She didn't suppose he waited gun in hand, ready to shoot her, but one never knew.

Besides, she was a civilized woman now, and it was more polite to knock.

"*Entrez,*" Valiant said, tossing a coin once more. So far, his throws had come up even—heads for Westerly to return alone, tails for Lucie. They both wanted to be rid of him.

This time it came up tails, and Lucie marched in, pointing a gun at him. "I would like to shoot you," she said in French.

Valiant spread his good arm, hand wide open. The other arm, swathed in bandages, lay in full view. The shape of the gun showed clearly under the sheet but far from his hand. "Behold me entirely at your mercy."

"Reminding me of the last time you said that will get you nowhere," she said.

Then why had he dreamed of her over and over in the past several hours? She was an expert at sending powerful erotic dreams—as good or better than he was—and if she'd intended to distract him, she'd succeeded. His cock was as helpless as the rest of him when it came to Lucie. He'd wakened hot and aroused, and throwing off all covers but the sheet hadn't cooled him down.

"It would if I weren't a little under the weather," he said. "I wouldn't let the leech cup me, though, so I should be myself again by tomorrow." God help him, he was ready for her right now. A vision of her climbing atop him made him shiver with lust. He buried that thought and waved a weary hand. "Once I am well again, you will be unable to resist."

Her bosom swelled. "I'm not so eager for death that I would put myself in your power."

He let himself enjoy the sight of her, remembered that chestnut hair spread upon the pillow, imagined cupping those lush breasts again and gripping that perfect behind… Plaintively he asked, "Not even the 'little death'?"

She didn't smile. "Why are you here?"

"That depends on why you're here."

She cocked the gun. Hell and damnation, she really meant it. Hard to believe that once upon a time she had said she loved him. "I certainly didn't come to visit Lord Westerly," he said. "We can't stand the sight of one another."

"Then why?" she snarled. "The war is over. You have had plenty of opportunities to punish me. Now it is time to leave me alone."

"I'm not at liberty to say why I'm here." Belatedly, it dawned on him that she was afraid. He'd forgotten about her fearfulness. She'd always put on a good act, but she hadn't liked being a spy, and she'd feared soldiers most of all—inconvenient during a war, to say the least.

She should know by now that she had no reason to fear him. He loved her and always would, whatever she was, whatever she'd done. If he'd been a true patriot, he would have killed her ages ago. "My mission has nothing to do with you. Believe me, Lucie, if I'd known you were going to be here, as well, I wouldn't have shot myself." He thought about putting on a seductive grin but decided against it.

She waved a dismissive hand. "I wish I could believe you, but you're a clever man. It could merely be a ploy within a ploy."

"And so could yours. I don't like being at a disadvantage any more than you do."

"You're at no disadvantage." She spat the words. "You are an Englishman in his own country and the son of a marquis."

Much good that did him. His father had long ago disowned him. His family wouldn't come to his aid, nor would they grieve if they heard of his death. A living spy was a regrettable necessity, a dead one hurriedly forgotten.

"You also have a loaded gun and a knife, and perhaps more weapons that I cannot see," she said.

"My gun isn't the only instrument that is loaded and

ready, as you've doubtless noticed by now." His cock had made a tent of the sheet, but there was no point telling it to desist. "If you are at a disadvantage—which I don't believe—it is by choice. You can lure any man you want to your bed. You could be a duchess by now if you wished."

She shuddered visibly. "I have had enough of husbands."

"Let's fence with buttons off, Lucie. Why are you here?"

"I'm no more at liberty to say than you are." She lowered the pistol. "But I had hoped to enjoy this English country Christmas. The holly and the ivy, the Yule log and the flaming pie."

"You like all that nonsense?"

"*Mais oui*, I like it very much." Her eyes widened with genuine surprise—something one rarely saw from her. She was delightful when she was being herself. "Don't you?"

"God, no. Can't abide it, but I didn't come here to spoil your enjoyment, and I swear upon my honour that I mean you no harm."

Immediately her guard went back up. "This is no coincidence. I don't promise not to kill you."

He nodded. Damned if he would let one of the master's schemes harm Lucie, but he couldn't protect her if she didn't believe him. "Pass me that sleeping draught, will you?" He indicated the glass on the table by the bed and watched her over the rim while he slowly sipped it all down. "I don't know what the doctor put in this foul concoction, but I expect I'll be dead to the world for a number of hours."

In other words, his life was in her hands. Her eyes, intent and suspicious, made it clear that she understood. She wouldn't shoot him, but there were ways of making a drugged man's death appear natural, and a spy like Lucie knew them all.

"When you decide to trust me," he said, "perhaps we can work out why we are really here."

He's the sort of man who gambles, Lucille told herself. She could have snuffed him out just like that, and no one would have suspected foul play. He knew it, and yet he'd risked everything on a throw of the dice. She had been like him once out of necessity, but it was no longer wartime, and she wanted to be a different Lucille.

And yet, one glance at him and she was lost. Incubi were born to make one breathless with desire. She had the same effect on men as he on women, but that wasn't what drew her to him. It was that he made her want to be herself, made her want it so badly that she couldn't help but give in.

He was so sure of himself, lying there with his erection pushing up the sheet, his come-and-take-me eyes mocking not only her desire but her love. It wasn't fair.

She hurried back to her chamber and climbed into bed, shivering with both cold and a combination of anger and dismay. It was bad enough that she wanted to make love with him, but that was only natural, an understandable phenomenon.

Far worse, she wanted to trust him, as he'd asked. She wanted to be safe with him again. How stupid! After what she had done to him, she could never be at ease in his presence, could never escape the fear and shame. If she hadn't been holding a gun on him, she wouldn't have been able to meet his eyes.

Yet now, as if England and France were again at war and spies were once more playing the game, he had thrown down the gauntlet—to taunt her, to make her take risks in return. But why? If he didn't want to kill her, why was he here?

She would not allow herself to think about Val. She dreamed about him, though—tantalizing erotic dreams that left her sweating even in the chilly night, aching and unfulfilled. Were these the product of her own imagination, or had he sent them? Was he really dead to the world, or had that been another ploy?

To hell with him. She could frustrate him just as easily, but she refused to combat fire with fire. Her job was to arouse Lord Westerly, not to play games with Lord Valiant Oakenhurst. She intended to fulfill her own mission and enjoy the English country Christmas.

Val woke from a drugged fog to find Lord Westerly standing by his bed.

He blinked the sleep away. Judging by the light seeping through the window curtains, it was morning. "I'm still alive." He managed to grin up into his host's cold, tired eyes. Westerly had been stiff-rumped as a youth, but the war had improved him, Val thought. "Have you come to kill me?" He certainly looked capable of it.

"I'm a soldier, not an assassin," Westerly said.

"Whereas I am an assassin," Val said. "Such a vast gulf between us."

Westerly shrugged. "Not really. We both served our country. Different jobs require different methods."

For a long moment Val lay suspended with surprise. "Charitable of you."

"No, it's realistic," Westerly said. "Don't be an ass, Oakenhurst. I used to be self-righteous, and you never had any morals, but I for one have changed. I have nothing against you as long as you leave Miss Southern be."

Val barely stopped himself from raising insolent brows. He was used to being an ass with members of his own class. It would require practice to change. In as polite a voice as he could muster, he said, "You have an interest in her?"

Westerly's face hardened even more. "She is both a guest and a valued friend. I won't have her discommoded."

Another long pause, during which Val made a decision. "That puts me in a pretty pickle."

Westerly grew even colder, quite deadly in fact. "For your sake, I hope you intend to tell me why."

"I'm probably not supposed to." Val sat up, wincing as the bandages shifted on his arm. "Not that I care about secrecy anymore. We're not at war." He sighed. "Someone wants Miss Southern to marry."

"What?" Westerly was understandably perplexed. "Which someone?"

"I don't know. Someone to whom my spymaster owes a favor. Hand me that cup of small beer, will you?" Westerly obliged. Val took a long swallow and made a face. "I could use something decent to drink."

"Later. Why would anybody care whether Miss Southern marries? Surely that's her business."

"Perhaps someone thinks she would be happier married than single. Most women are. My spymaster refuses to reveal his identity, but he's of our class. I assume he knows someone who's related to Miss Southern and cares about her." He blew out a long breath. "My ridiculous mission is to arouse her interest in sensuality in the hope that she will choose to, as my spymaster put it, fall in love and marry. I have been forbidden to so much as kiss her."

There was a silence, whilst unreadable emotions chased themselves across Westerly's face. "You're serious, aren't you?"

"I couldn't make up anything so absurd," Val said. "You needn't look as if you'd like to murder me. She's not my sort of woman at all."

"Which brings me to my other concern," Westerly said. "Madame Beaulieu, who I would say is your sort in more ways than one. Who is she?"

Val grimaced. "A former spy."

"I thought so." Westerly paused. "I've met her before, although I don't recall quite where. I think perhaps she was not French at the time, but Spanish."

Val nodded. "She is French by birth, but after losing her parents she was fostered in Spain and eventually sent to England. She can play a convincing Englishwoman or Spaniard if she chooses. She worked for our side, if that matters to you." This might not be the truth. She'd certainly been working for France when she had destroyed Val's mission. He'd watched her after that until the war was over, dreading the prospect of having to kill her, but she had never trespassed again that he could see—in fact, she'd done some damned dangerous and highly efficient work for England. He still didn't understand what game she'd been playing.

"I don't care who she worked for," Westerly said. "She's not the sort of woman with whom I want Miss Southern to associate."

"Surely Miss Southern's friends are her business?" Val suppressed a laugh at Westerly's glower. "Maybe she's bored with being a pure, untouched virgin. Maybe she enjoys the titillation of having a worldly sort of friend. Maybe whoever thinks she should marry is entirely right about her needs and desires."

"And maybe you should mind your tongue before I lose my temper," Westerly said. "There's something damned havey-cavey going on here. I don't believe the story of a carriage breakdown in front of the vicarage any more than I did your tale of highwaymen."

"I don't believe it, either, but she refused to tell me why she's here." He laughed. "Has she tried to flirt with you? Maybe someone wants you to marry, too."

"Then they can go to the devil. I'll let you stay here long enough to convince your spymaster that you did your best, but in return you'll have to do something for me."

Christmas Eve passed quickly. Lucille helped Theodora make table decorations with holly and rosemary. They all tramped into a nearby wood for a ceremonious cutting of the Yule log, which was dragged to the house by servants and placed in the great hearth. The guests arrived—five chattering young women with their parents, as well as a few unprepossessing men to keep the numbers even. Lord Valiant descended from his sickroom, raven-haired, brooding, and irresistibly romantic-looking with his arm in a sling. The young ladies whispered and sighed.

Their parents whispered, too. Fathers scowled at Lord Westerly and mothers sent shocked or reproachful looks at his aunt. On the way downstairs, Lucille caught the sound of raised voices in the bedchamber next door to hers and stopped to eavesdrop.

"Lord Valiant is the worst sort of lecher," a man's voice

growled. "God knows why he has such an effect on women, but he's extremely dangerous. Have your maid pack your things. I won't have my daughter in the same house as him."

"But, dearest, we've just arrived," said his wife. "I had hopes that Lord Westerly would fall in love with our Anne." Ah, this was Lady Shaw, a pleasant matron Lucille had met once or twice during the Season.

"He won't fall in love with any girl who's making eyes at Oakenhurst," said her husband, Sir Digby, an old roué with a big belly and a roving eye. "I'm beginning to have my doubts about Westerly, too, allowing that libertine under his roof."

"But, darling, Lord Valiant was shot by highwaymen. Lord Westerly couldn't leave him bleeding to death on the doorstep."

"Nothing wrong with the fellow today, as far as I can see. I shall speak to Westerly now. Either Oakenhurst goes, or we do." At the sound of irate footsteps, Lucille hurried away down the passage, but not quickly enough to escape Sir Digby, who did his best to paw her before descending upon Lord Westerly.

A half hour later Sir Digby and his wife and daughter got into their coach and drove away.

Theodora, it transpired, had heard the entire row. "Lord Westerly seemed to enjoy it," she told Lucille. "He asked Sir Digby if he feared his daughter's morals were as lax as his own. I don't know how I managed to keep from bursting out laughing." For an innocent, Theodora wasn't easily shocked.

Everyone gathered in the drawing room before dinner. Lady Westerly floundered through excuses for the abrupt departure, but Lord Westerly put up a hand to silence them.

"Nonsense," he said. "They left because I refused to send Lord Valiant away. I could not in all conscience do so. In the first place, he is still recovering from his wound, and in the second place, it is Christmas Eve."

"Indeed, it would have been wholly contrary to Christian charity," Theodora said.

"Instead you sent Sir Digby and his family away!" cried Lady Westerly. "That isn't Christian charity. Think of his poor wife and daughter. Night was falling, and there are highwaymen about."

"I didn't *send* them," Lord Westerly said. "Sir Digby chose to leave, and there is a respectable inn only a few miles away." When Lady Westerly began to remonstrate, he interrupted, his tone harsh and clipped. "I suggest you drop the subject. You would not wish me to lose my temper and drive away the rest of our guests."

At this precise moment, Lord Valiant strolled in. No doubt he had been listening outside the door. "What a pity that would be." He cast an appraising glance about. "Such beautiful young ladies and their delightful mothers."

Amidst the sighs, blushes and wrathful mutterings that followed this entrance, Val sidled over to Lucie. "It's Christmas, darling," he whispered in French. "Let us call a truce."

"One only calls a truce during a war," she retorted. "Are we in a war?"

"Not of my making," he said.

"Nor mine," she snapped back.

"No? You seemed rather warlike last night. I wasn't the one waving…pistols…about."

She struggled to keep her smile in check. She wished… But wishing was no use.

"Come now, Lucie," he said. "For old times' sake. You want it as much as I do."

She shrugged and walked away, not because she thought it would fool him, but because she needed to think about practical matters such as life and death, rather than how much she wanted to crawl on top of him and make him hers.

"What a dreadful man," said Lady Westerly in her ear, startling her. "Did he make a lewd suggestion to you?"

"*Bien sûr,*" Lucille said. "Of course, and so did the hypocritical Sir Digby. But you must not think it bothers me. I am a widow, so I am not easily discomposed." She smiled kindly at Lady Westerly's visible struggle between embarrassment and her desire to be thought an equally worldly-wise widow. "What did Lord Valiant do that has given him such a dreadful reputation?"

"He ruined an innocent young woman." Lady Westerly lowered her voice to a shocked whisper. "When he was only fifteen years old!"

Lucille gave an appropriately scandalized murmur.

"His father, the Marquis of Staves, found a husband for the poor girl. Not that I approve of her behaviour, mind you, but one has but to look at Lord Valiant to realize it was all his fault. I can't think what my nephew is about to allow him to stay."

"Lord Valiant is no longer a foolish schoolboy," Lucille said. "Surely he knows better than to seduce innocent maidens."

"His father has disowned him," Lady Westerly said darkly.

Lucille didn't need to feign surprise. "Oh, surely not!"

"The Marquis of Staves is an upright and proper nobleman. He would not do such a thing if he did not believe his son had gone beyond the pale. I have heard the most dreadful rumours… Oh! I have an excellent notion." A crafty look crossed her pinched features, but the butler appeared to announce dinner, so Lucille didn't get to hear what the excellent notion was.

It soon became apparent. Lady Westerly, at the foot of the table, disregarded good manners and spoke loudly and over everyone else about her nephew's praiseworthy career, painting him as a noble war hero.

"Enough, Aunt," Lord Westerly said. "I am merely one of the lucky ones who emerged from the slaughter alive and in one piece."

"It seems Lord Valiant was lucky, as well," she said. "Dear Lord Valiant, you were away from England during recent years, too. Tell us, what did you do?"

Val leaned back in his chair. His wonderful long eyelashes—oh, how Lucie loved those lashes—hid the challenge in his eyes. "I was a spy."

Shocked whispers went around the table. Lady Westerly's smile turned smug.

"And on occasion, an assassin," Val said.

One of the indignant fathers surged to his feet. "This is unacceptable!"

"All in the service of God and country," Val murmured.

"Necessary, no doubt, but most ungentlemanly," said a ruddy young man. "Such work should be left to the low fellows to whom it comes naturally."

"Oh, it came quite naturally to me," Val said with an utterly charming grin. Again, it took all Lucie's control not to smile.

"No wonder your poor father disowned you," a second

father said. "How can you blatantly admit to such infamous work?"

"Why wouldn't I? It's the truth," Val said.

"But not a suitable topic for ladies," said a third father, more mildly.

"Why not?" Lord Westerly interposed. "Perhaps ladies should know what Englishmen have done in the service of their country." His narrowed eyes and clipped tone betokened anger, rigidly suppressed—but not anger at Val. "Perhaps, instead of thinking only of balls and gowns and jewels, they should be made to understand what those men have suffered and sacrificed for their sake."

"Definitely not." The second father shook his grizzled head. "It harms their delicate sensibilities."

"I don't mind knowing," Theodora said. "I would much rather possess knowledge than delicate sensibilities."

"I think I would, too," one of the young ladies said shyly, and was immediately shushed by her mother.

"Perhaps, my dear, but not about spies and assassins," her father, the milder one, said.

If Lucille hadn't known Val in the past, she might not have realized that under his insolent front, he was not enjoying himself much at all.

He came to her at midnight, silent and dark, intent as a panther. Swathed in her nightclothes, she clutched her wrapper tightly against his approach. What had happened to her? She had once been bold with men, never at a loss. She'd been bold with *him*...

No longer. She loved him, but she had made a choice long ago, a choice that meant losing him but keeping her honour, and living with that had turned her into a shadow of her former self.

He had his own notions of honour. She didn't think he would break a truce.

He slipped into her bedchamber, shut the door and leaned against it, watching her. Even as her heart beat heavily and desire pooled in her loins, anxiety and regret gnawed at her. "Why did you do that?" she asked. "Why expose yourself to their unkindness?"

He grinned, all mischief now. "I'm not at liberty to say."

He was trying to rile her. She managed a mocking laugh. "If it was to gain my sympathy, it worked. I wanted to slap them." As always, he stole her breath, her resolution, her very soul. She had to decide *now*.

He prowled forward and took the decision, illusion that it was, out of her hands. "I didn't come here for sympathy." He pulled her against him and kissed her hard. Pleasure washed through her, the same as always, dark and hot and irresistible. No other man had this effect on her. Oh, how she had missed him. She gave a tiny sob and twined her arms about his neck, drinking him in like a parched wanderer in the desert who has finally found the oasis.

After drinking one's fill in the desert, one moved on.

But she didn't want to think about that, so she set herself instead to doing. She unbuttoned his waistcoat and pulled his shirt gently over his head, skimming it over the bandages on his left arm. She knelt, unbuttoned his pantaloons and pushed them down. He stepped out of them, and she went for his smalls.

His member sprang out, thick and heavy and ready for her. She took it in her hand, inhaled its musky scent, and gave it a long, slow lick. He shuddered, but slid his hand into her hair and raised her to her feet.

"Lovely Lucie," he whispered, "as sweet as cherry wine." She quivered at the sound of his voice. He wasn't like other men, silent and panting or blurting obscenities. While making love, Val murmured of passion and wooed with possessive heat. She had always thrilled to the sound of his voice. Like no other, she thought, the reminiscent pang sending a tiny, cold arrow into the heat of desire.

He began on the buttons of her wrapper, and she knew he would have undressed her slowly, painstakingly and tantalizingly with his one sound arm, but she was afraid to pause for fear that the arrow would force its way in, that the cold would take over and destroy what little was left to them. She let the wrapper fall, ripped the nightdress over her head, and pushed him onto the bed.

She crawled up after him, drinking in his virile beauty. *I love you*, she thought, but she didn't say it, because he wouldn't believe it, probably didn't even want to hear it.

She mustn't think about that, must merely lose herself in pleasure for this short, sweet truce. She played with him, rubbing him against her core, pulsing unbearably, and he pulled her face to his and kissed her again, possessive and sure. She broke away, panting, to guide him inside her.

Ah. She had done this with many men, but with Val it was different. It was right.

One arm lay gently against her hip while his other hand roamed. Skin to skin, mouths and arms and hands, her breasts against his hard chest, his every thrust a caress, their every rise and fall an exchange of ultimate pleasure. Of love.

No, it wasn't love anymore. It couldn't be, but she didn't

have the strength to resist, and then their pace quickened, and she couldn't think anymore. Dazed with the heat of their joining, she rocked over him, mindless, riding up the crest to pleasure. He pounded up into her, and she sensed his climax and let herself explode with bliss.

As she lay in his arms afterward, the pulsing gradually slowed, and realization hit her. Except for that first endearment, he had said nothing to her. No whispers, no murmurs or growls or...anything. Contentment drained from her.

There was nothing right about this. She'd been a fool to think it meant anything more to him than a quick tumble.

She rolled away. "Just this once for old times' sake, but I cannot do this anymore. As you say, it is no longer wartime. I cannot be a succubus without good cause."

His brows drew together. "You're not being a succubus with me, any more than I'm being an incubus. We're just Lucie and Val."

"No," she said, "there is too much between us for that."

He slid off the bed, lean and strong and beautiful. "We're here together. There needn't be anything between us except...this."

Two naked bodies and two guarded souls. They could never trust one another, and without that there was only this pleasure—which, while wonderful in its way, no longer held any appeal for her without love. She wished she could be innocent like Theodora, who had opted for true love or nothing.

She retrieved her nightdress and pulled it over her head. "That's like being a succubus. I don't want to do that anymore."

He picked up his clothing but didn't put it on. Perhaps it was too difficult with only one sound arm, but she couldn't offer to help. She wouldn't risk touching him again. "From now on, I want to use my power to send dreams to help people, to do only good," she said. "I shall concentrate on my mission."

He shrugged, indifference in his posture and his gaze. He was a competent actor, but she feared this was no pose. "I hope it's less ridiculous than mine," he said. "It's no secret worth keeping. My spymaster sent me to arouse the sensual feelings of Miss Southern."

Lucie halted midway through donning her wrapper. "What? Why?"

"Someone to whom my spymaster owes a favour wants Miss Southern to marry and believes that if she feels the pull of sensuality, she will be more likely to fall in love." He chuckled unpleasantly. "You needn't look so appalled. I won't seduce her. She's not my sort of woman, and even if she were, I've been ordered not to."

"Your mission had nothing to do with me? You were not ordered to kill me?"

He rolled his eyes. "As I already told you, I didn't know you would be here."

"That does not reassure me," she said. Even if he was telling the truth, it didn't mean that he wouldn't soon be ordered to kill her. It didn't mean that this wasn't a test of his loyalty to England. "My mission is much like yours. I am to arouse Lord Westerly's interest in the female sex, in the hope that he will wish to marry and carry on his name."

Val wrinkled his nose in a sneer. "You intend to seduce him?"

What business was it of his? He couldn't possibly be jealous. "No, because I think Theodora loves him. Even if he has no interest in her, it would be too much like betraying a friend."

His sneer turned bitter. "A friend you cultivated in order to come here."

"She is my friend nonetheless," Lucie said, aching with the pain of all she couldn't say. *I didn't want to betray you. I had no choice.*

"You're wasting your so-called loyalty," he said, going to the door. "Westerly asked me to try to make his guests uncomfortable. He didn't invite them and doesn't want them here. He's not interested in marriage."

A brief sadness for Theodora flitted through Lucie's heart, and then it filled again with her own misery. "You know nothing about my loyalty," she said.

He shrugged again. "I know enough." He left.

She locked the door behind him, threw herself onto the bed and wept her heart out. What a strange expression, she thought, when at last she reached the stage of exhaustion. Her heart still resided in her breast, and it didn't intend to change its mind about loving Val.

She should have known better than to bed him; it had only opened old wounds. He despised her. He didn't even *want* to understand.

What an idiot he'd been. He'd believed nothing remained between them but animal attraction. He'd thought to share some pleasure with her, nothing more. He should have known better than to think they could indulge their physical passion without emotions elbowing their way in and spoiling it.

She didn't love him. He already knew that; had known for years. An incubus shouldn't be so susceptible, shouldn't care so much, but the fact remained that he'd fallen in love once and for all, and nothing would change that.

Once he'd realized the hopelessness of it all, he should have reverted to logic. Considering the agony he'd gone through, first because of the betrayal and then in fear that he would have to kill Lucie, he should have leaped at the chance of an explanation—a cool, rational discussion of what she had done and why. Instead, his bruised heart had taken charge and he'd sneered at her.

And upset her. Tears had glimmered in her eyes as he'd left. She no doubt deserved it, but that didn't mean he liked being the one who'd made her cry.

He'd thought her dead to all tender feelings. After the betrayal, she had shunned him entirely. She'd refused to even look him in the eye—a fool's move, since it made her as good as a traitor confessed. Could it be…that she'd avoided him from a sense of shame?

Why would she claim loyalty unless she felt he'd misjudged her? Or was this claim merely another act?

Oh, hell. How should he know? Maybe he should get it over with and just leave.

Or maybe he should find out what was really going on. Hope, massive and most likely unjustified, swelled with him. He would stay a little longer—at least until he knew the real reason he'd been sent to Westerly House.

Eventually, Lucille fell asleep. She woke on Christmas morning determined to make headway with her mission, but even a traitor and former spy couldn't attempt to send dreams in church—even though many people tended to nod off during the sermon. She chuckled at the thought of the mischief one could create. What a pity she couldn't share the jest with Val, but she had to stay away from him. She dressed and went with the rest of the party in a pious and subdued frame of mind.

Val didn't come. He stayed in his bedchamber, citing his wound as an excuse. "Entirely appropriate," said one of the obnoxious fathers. "Such a man should not be allowed across the threshold of a church."

Lucie couldn't contain her indignation. "Why not? He did his duty. You have no right to judge whether he is beyond redemption."

"Everyone should be welcome at church," Theodora said. "They certainly are in my father's parish."

"As they are here," Lord Westerly said, silencing everyone.

The old stone church, all that was left of the abbey from long ago, was decked in greenery, the choir enthusiastic if somewhat off-key, the vicar a gentle sort of man. Lucille found herself pondering the meaning of Christmas. *On earth peace, good will toward men.* Shouldn't this be a time for forgiveness? For new beginnings? But there could be no new beginning with Val.

As they returned home, she thought about sending dreams to Lord Westerly. She didn't want to. Perhaps in a few days she would manage to drum up the necessary interest, but she doubted it. She might be a succubus by birth or magical talent or whatever it was that gave one such powers, but she was no longer a succubus at heart. Not that that stopped every other man in the house—guests and servants alike—from eyeing her with helpless lust. Except Val, who took to fixing his dark, smouldering gaze on the remaining younger ladies, with the result that another family found an excuse to cut their stay short.

Lucille threw herself into the pleasures of the season: food and drink, charades, rides in the countryside, walks in the grounds, and a visit to the abbey ruins. Lord Westerly had discovered the remains of a Roman villa under the ruins, and had dug a great hole near one of the walls. He neglected his duties as host, spending every spare moment there. But the weather was crisp and clear and the company pleasant for the most part. It was almost like the Christmases she had spent in England as a girl.

If only she could sleep well! Dark dreams invaded her mind—memories of the Revolution, of soldiers taking her parents, of her life as a foster child in France, Spain and England, of five dead husbands as a spy…and, over and over, of Valiant's sneer and his scornful eyes. He was ruining everything! If it hadn't been for their senseless, futile missions, he wouldn't have been here, and she could have enjoyed herself… They'd never been asked to do anything so ridiculous before. It felt like a cruel jest. It was certainly a waste of time.

After a night or two, better dreams began to nudge their way into her sleep. Their gentle eroticism comforted her, reminding her of the leisurely days and nights after she'd nursed the wounded Valiant back to health. If they were from him, what was he trying to do? He was supposed to be sending dreams to Theodora, so why would they come with such force to Lucille instead? Some effect on others was to be expected, since succubi and incubi tended to inflame everyone in their vicinity—but not to this extent. Besides, he felt only contempt for Lucille. He wouldn't send her thoughts and images suffused with tenderness and love.

One night, she found herself trapped in a dream so fraught with memory that it could only have come from Val. They were in Paris, a city perilous to them both, and he'd laughed at the danger and made her laugh, too, infecting her with a mad, delirious joy. She gave in to the dream as she had to the reality, letting his hot, skilled hands and relentless tongue carry her to ecstasy again and again.

How could she resist such a contrast to her nightmares, such seductive power and utter abandonment to vibrant, sensual life? During her wakeful hours she couldn't stop thinking of him, recalling their times together, reliving the heady excitement of forbidden lovemaking, remembering with both joy and tears the languorous pleasure of weeks they'd spent on leave in a villa in southern Spain, playing at being husband and wife.

Then she realized she wasn't just remembering—she was responding to the dreams he'd sent her, offering him her memories, reminding him of their love, if only in *his* dreams. He would recognize what she was doing and scorn her for such tactics. She stopped herself at once.

The last day of the year was filled with plans for a most bizarre event. "We perform two wassail rituals here," Lord Westerly explained. "The first is on New Year's Eve. Men from the village and nearby farms come to cleanse the house of evil spirits."

Lord Valiant rolled his eyes. "They do the same at my father's estate. A pack of idiots stomp about the house, then gorge and drink themselves into oblivion. My mother hated all the dirty boots and loud, uncouth behaviour, but because it was the custom, she had to put up with it."

"I understand your poor mother's feelings, but one must keep up the traditions," Lady Westerly said. "As one must carry on the family name." She cast a darkling glance at her uncooperative nephew.

"What is the other wassail ritual?" Lucille asked.

"That one takes place in the orchard on Twelfth Night, to drive the evil spirits away from the apple trees, where they have supposedly fled after leaving the house." Lord Westerly gave one of his rare grins. "Muddy boots and uncouth behaviour are a young boy's delight. As a child, that was my favorite tradition of all."

"In our village we have a similar ritual going from orchard to orchard," Theodora said. "Our trees bear well and the cider is excellent, so one must assume it works."

Valiant rolled his eyes again, but he had taken on a mischievous look so reminiscent of the past that Lucie knew an urge to weep. He'd revelled in the risks of being a spy.

She hadn't.

She threw herself into decorating the Great Hall with fresh greenery and adding spices to two huge cauldrons of ale. She intended to enjoy every bit of this Christmas, no matter what.

It was time to take action. Val had been patient for almost a week, and he'd had enough. Obedient to his host's request, he had flirted with the remaining maidens, but they or their parents were made of sterner stuff than those who had departed. One young woman, a tempestuous redhead, found herself some mistletoe and did her best to trap him in an alcove. He obliged her with a kiss, but also warned her not to try the same tactic on Lord Westerly. "He's a very particular fellow. He won't marry a woman who pursued me." She flounced off in high dudgeon. Val rather liked one of the others, a Miss Wedgewood, who seemed to have both a brain and a sense of humour.

He'd tried to send dreams to Miss Southern, but memories of Lucie kept getting in the way. He gave his erotic imagination wings to fly to her in the night, and if some of his thoughts ended in Miss Southern's dreams instead— well, that would have to suffice. He thought Lucie might be responding in kind, but if so, her sensuality was studded with melancholy and pain.

Since Christmas day, he'd tried to bring up their missions, but Lucie had refused to speak to him. She didn't believe in coincidences any more than he did, but she was ignoring this one as if it didn't matter. That wasn't like her; she'd been an efficient spy at one time.

Val would have to think for both of them. The offices of the succubi and incubi appeared to operate separately, but he had long wondered if this was yet another front, another method for keeping the identities of the master and mistress a secret. If they both knew what was going on, what was their true purpose? Westerly was a lost cause, and even if Theodora Southern began to want to fall in love, she would have to go someplace else to do it.

If the master and mistress knew about Lucie's betrayal, they could have taken care of the matter themselves. If they knew Val had fallen in love with her and refused to betray her in turn, they could have disposed of him, as well. If they didn't know either of the above…then he didn't know what they were about, but these so-called missions gave him an excuse to work with her again.

If Lucie thought she was done with him, she was sorely mistaken. If she'd acted from loyalty, he wanted to know…

to what. Or to whom. If she possessed a sense of shame, he wanted to know. If she still loved him...

He was getting too far ahead of himself, but that was how hope worked. Like a seed, it put out leaves and grew, heedless of the possible drought to come.

He needed an opening, a way to force her to deal with him. He'd never been one to wait for an opportunity, so he set about creating one. He considered his host's feelings and dismissed them. He considered Lucie's feelings, too, and decided the end justified the means. He sidled away to charm Westerly's aunt.

Evening came, with trestle tables and benches set up in the Great Hall. The room was festooned with greenery, and after the wassailing, the visitors would be regaled with food and hot, spiced ale. Val had to admit that due to the combined efforts of Lucie and Theodora, the Christmas celebrations had truly taken on a festive note. If he and Lucie had been on good terms, he might actually have enjoyed himself.

Only Lord Westerly seemed less than pleased. He glowered at Lady Westerly, who was beckoning him over to the massive front doors where he would greet the wassailers.

"She's still trying to paint me as a war hero," he growled to Val. "She has persuaded the villagers, who include a couple of soldiers from my regiment, to add a military note to this year's ritual in honour of my so-called glorious return from battle."

"Humour her," Val said, playing the innocent. "Then send her to live in one of your other houses once this party is over."

"The only way I'll get rid of her is if I marry, thus saddling myself with another ignorant female," Westerly said.

"To think I used to enjoy this tradition." Still scowling, he stalked over to the doors.

Val slid up to Lucie and murmured in French, "*Chérie*, I don't think you're going to like this particular Christmas custom."

Her bosom swelled. "Must you ruin everything for me? Go away."

"Lucie, this is important. I'm trying to warn you, believe it or not, out of the kindness of my heart. Listen to me this once."

The kindness of his heart? No such sentiment existed. She shook her head and moved away. Why shouldn't she enjoy this tradition? Annoyed, she went over to Theodora, who was making a last-minute check of the tables where the revellers would be plied with food and drink once they had driven away the evil spirits.

Lucille certainly didn't like that aspect of the ritual. She didn't believe in evil spirits, but many people, if they knew about the dreams she could send, would see her as one. Could that be what Val meant?

She shivered in the draft, which would become worse once the doors were opened wide. The wassailers had not yet arrived; surely there was time to fetch a shawl. She headed toward the great staircase.

"Where are you going?" Theodora said. "They'll be here any minute."

"For a shawl," Lucille said.

"Very well," Theodora said with a worried look, "but be quick. The whole household must gather here."

Lucille nodded and hurried up the stairs. She had barely reached the top when a shout went up outdoors. "Wassail,

wassail, let us in!" She sped down the corridor to her bedchamber, dug in her belongings for a shawl, wrapped it
about herself to the distant sound of singing, and returned
to the passageway.

The sound of marching boots froze her in her tracks.
Shouts, peremptory and military, paralyzed her. Soldiers
were here!

Stunned, her mind a desperate whirl, she backed into
her room and armed herself. Was it all a plot? Did they all
know who and what she was? Was the house party a trap
and the wassailing a fraud?

Val raced up the stairs. She was playing into his hand
even better than he'd planned. The one and only time he
had seen Lucie lose control was when French soldiers had
marched into the town where she'd then lived as a recent
widow, awaiting her next assignment. He'd held her shaking in his arms until they'd gone, and she'd told him about
the day the soldiers had taken her parents away.

"Ho! Where are you off to?" called the leader of the revellers. "Everyone's to stay here, safe from the evil spirits."

"I *am* an evil spirit," Val called back, and kept on going.
That raised some cheerful shouts. Wassailers loved having
someone real to pursue. He raced into the corridor, tried
Lucie's bedchamber, then tried a few others.

Below, Westerly started his obligatory speech, but it
wouldn't last long.

"Damn it, Lucie, where are you? Let me take you outdoors, away from these fools." Silence greeted him. "Lucie,
they're not real soldiers."

He caught it then, the faintest sigh behind him. She stood

just inside the doorway of another room, a pistol in one hand. At least she wasn't aiming the gun at him this time.

"I know that," she said, but her voice shook. "It's fortunate, because I'm too big to fit in a valise." She'd hidden in a valise on that fateful day when her parents were seized, and one of the servants had made sure no one found her.

Val laughed and plucked the gun from her resistless hand. He grabbed a cloak from behind his door and towed her toward a secondary staircase at the rear of the house.

"After them!" came a roar from below, followed by a horrendous din.

"What's that?" She quavered and then gathered her composure. "I know. Not sticks and swords and bayonets, but pots and pans and such. Theodora told me."

"And gongs and mallets and tongs," Val said, hurrying her down the stairs, through the kitchen and into the night.

It took Lucie far too long to realize that Val had planned this escape. She should have known from the start. "Where are we going?"

"Into the orchard, like good little evil spirits," he said, "and then somewhere warm."

He knew exactly where he was going. He slung the cloak across her shoulders and hustled her through the dark orchard, then took a sharp turn, bringing her across the meadow to the abbey ruins. He strode confidently through the gloom, jumped into the pit Lord Westerly had dug, and swung her down after him.

At one side of the pit, a charcoal brazier glowed. Two wooden chairs sat cozily before it. He set her down in one of them.

She stood again. "You planned this escapade." Fury bubbled up.

"Only the military part," Val said. "The rest—you running about upstairs instead of merely clinging to me—was fortuitous. Incubus's luck."

She huffed. "The brazier? The chairs?"

"Westerly comes here at night. There used to be only one chair." He winked. "I wonder where the second one came from?"

She wanted to punch him. "Not content with playing a stupid trick and depriving me of enjoying a Christmas tradition, now you lie to me." She stomped to the edge of the pit and heaved herself up onto the turf, getting tangled in her skirts.

He leaped up beside her. "I didn't lie." He offered a hand.

She refused it, sorting out her skirts without his help, getting to her feet and brushing herself off. "You took advantage of what you know of me."

"Come now, Lucie. You were a spy for years. It's what spies do."

"We're not spies anymore," she cried. "You're the one who said the war was over."

"It is, my lovely, but I am the same Val." He pulled her into his arms, kissing her hard, nipping at her ear, nuzzling her neck, his hot breath burning her in the chilly night. She melted into his heat, throwing her head back, shivering as his tongue trailed lower and her nipples hardened in response. "I will always do whatever it takes," he whispered.

She wrenched herself away. "Wasn't it enough punishment to torment me for years? To follow me and have me watched and constantly threaten me with death?" She stormed away across the meadow.

He pursued her. "What choice did I have? I couldn't let a French agent continue to operate."

He'd thought she was a French agent? Of course he had. What other conclusion was he to draw? "Then why didn't you kill me and get it over with?"

"Unfortunately, I was in love with you. I couldn't just cold-bloodedly murder you."

She knew he didn't love her anymore, but this hurt. She would never regret falling in love with him.

"You think *you* were in torment?" he said. "What about me, waking up every morning wondering if this was the day I would find that I no longer had a choice? That you had handed some information to the French, and therefore I had to kill you."

"I—I never thought about it that way."

He blew out a breath. "I had nightmares about it, Lucie."

"I'm sorry, Val. I had nightmares, too." She imagined them in their separate beds filled with bad dreams. "For an incubus and a succubus…"

"Ironic, isn't it?" His grin was lopsided and rueful.

She nodded sadly. "But the war is over now. Everything is over. Why can't you leave me be?"

"I *was* leaving you be," he said. "But here we are, each with a ridiculous mission. Don't you want to know why?"

"Not particularly. I'm done with playing games." Thank God they were approaching the house. "But I apologize for causing your nightmares. You are right to despise me."

"I don't despise you," he said cheerfully. "Admittedly, I was disappointed, even broken-hearted at the time, but now I'm all admiration. It's not easy to play both sides. I mightn't have caught you at all if you hadn't avoided me so pointedly, and I never did catch you again."

She opened her mouth to correct him, but they had already arrived at the house. Val rapped on the great front doors.

Too late, she thought. She had never played both sides and wouldn't have even if she'd been as clever as he supposed. How cool and unemotional he was. How practical. He had left heartbreak and war behind as if neither had ever mattered. She couldn't be like that. Everything she'd done, she'd done out of passion or obligation.

She gathered his cloak about herself and her composure with it.

"Oh, thank heavens," Theodora said when a footman opened the doors and let them in. "I was worried about you. They couldn't find you anyplace upstairs."

"We were possessed by evil spirits," Lucille said, laughing as she entered. It was a very good laugh, worthy of a former succubus and spy, not a confused, lovelorn fool.

"But we outwitted them," Val said. "We brought them to Lord Westerly's ruins."

"Where there was a chair for each of them," Lucille said, passing Val's cloak into the footman's hands.

"To sit by the brazier and keep warm," Val said. "And there they stayed."

Everyone laughed and cheered, and Lord Westerly narrowed his eyes at Val, but Theodora served them hot, spiced ale.

So far, so good, thought Val, but not good enough.

But in many ways it was very good indeed. Lucie had spoken to him, and not only that, she had worked with him even though he'd overset her. When they'd entered the house, she'd taken the lead like a professional. This was the Lucie he knew of old.

She hadn't risen to his other bait yet. Yes, he had a certain admiration for cleverness, but he wasn't bereft of honour, nor had he forgiven the past. If he let himself dwell on it, he was as furious as the day she'd let the French spy escape.

Had she truly been working both sides? She hadn't denied it…but had she been on the verge of doing so when he'd knocked on the door?

There were at least two other possibilities. Option One, that she'd been entirely on the French side—but he found that hard to believe, because her excellent work for the English had far outweighed the one mission she'd spoiled for Val. Not only that, why hadn't she returned to France after the war? Why was she still accepting missions from her English spymistress?

Option Two, that she'd been working only for the English, in which case destroying his mission had been a personal matter. Either she'd wanted revenge on him—although for what, he had no notion—or she'd fallen in love with the French agent he'd planned to kill.

He laughed at himself—an incubus fussing because a succubus had been unfaithful. He was thinking like an ordinary, jealous man.

Could he trick her again? He rather doubted it, but that wouldn't stop him from trying.

He settled into getting through the evening. Strange how pleasant the Christmas season could be without one's father making autocratic pronouncements and insisting on being obeyed whilst one's brothers meekly acquiesced, one's mother attempted to keep the peace, and one's sister, who wasn't allowed to play an evil spirit, ran to her bedchamber in tears.

Lord Westerly had got over his ill humour and now put himself out to deal cordially with his dependents. Unlike Val's father, whose haughty manner magnified the distance from the lower classes, Westerly's genuine concern lessened it. Merriment and... Val could think of no word for it but Christmas joy—filled the Great Hall.

An unexpected and entirely unfamiliar contentment came over him. The greenery was truly festive, the plum pudding and mince pies a savoury delight, the hot, spiced ale superb, and when he raised his cup to Lucie in a silent toast, she didn't turn away.

Lucie toasted him in return. Whatever had come between them in the past, they were old friends, and it was Christmastide.

Besides, she wanted him. In bed. Again.

This was one of the great inconveniences of a being a succubus. Not that ordinary women didn't experience lust—of course they did—but it was an integral part of a succubus's being. She invited it when she didn't want it, and when she did, it got in the way of common sense.

Rather like many men, actually. It must be even more difficult for an incubus. She glanced at Val. The redhead was fluttering her eyelashes at him. Even the sensible Miss Wedgewood's lustful thoughts were written on her face. Val rolled his come-and-save-me eyes at Lucie. She huffed.

He'd infuriated her regularly, and in spite of the risks to both their missions, she'd just as regularly ended up in bed with him.

At last the revelry ended, the wassailers left, and everyone retired for the night. She donned her nightclothes, tip-toed down the passageway and tapped on his door...no answer. Was he asleep? Not there? *With another woman*?

How disconcerting. In wartime, she would have taken his seduction of another woman for granted. One did whatever was required. Now the very idea appalled her.

She mustn't allow herself such feelings. He certainly had none for her, and an incubus liked his pleasures. He might have decided to give in and deflower the redhead or that progressively less sensible Wedgewood girl.

He opened the door just enough to peer through. "Oh. It's you." He motioned her in with a jerk of the chin.

Desire slammed into her. How could a simple, insouciant movement of his chin have such an effect?

"Who were you expecting?" She tried to sound cool and unaffected, while her heart thudded and heat pooled in her core.

He shut the door. "That redhead is making a nuisance of herself." His lip curled as if both jealousy and desire were written on her face. How annoying, regardless of whether he saw through her or merely pretended.

"Which would you like tonight, my love?" he drawled. "Shall I be at your mercy, or you at mine?"

She was completely at his mercy, and his eyes showed he knew it. Pride reared up within her. "Neither. I have come to set matters straight." Damn him, it took all her control to remain still. She was well nigh writhing with desire.

His brows rose. "Oh?"

"I have a confession to make," she said. "I am not as clever as you think me."

"My cock is indifferent to cleverness." He pulled her hard

against him, making his member's priorities scintillatingly clear. "It prefers tight, wet heat."

She shivered at the thought of his cock thrusting inside her and her answering throbs. She slid her hands up his chest and twined her arms about his neck. Perhaps she should simply give in and forget about the truth. Their lips touched, their breath mingling. "Is it entirely amoral?" she asked against his mouth, her voice husky.

"Sadly, yes," he said. "Do you mind?" He raised her nightdress slowly to her hips.

"My wet heat is as bad," she said and then blurted, "but I never played both sides."

A pause, barely perceptible, and then he asked, "Shall I play *you* from both sides?" His hands slipped between her legs, one in front and one behind, spreading the evidence of her desire.

She writhed and panted. His sliding, stroking fingers drove her mad... Which was precisely what he wanted, for he whispered, "Which side did you play, love?"

She twisted away but flew at him immediately, tugging his shirt from his breeches. "What does it matter? The war is over now."

He tossed his shirt over his head. "So they say," he said between his teeth, and removed her nightdress. He kissed her hard, an assault to the senses and to her control. As if he owned her. As if she was wholly his. "Darling Lucie, delight of my heart." He cupped one breast and fondled it. "Sweetest Lucie, treasure of my soul." He stroked her nipples until both breasts swelled and tingled and ached. Until her heart and soul swelled, as well...

"Which side?" he asked again. No, not asked—demanded, even as he kissed one breast and then the other, sucked one nipple and the other, back and forth, murmuring, "This side…or that?"

Fire with fire. She undid his buttons and took his member in her hand, arousing him to insanity in return. "Surely that is obvious to a clever man."

He freed himself from her stroking fingers, shucked his breeches, and pushed her onto the bed. "Not if the woman is far cleverer," he growled and kneed her legs apart, nudging her privates with one powerful thigh. "Not if her work for the French is not only invaluable but invisible."

She guided him into her core with a moan of ecstasy. "I already told you," she panted. "I'm not that clever."

He began to move in and out of her with slow, strong strokes. "No? Then what are you, my love, my angel, my soul?"

She kissed him, caring so much it hurt, and told him the truth. "I am a woman who pays her debts."

He let that ride for a while, let them ride one another, and then said, "What else?"

"I am loyal." She answered his thrusts, caressing him with her core, willing him to understand.

"To whom?"

To you, always and forever. But if she said it, he wouldn't believe. She tried to show him with her every move, her every cry of pleasure. "Oh, Val." In the throes of ecstasy, she'd never been able to say anything but his beloved name.

His thrusts quickened. His breathing grew harsh, his voice insistent. "To whom?"

She writhed beneath him. She thrust at him. *To you.* Thrust again. *You, Val. You.*

He was racing to climax and so was she. "To whom?"

Racing hard, racing to win. "Tell me, Lucie. Tell me *now*. To *whom*?"

"To those I love," she said, and soared.

He gave up and let go, burying himself wholly inside her. There would never be any other woman for him, but at least he hadn't said so.

Stalemate. A tie. Damn, she was good.

Those she loved. He rolled off her and pulled himself together. "Did I do something to upset you? Was that when it all went wrong?"

She turned to face him, her brow furrowed. "You upset me often, but it was good for me. A challenge. It's one of the things I love about you, Val."

Love, not loved?

"But you loved someone else more." He sounded to himself like a spoiled, sulky child. He almost rolled over and away, almost covered himself with the blanket and forced himself to sleep. To forget—at least until morning.

"No!" she said. "Whatever gave you that idea?"

"You betrayed me," he said, turning onto his side to face her instead, determined to dig out the truth once and for all. "You told that accursed Frenchman that I was on to him. You let him get away."

"You were going to kill him. I had no choice."

"No choice? It was my job to kill him."

"It was mine to save him," she said. "I pay my debts."

He stared at her. She hadn't been in love with the French spy? "What damned debt?"

"Life," she said. "I owed him mine. He was the servant who saved me when the soldiers took my parents away. Not only that, he took me to his mother, who fostered me, who found me a safer haven in Spain, and who eventually arranged to have me sent to England. I owed them everything."

He rolled onto his back, staring at the shadows on the ceiling. She hadn't been in love with the bastard. He let out a long, ecstatic breath. "Oh, Lucie. Why didn't you tell me?"

"How could I? You would still have killed him."

He thought about it. Shadows shifted in the candlelight and sparks popped in the hearth. "Yes. I would have had no choice."

"I stayed awake all night, trying to find another way out, but there wasn't one. I knew you would hate me forever, but I would have hated myself more if I had let him die."

"Understandable," he said, tilting his head to savour her lush, chestnut hair and violet eyes. "Loyalty, indeed. I apologize for believing anything less of you."

"You needn't," she said. "I could have pretended innocence with anyone else, but not with you. I couldn't even bring myself to meet your eyes. I expected you to kill me, but it didn't matter at the time. I was dead inside anyway."

"I never hated you, Lucie," he confessed at last. "I couldn't, no matter what."

"I tried to make it up to you and to England," she said. "I terrified myself with some of the lunatic missions I took on."

He shivered at the thought that he could so easily have lost her, that he could so easily have never learned the truth. "And I terrified you further by pursuing you constantly. War played havoc with both of us and countless others." He rolled to face her again and pulled her into his arms. "Sweetheart, I've always loved you, and I always will."

"Oh, Val," she said, settling against him, their bodies

entwined, a perfect fit. "I love you, too. We—we belong together. It's always been that way."

"Indeed it has, my love… But it's different now. We don't have to steal our moments of passion. We don't have to play the game anymore." Finally it dawned on him. "Oh, hell. We've been such fools. That's why they sent us here."

Drowsiness had begun to claim her, but she blinked it away. "What?"

"Er…did your spymistress happen to mention anything about marriage?" He tightened his arm about her. "Not Lord Westerly's, but yours."

"Only that…" She came fully awake again at the sparkle in his dark eyes. "She said marriage might relieve my boredom, and that I could choose my own husband this time." Within her, something blossomed and grew. "Oh. What did your spymaster say?"

"Much the same—that marriage might be just what I needed—and of course he was right. He always is."

"So is my spymistress," Lucie said. "Do you think— Do you think they know everything?"

"Maybe," he said, "but I for one don't care. They've achieved their goal. Lucie, could you put up with another husband—a permanent one this time? Let's go away from this tedious party and find a place of our own."

A fountain of joy overflowed inside her. "I should like that, Val, but…"

"But what?" he demanded. "There are no buts. You're mine." Pause. "And I'm yours, and if we value our skins, we'll obey what are clearly orders from above."

"Yes, which means we can't ignore our missions entirely. My spymistress told me that now I could use my magical abilities in peaceful ways. I think the war has damaged Lord Westerly, and a wife—the right wife—is just what he needs. And I have become close to Miss Southern, and I believe we must try to help her, too."

"Very well," Val said. "I'm game if you are. Any more buts?"

She smiled at him. "Yes, my darling. You will have to put up with a few Christmas traditions. You may even learn to enjoy them." She would make certain he did.

"For you, I'll even do that," he said. "But you won't tell our daughter she mayn't play an evil spirit, will you? My father did that to my sister every year."

"Of course not," she said. "We'll even invite your sister for Christmas so she can play one now."

He grinned. "And you won't tell our son he can't climb on the roof to taunt the wassailers?"

She pulled away. "I can't promise that, Val."

He chuckled and drew her close again. "I can't promise it, either. Will you marry me, Lucie?"

"Yes, Val, I will." She wrapped herself around him and let out a deep sigh. Once, long ago, she'd thought of him as her harbour, her not very safe but perfect haven, but it seemed that he'd always been as adrift as she. Now she could be his harbour, too.

On earth peace, good will toward men...

The new beginning she'd longed for had come.

* * * * *

Under a New Year's Enchantment

BARBARA MONAJEM

Many thanks to Kathy Payne for discussing Roman hoards and ruins in Britain with me and for directing me to websites where I spent a great deal of time puttering happily. What better friend than one who gives one cause to putter?

Hampshire, January 1816

*T*hank God there's no mistletoe. Theodora Southern swerved to avoid one of the rowdy guests at the New Year's Eve celebration at Westerly House. She had had enough of the worst Christmas house party ever.

She glanced behind her, but Maynard Buxton, the bane of her existence, was doing his best to coax one of the serving maids into a corner for a kiss without the benefit of mistletoe. Garrick, Lord Westerly, whom she had known since childhood but seen rarely during the war years, had forbidden mistletoe this Christmas, except in the servants' quarters. At first, Theodora had been dismayed—she'd hoped for a kiss from Garrick. But on the other hand, it meant less of having to be on one's guard.

Or it should do, but something was most peculiar about this party. There was always some illicit behaviour at house parties, and this one was a fortnight long, making a few *affaires* unavoidable. But this year Westerly House seemed to sizzle with sensual desire.

Thank heavens the first wassail ritual, in which the villagers made a lot of noise and clamour to rid the great house of evil spirits, was over. The guests, high and low alike, mingled in the great hall. Ladling the wassail—hot, spiced ale—into the cups of the thirsty throng was Theodora's responsibility, but when her friend Lucille had offered her some respite, Theodora had taken advantage of the opportunity to escape.

She hastened upstairs and down the passageway to her bedchamber. Judging by the grunts and moans from one of the rooms, some guests had already left the great hall and were once again indulging their baser instincts. "One would think this was a bawdy house," she muttered. She was unwed and therefore a virgin, so she couldn't risk indulging herself with an *affaire*. Usually, she didn't even wish she could. She had a completely satisfying secret life—daydreams in which a handsome lover pleasured her in multiple ways. She had long ago decided she didn't need a real flesh-and-blood man.

But something about Westerly House this Christmas made her feel as if she did.

Not Maynard Buxton, though.

At the moment, Theodora had better things to think about than lust. She grabbed a cloak from a hook in her bedchamber, slipped downstairs and through a corner of the great hall, and hurried down a deserted corridor. In the gun room, she found and lit a lantern. She pulled the hood of the cloak over her hair and set out through a side door into the cold night.

She crossed the meadow toward the abbey ruins, thankful for the chilly wind, which meant no one would venture outdoors. Ever since she'd learned that Garrick had discovered the remains of a Roman villa under the ruins, she'd been dying to take a look. A proper look, not a glance as one of a gaggle of young ladies whose only interest was in batting their eyelashes at his lordship. She'd thought about asking Garrick for a brief tour, but he'd been in a withdrawn, unfriendly mood since her arrival a week earlier. He'd spent much of his time alone in the ruins and hadn't even tried to hide his annoyance when Lady Westerly had shepherded the ladies up to gawk at him. Very well, then! Since he had returned from the war a complete curmudgeon, Theodora would visit the ruins by herself.

She made her way through the overgrown sanctuary and across a strip of flagstones to the site of the old refectory. A pit the size of a small bedchamber, but only a few feet deep, yawned near the tumbledown stone walls. A makeshift canopy covered it to keep out the rain. She jumped into the pit and made her way carefully around the picks, shovels and trowels, past the brazier and a couple of chairs to where several pillars had been unearthed.

She squatted, aiming the beam of the lantern. She knew what the pillars were. She'd seen a drawing in one of Papa's books. They were the remains of a hypocaust, which—

"What the devil are you doing here?" said a voice of pure rage.

Theodora started violently, dropping the lantern. It hit the ground with a clatter. The glass broke and the candle went out, plunging her into darkness. She uttered a mew of distress.

"It serves you right." It was Lord Westerly speaking, she

realized. "I don't intend to wed you or any of the others, as I trust I've made plain by now."

She stood, disbelieving, staring into the blackness. He thought she'd come out here to trap him!

"Even if I did, this sort of ploy wouldn't work," he said. "I won't be forced into marriage."

Mortification washed through her. As if she would! Much as she liked Garrick, she wasn't one of those ninnies his aunts had invited in the hope that he would fall in love with them. She had come, as she did every year, to help out as a sort of secondary hostess. She'd known Garrick Westerly for years. She'd followed him about when she'd been ten years old to his fourteen. She'd been desperately in love with him at fifteen. She'd prayed for him when he was away at war, and she'd looked forward to seeing him again.

He wasn't the same man. He had returned hard, bitter and frequently rude.

"Let this be a lesson to you, before you ruin all your chances," Lord Westerly drawled. "Gentlemen use some rather unpleasant words to describe the sort of woman who chases a man. I assure you, nobody wants one of *those* as his wife."

Shaking with anger now, Theodora made her way slowly away from his voice and toward the edge of the pit. It was all she could do not to shriek at him. *I already did that, remember? I wouldn't chase you now if you were the last man alive.* Theodora's half boot encountered a trowel. She muffled a curse and bent to pick it up. *And I'll certainly never use you as a daydream lover again.*

She hurled the trowel in the direction from which his voice had come. It met something with a clang—fortunately not Garrick's head, which wasn't made of metal, although evidently he had returned from the war about as intelligent as a lump of lead.

"You disgust me," she said. She picked up her skirts and stormed away without another word.

Garrick Westerly stared into the night. *Dora?* Damnation, what had he just done?

Her footsteps died away. The chilly breeze flapped the canopy overhead, and in the distance a fox yowled. He should go after her and explain. He set out in pursuit, but as he exited the far side of the ruins, the sound of voices stopped him short.

"Miss Southern?" asked a female in sharp, disapproving tones. "Whatever are you doing outdoors at this time of night?"

"It's just as I told you, Mother." That was the vain, red-headed Miss Concord, the most persistent of the female guests at this disaster of a house party. So far she had stalked him in the corridors day and night and even hidden in his bed in the hope of trapping him into marriage. He'd managed to get rid of her each time, but it had been a close-run thing. "She followed Lord Westerly out here. She tried to steal him from me."

"Don't be ridiculous," Theodora said. "I'm not the slightest bit interested in Lord Westerly."

That stung. Theodora wasn't one of the too-young ladies assembled to tempt Garrick into marriage, but he'd known her forever. He liked her, and she'd had a *tendre* for him long ago. The one woman Garrick cared about in the entire household, and look what he'd done. He couldn't have blundered worse if he'd planned it in meticulous detail, copied it in triplicate and passed it to the most inept of his commanding officers for approval.

"Then why are you out here?" Mrs. Concord demanded.

"To see the remains of the Roman villa," Theodora said.

He let out a breath. This was just the sort of thing Theodora Southern would do, but if he made his presence known, it would only serve to confirm their absurd suspicions. Best to pretend he'd never been outdoors at all. He wouldn't have been if his friend Lord Valiant hadn't spotted a lantern bobbing its way toward the ruins. Garrick didn't want anyone messing about up here, so he'd followed straightaway.

"Nonsense," Mrs. Concord said. "No respectable woman would venture out alone at night to look at a bunch of mouldy old stones."

"They're not stones, but pillars of tile for an under-the-floor heating system," Theodora said. Garrick had forgotten that she knew something about the Romans, thanks to her scholarly father.

Mrs. Concord made a rude noise. "Surely you don't expect us to believe that. It's obvious why you were here."

"Everyone knows I decided long ago to marry only for love, so your supposition is absurd," Theodora said. "However, believe what you like. I certainly don't care what you think of me."

Miss Concord muttered something which Garrick didn't catch.

Theodora's voice came clear and crisp on the night breeze. "You are entitled to your opinion, Miss Concord. Now it's your turn to listen to mine. Stop angling for Lord Westerly. He is a rude, unpleasant man who has made it clear that he doesn't wish to marry you or any of the others.

If you ruin your reputation trying to catch him, you will suffer the consequences. He simply doesn't care."

That this was true didn't make it any more palatable from the lips of Dora Southern, who had once been his friend.

Theodora felt the repercussions of her unwise comment almost immediately after returning to the great hall. Mrs. and Miss Concord had arrived a little earlier and set the gossip in motion. Several heads turned to stare at her. Someone pointed at her gown. When Theodora glanced down, she saw to her dismay that she had acquired a sizeable mud stain, no doubt when she'd fumbled her way out of the pit. One young woman giggled behind her fan. Maynard Buxton leered, but since he always did so, that was no surprise.

Her heart was thumping unhappily by the time she reached the wassail bowl, where Lucille Beaulieu ladled spiced ale to a queue of amorous villagers. Something about Lucille made men clamour for her, and it wasn't merely her exotic appearance and violet eyes. Lucille fended them off with aplomb; she didn't seem to mind being leered at.

Theodora minded very much and noticed to her alarm that Maynard Buxton wasn't the only one doing it. The notorious Lord Valiant Oakenhurst, who had spent the war as a spy and assassin, was the only man with kindly rather than curious eyes. No doubt he sympathized, because although the women sighed over his sensual beauty, most of the gentlemen avoided him.

"What are they saying about me?" Theodora whispered in French.

Lucille shrugged in her typically languid way, and the queue of wassailers breathed a collective sigh. "There are two stories going about. Which would you like to hear, the bad or the worse?"

"Don't tease me, Lucille. What are they saying?"

"That you tupped Lord Westerly in the ruins. That was Miss Concord's story."

Theodora felt herself go as red as the holly berries on the table decoration.

"You are now a scarlet woman, both literally and figuratively," Lucille said with a little chuckle.

"It's not funny," Theodora said, as a visitor who had been the soul of politeness in the past glanced knowingly down the bodice of her gown.

Lucille smiled at the man, whose attention fixed immediately on her instead. "Miss Concord is a fool. Does she not realize that if Lord Westerly had really taken your virginity, he would feel obliged to marry you? Her mother shushed her, saying that your only folly was setting your cap at a man who doesn't want you. She said that when you went to the ruins, he spurned you immediately."

Theodora groaned. Either way, the consequences were likely to be unpleasant, but she would almost rather be seen as a wanton than a desperate spinster. She had inherited a small fortune from her godmother and therefore didn't need to wed. After a brief engagement, forced upon her by family members and terminated when her betrothed died in a hunting accident, she had decided to marry only if she fell in love. Her family had accepted this decision, but most others, such as Mrs. Concord, refused to take her seriously. To them, marrying only for love made no sense at all.

"What do you care what these obnoxious Concord people think of you?" Lucille said.

"I don't, but I shouldn't have said so when they accused

me of setting my cap at Lord Westerly. A mistake, but I was already overset, and my tongue took over for my common sense."

"You were upset? Why?"

"Because when Lord Westerly found me at the ruins, he *did* accuse me of trying to trap him into marriage."

"With so many women wishing to marry him, what else is he to think?"

"He should know me better than that! He used to be my friend, but it never even crossed his mind that I might be there for scholarly reasons. It is so *mortifying.*"

Lucille gave a very Gallic shrug. "What he thinks of you is his problem, not yours. Why let it disturb you?"

Theodora's face heated again. "Because once upon a time it was true." At Lucille's inquiring look, she added, "I fell madly in love with him at fifteen—almost sixteen. He was twenty and about to go off to war. I asked him to marry me before he left, and—"

"*You* asked *him* to marry you?"

Theodora nodded shamefacedly. She swallowed her embarrassment. It was ridiculous to mind so much after more than ten years.

"How delightfully forward of you," Lucille said.

Garrick made his way through the throng of villagers, tossing a few jests this way and that, bidding them goodnight one by one. He would be more cordial from now on if it killed him.

If rage could kill, it might well do so. Since his return from the war, he'd found himself infuriated at everyone—at their smug indifference to anything but their petty concerns. At their utter lack of gratitude for the sacrifices made by thousands of soldiers. At their unwillingness to lend even a helping fingertip to those who had survived.

Theodora wasn't like the others. He must apologize to her and would do so when the opportunity arose, but for the moment her indictment of him rang in his head like a death knell: *rude, unpleasant, doesn't care.*

He had returned to Westerly three months after the battle of Waterloo, weary and sick at heart, to take up his inheritance. Instead of the peace and quiet he'd longed for, he'd been plagued by a recurring nightmare and his aunt, Lady Westerly, with her plans for the rest of his life.

She had advised him ceaselessly on how to run the estate. She had planned a Christmas house party against not only his wishes but his express orders. She had invited several eligible young ladies, even though he didn't intend to marry anytime soon, if ever. She'd had the servants put up an ungodly amount of mistletoe in the hope that he would sample the kisses of all the prospective brides.

Strangely enough, he'd remained patient through all the nagging and unwanted advice. He'd even put up with her flagrant disregard for his wishes, but the mistletoe was the last straw.

To hell with civilized behavior, which several years of horrors had taught him was merely a facade. If war had rendered him unfit for polite society, so be it. He ordered all the mistletoe taken down, and when the notorious Lord Valiant Oakenhurst arrived unexpectedly, he asked him to stay. If his aunt's guests didn't like Oakenhurst, they were welcome to leave, and some had done so. If the young women compromised themselves trying to trap Garrick, they would indeed suffer the consequences, just as Theodora had said.

Now that he'd made his point and his aunt had learned her lesson, he must strive to reacquire a civilized front, but how? He seemed to have utterly forsaken the tenets of his upbringing. One needn't be rude to get across a point, but he didn't seem capable of anything else. The mere thought of pretending to be as asinine as his guests aroused his simmering rage.

And yet, good friends were rare; he'd already lost too many to war, and he couldn't afford to lose Dora, as well.

"More women should do the asking," Lucille said.

Theodora stared. She spoke French quite well, but surely she had misunderstood. "I beg your pardon?"

"The prevailing method is so inefficient, with women obliged to wait and hint and wait some more until men get up their courage."

"That's easy for you to say," Theodora said. "Any man you asked would jump at the chance."

Lucille snorted. "Most of them want to bed me, not wed me." She ladled wassail for another amorous guest. "I gather he declined."

"Yes, very kindly, but it was mortifying all the same. I did it out of desperation, because I was so afraid he would be killed. I wanted to be...to be truly his before he went away." She sighed, as the memory of that grief whispered through her. "I accepted his refusal and said farewell with a good grace." She'd cried her heart out afterward, alone in her bed.

"You were very young," Lucille said. "Even if he had agreed, your parents would most likely have refused permission."

"I'm sure you're right." Theodora glared as Garrick threw

his head back and laughed at some villager's jest. How dare he be so carefree after dealing her such an insult? "In any event, it's ancient history now." In which case, why was she so irate? "I've scarcely spoken to him all week because he's been in such a forbidding mood. He should have known I wasn't angling for him."

Smiling at a besotted villager, Lucille ladled more spiced ale.

Theodora gritted her teeth. "He makes me so angry that—that I would like to *kill* him."

Lucille tutted. "No, you would like to bed him."

"What?" Theodora squeaked, thankful no one understood them. "I certainly would not!" Sometimes she found Lucille's conversation a little too scandalous. She didn't know the Frenchwoman well—wasn't sure she'd ever met her in London—but they had friends in common, and when Lucille's coach had broken an axle in front of the vicarage, Theodora's parents had taken her in. Since the axle would take more than a week to fix, Lucille had asked if she might attend the Westerly house party.

Theodora had agreed, thinking Lucille, who had a worldly air, would be an entertaining companion. *Worldly* was an understatement. Lucille wasn't the least bit discomposed by the sensual atmosphere and seemed to expect Theodora—a respectable spinster—to feel the same.

The Frenchwoman rolled her eyes. "You cannot fool me. I have seen the way you look at him."

Perhaps Theodora had looked at Garrick with lustful appreciation the first few days of the party. Why wouldn't she? He still had the dark golden hair and masterful chin of his youth. Once she had recovered from her girlish attachment to him, she'd used him as a daydream lover from time to time.

"As if I would like to strangle him?" she retorted.

"As if you have suffered a severe disappointment," Lucille said.

Theodora couldn't deny that. "Of course I am disappointed. I have known Lord Westerly since he was a boy. He was… He has changed greatly."

"What did you expect? He spent years at war. He risked his life, he killed others and he saw savagery and devastation such as you cannot imagine."

Something in her voice told Theodora that Lucille wasn't speaking only of Garrick. "You were on the Continent during the war, were you not?"

Lucille nodded.

"You have seen some of the same horrors."

Lucille squeezed her eyes shut and opened them again.

"Yet you are polite and charming," Theodora said. "Lord Westerly has been consistently unpleasant since we arrived."

"War affects each person differently," Lucille said. "I try to forget. Lord Westerly is determined not to."

"Yes, but must he shove his opinions down everyone's throats?" She agreed with most of those opinions—such as the need to employ former soldiers—but not his method of delivering them.

"Perhaps he hopes to shock people out of their stolid Englishness," Lucille said.

Theodora certainly understood that. Over the past few years, she had become more and more frustrated with stolidity. With people's refusal to believe anything but what they already understood. With rules and standards of behaviour, which were like fences and hedges one could see over, but through which one must never pass, particularly if one remained unwed. "Perhaps I have misjudged him, but that doesn't mean I want to..."

"You cannot fool me, *chérie*. You want it so badly you cannot even say it."

"It doesn't matter what I want. I'm a respectable virgin."

Lucille indicated the hostile eyes of the ladies and the lustful ones of the men. "Not anymore," she said.

"Forget about apologizing," Lord Valiant Oakenhurst said. He and Garrick were sharing brandy and a quiet moment in the library now that the villagers had gone and the guests had retired. "Take Miss Southern to bed."

This was typical of Valiant, who was what the espionage world called an incubus—a man with unusual powers of seduction and the ability to send erotic dreams. When Garrick had first become embroiled in espionage, he'd thought this ability pure fantasy, but eventually he'd been forced to accept it as the simple truth. It was a useful quality in spies, but in a friend it could become tiresome. For every problem, Valiant suggested a sensual solution.

"Be reasonable, Val. Miss Southern is an innocent."

"All the more reason to seduce her. Like every unmarried lady, she's a volcano of unsatisfied desires, hot and smoking and ready to erupt."

"That's no way to speak of a virtuous woman," Garrick said, but he couldn't suppress a grin at the image Val's words had conjured up. "In any event, it's absurd. Theodora is..."

"Very pretty," Val said.

"Calm, capable and a spinster by choice," retorted Garrick.

"She has a mighty trim figure," Val contributed.

Including a particularly attractive bosom, but Garrick's appreciation of it had nothing to do with Theodora's hypothetical desires. "Many women have good figures. If I've noticed hers, it's your fault for stirring up the entire household—you and that damned succubus."

"That's no way to speak of Lucie," Val said, suddenly not the least bit amused. "She can't help what she is." Lucille Beaulieu, like Val, had been a spy for years. With the two of them in the same house, extraordinarily sensual by nature and most likely sending dreams about like shuttlecocks, it was no wonder the party had become so erotically charged.

"I don't suppose she means any harm, and nor do you, but this party is beginning to resemble an orgy," Garrick said. "Maynard Buxton is chasing—and frequently catching—everything in skirts, and if I'm not mistaken, even my aunt is indulging herself."

Val laughed. "Yes, with Mr. Wedgewood, the only available widower."

"It's unlike her—she's one of the starchiest women I know—and it's all your fault," Garrick said. "If you've been sending dreams to Theodora, stop it."

Val grinned. "Only the first night I was here." Lord Valiant had come to Westerly on a bizarre mission for the Office of the British Incubi—to arouse Theodora's interest in sensuality in order to encourage her to marry. Evidently, one of Theodora's relatives had influence with the incubi and wanted her wed before she became a confirmed old maid. It was damned officious, in Garrick's opinion.

"Since then, Lucie and I have been sparring with dreams," Val said. "Or rather, I've been sparring openly and she's been pretending not to. But it's not like shooting or archery, old fellow. One conjures up erotic images and aims them at the intended recipient, but thoughts don't necessarily go straight to their destination and stop there. They tend to diffuse and affect everyone."

Garrick had seen this effect during the war—it definitely had its uses—but he didn't want it here in his house. "I've no interest in women at the moment, so it's a bloody nuisance."

"Tsk," Val said. "A woman is just what you need." Trust Val to exit on a typical parting shot. "I'm off to a warm bed. Enjoy your cold one."

Very well, I do want it, Theodora admitted to herself a few hours later as she lay in bed. If people were going to call her a loose woman when it wasn't true, why maintain her very proper, very boring innocence? Sometimes she became so frustrated she felt she would burst. She longed to escape the tedium of many aspects of her life, but there was no place to go. However…why not find a lover and have an *affaire?*

Not Garrick, though. Perhaps Lucille was right and the war had affected him badly, but Theodora would never forget how horridly he had treated her tonight. She would have to find another candidate. She considered the other males at the party and dismissed them with a shudder. She ran through a list of attractive men she'd met in London— even a particularly brawny coal-heaver, unfortunately impossible—but her mind kept returning to Garrick. She fell asleep thinking of him.

She woke sweating and aroused, touching herself. She'd been dreaming of Garrick. His hot, sensual eyes devoured her through the thin fabric of her nightdress. Her nipples were hard against the fabric. More than that, they were visible, and he smiled and brushed them with his hand.

Her heart thudded with the power of the dream. This was nothing like the daydreams she'd had of Garrick or other men. Her imagination had never—*could* never conjure up anything so—so overwhelming. So intoxicating. So very *real.*

She reveled in the slick heat of desire. The temptation to satisfy herself by dwelling on the dream was too much to resist....

No, it wasn't. She didn't want to think that way about Garrick anymore. Perhaps she shouldn't have looked at him with lustful eyes. Perhaps she shouldn't have daydreamed about him on and off over the years, but she'd seen no harm in it. She'd rarely seen him during the war years, so he'd become almost a creature of her imagination.

The real Garrick was entirely different, and although much of her anger had drained away, thinking of him now made her sad and sore at heart. Conjuring up another imaginary lover didn't feel right either, so she clasped her hands about her pillow and thought about...oh, onions. There was nothing erotic about onions. Or asparagus pudding.

Bit by bit the throbbing retreated, but it seemed like hours before she fell back to sleep.

Garrick dreaded sleep because of the recurring nightmare in which he failed to save Will Cooper.

Tonight was different. He woke soon after falling asleep, harder than he'd been in ages. His response to attractive women had been lackadaisical at best in recent months. Even the sensual atmosphere permeating the party had hardly affected him, so this arousal was a surprise. Better than a nightmare, but it had probably been brought about by that succubus Theodora had brought into the house. He didn't want to bring himself to orgasm while thinking of Madame Beaulieu. He would much rather imagine kissing Theodora, licking and caressing and thrusting into her....

Confound it, what was the matter with him? He'd never had a lascivious thought about her before this blasted party. He'd always found her very pretty. He'd kissed her once under the mistletoe—at Christmas long ago, when she was fifteen or sixteen years old and had driven over with her parents for the Twelfth Night wassailing, just before he'd gone away to war. She'd been so afraid he would never return that she'd begged him to marry her before he left. He'd tried to reassure her and kissed her goodbye, but as for genuine lust—no. A proper gentleman didn't allow himself to think that way about a respectable lady unless he intended to marry her.

Damn Val for prodding him into thinking otherwise. He couldn't even consider marrying Theodora. War had rendered him entirely unlovable and unsuited to marriage. His unrelenting bad temper made that clear.

No, she wouldn't marry him, but with luck, he might be able to convince her to remain his friend. He punched the pillow and willed himself back to sleep.

And woke again, heart hammering, dripping with sweat even in the chilly winter air. As always in this dream, his boots were stuck in mud which slurped and sucked vilely. By the time he wrenched himself free, Will Cooper was as he'd found him on the battlefield—as aloof and indifferent, as coldly accusing in death as he'd been warm and kindly in life.

The blasted dream, which assailed him almost every night, was another reason he would make a poor husband. Shivering, he fell asleep, but his rest was fitful at best, and he woke late.

Whilst he was dressing, his Aunt Esther, Lady Westerly, burst into his bedchamber. "Did you or did you not dally with Theodora in the ruins last night?" she demanded in her habitual bellow.

His valet tried to withdraw discreetly, but Garrick stayed him with an upraised hand. "My dear aunt, how dare you suggest such a thing of Theodora?"

Aunt Esther glared. "I wouldn't if it weren't for the talk that's going round. I have the greatest respect for Theodora, but where there's smoke there's fire, and—"

Valiant had told him there was gossip going about, but Garrick had dismissed it as irrelevant. "The rumor was invented by those spiteful Concord women—*your* guests, may I remind you."

She pursed her lips. "They wouldn't invent something like that. Mrs. Concord says they caught her scurrying away from the abbey ruins in pitch-darkness!"

"And what, may I ask, were *they* doing outdoors last night?"

"I'm sure it's none of my business if a mother and daughter choose to go for a breath of fresh air. A young woman alone, however…" She tsked. "What were they supposed to think?"

"One, that Theodora went to see the remains of the Roman villa when I wasn't there—which is my fault for being unfit company this past week. Two, that her lantern went out and she had to grope her way back in the dark." He accepted a cravat from his valet. "And three, that no woman in her right mind would dally with a lover in the bloody cold ruins when there's a whole houseful of rooms with fires and warm beds. Most of the others guests have been doing so for days."

Two red spots bloomed on her cheeks. "That must be the influence of your dreadful Lord Valiant. His air of decadence affects everyone he meets. If you had sent him away the day he arrived…"

"But I didn't." Garrick turned to tend to his cravat. "And I won't."

"I'm beginning to think that friend of Theodora's is just as bad. Have you noticed the way every man in the house looks at her? Even the footmen can't keep their eyes where they belong."

"Madame Beaulieu is a beautiful woman." Garrick centered the cravat behind his neck. "And no, I won't send her away, either. Knowing your so-called friends, she's probably the one female guest still willing to speak to Theodora."

"It's Theodora's own fault. She refuses to deny the rumors. She hasn't said a word except that people should mind their own business."

Good for Theodora. "Quite right."

"How she can calmly eat breakfast while people whisper amongst themselves about whether to cut her acquaintance is beyond me."

Garrick knotted the cravat, tucked the ends into his waistcoat and retrieved his signet ring from the dressing table. "Theodora is behaving rationally, as always. Unless you are willing to send the Concord women packing, I suggest you follow her example and ignore the gossip." Pointedly, he turned away, and Aunt Esther stalked out in high dudgeon.

Only five more days, he told himself on the way down to breakfast. After Twelfth Night, the guests would leave. Surely he could manage a little cordiality and convince Theodora to remain his friend.

The atmosphere in the dining room was thick with uneasiness. Theodora sat between Lucille Beaulieu and Lord Valiant, placidly eating coddled eggs. Mrs. Concord and her daughter spoke loudly of their plans for the coming season while the other guests glanced at Garrick, at Theodora, then at nothing in particular—except Maynard Buxton, who quite frankly leered. Garrick gave them a hearty good-day, making a mental note to keep an eye on Buxton, and helped himself from the sideboard. Behind him, Madame Beaulieu was telling Theodora about the Roman aqueduct in Segovia, Spain.

"It sounds wonderful," Theodora said. "I should love to go there one day."

"And so you must, now that the war is over," Madame Beaulieu said. "And Rome! Everyone must see Rome at least once."

"It has been a dream of mine ever since I was a child," Theodora said. "My father went to Rome as a young man, and he still speaks of it."

"And Venice," Lord Valiant said. "That's a fascinating city."

Garrick could have been the one telling Theodora about places he'd visited on the Continent if he hadn't been a fool last night. He poured himself a cup of coffee and took a seat across from her.

She raised her eyes to his. She had remarkably fine grey eyes. He was surprised he hadn't noticed how fine before now. "Good morning, Lord Westerly," she said, her voice even and cool. "I trust you slept well?"

A titter came from the other end of the table. Theodora showed no sign of having heard.

"As well as can be expected," he said.

Valiant snorted, and Madame Beaulieu's lush lips curled into a tiny, feline smile—tantamount to admitting she'd sent sensual images to his sleeping mind.

Garrick refrained from snarling. "And you, Miss Southern?"

"Perfectly well, thank you." Her words felt like darts, and the shadows under those fine eyes betrayed her. She was too well bred to show it, but the gossip had certainly upset her.

"No dreams?" Val said, and Garrick knew an urge to toss him through the window. Lucille Beaulieu's smile grew even more catlike.

Theodora went pink. "None that I care to remember." With sharp slashes of her knife, she cut a slice of ham into strips.

She'd probably had an erotic dream, but if it was about him, she hadn't enjoyed it, and who could blame her? A pity, because despite his good intentions, he liked the idea that there might be some passion buried inside her.

He cleared his throat. "Miss Southern, I'm told you ventured into my excavation of the Roman villa last night."

Theodora shot him an incredulous glance, but how the devil else was he supposed to mend matters? "I'm sorry you felt obliged to go there after dark," he continued. "It doesn't hold a candle to what one finds on the Continent, but please feel free to visit it in daylight anytime you like."

"How very kind," she said frostily and buttered a slice of toast.

"On the contrary. I have been most remiss, or I would have suggested it before. I had forgotten that you share your father's interest in antiquity."

She raised elegant brows. "Had you indeed?"

Didn't she believe him? "Perhaps, after the party is over, you might like to ride here with him someday."

"*He* might," she said flatly. "I saw quite enough last night."

This provoked a flurry of titters from Miss Concord, her mother and one of the other young ladies, and an even more explicit leer from Buxton.

Theodora reddened. "Certainly enough to know that my father will be delighted at your invitation," she elaborated testily, and returned to eating her ham. Val gave Garrick an I-told-you-so look.

Garrick began to be annoyed, but he didn't intend to show it. No displays of temper, no more rudeness and unpleasantness, no more *simply doesn't care*.

Theodora took a bite of toast. Garrick found himself noticing her teeth as she bit, watching her tongue as she licked the butter off her lips.

The idea of bedding her seemed to have fixed itself firmly in his mind. It was a pleasant change from ignoring women altogether, but he was a gentleman, and regardless of what Val said, he intended to apologize to Theodora. Not only that, he couldn't—simply *couldn't* seduce her.

No matter how much he was beginning to wish he could.

The instant she finished her ham and toast, Theodora rose and excused herself. Five minutes later, she left by the kitchen door. While Garrick was safely at breakfast, she would make a quick trip to the ruins and sketch the hypocaust for her father.

How could Garrick *still* think she hoped to trap him into marriage? There was no other conceivable reason to pretend he hadn't been in the ruins last night. She didn't like him at all anymore. How could he have changed so much over the years? During the past week he had embarrassed his aunt and insulted his guests, turning the house party from the usual pleasant, well-run affair into an erotically charged catastrophe.

Not that the erotic aspect of it was his fault—how could it be?—but he shouldn't have permitted Lord Valiant to flirt shamelessly with the prospective brides, creating havoc and causing some guests to leave. As for Garrick himself, he hadn't shown the slightest interest in any of the women. He'd been colder than the highlands of Scotland in January. If he didn't want to marry any of them, why had he invited them?

She crossed the kitchen garden, sketchbook and pencil in hand. The morning was brisk, with frost still on the meadow and a pale cloudless sky. She made up her mind to enjoy the crisp, clear weather and a proper look at the excavation.

She soon arrived at the pit. She carried one of the chairs to where Garrick had unearthed the tile pillars. The Romans had been advanced in so many ways! She'd often thought how lovely it would be to have a house heated from underneath, or at the very least a bathhouse.

What a pity the coals in the brazier had gone cold, because even with gloves on, her fingers were nearly numb.

It didn't make for good sketching. She blew on her fingers to warm them up, sketched a bit and blew on them again.

Footsteps sounded behind her. She started up, whirling. It was Garrick. "Oh. It's only you." She didn't want to see him, but at least it wasn't Mr. Buxton.

"Only me." Garrick carried a bucket of hot coals over to the brazier. "Whom did you expect?"

"No one," she said crossly, as awkwardness rushed in. "It's far too cold to be out here."

"I thought you might need some warmth for your sketching." Garrick emptied the coals into the brazier and set it beside her.

He'd suddenly decided to be thoughtful? She didn't understand him at all! "Thank you," she muttered, sitting again and holding her hands over the blessed heat.

"You're welcome." He shucked his gloves and dug in his pocket. "I thought you might like to sketch these, as well." He held something out.

"It's a comb," she said, relieved to have something so unemotional to discuss.

"Made of bone. It's missing a few teeth, but otherwise intact."

She set her sketchbook aside and took the comb, which had two sets of teeth along a central shaft, with circular designs carved into the ends. One set of teeth was much finer than the other. "How strange to think that a Roman woman once used it."

"I expect the narrower teeth were for nits and lice," he said.

"Ugh." She passed it back.

"And this." In the palm of his hand lay a coin. "Go ahead. Pick it up."

A quiver went through her as her gloved finger touched his palm. How absurd! She reminded herself firmly that he had insulted her both last night and this morning, and read the words engraved on the coin: *IMP CAESAR VESPASIANUS AVG.* "The Emperor Vespasian. Heavens, this coin must be…what, fifteen hundred years old?"

"More than seventeen hundred," Garrick said. "I found others as well, but they're all more recent."

"How astonishing to unearth them after so long. Where were they?"

"In a clay pot under the old abbey walls. Someone's hoard, I suppose, for which he never returned. My favourite piece is a brooch called a fibula, used as a clasp for a soldier's cloak."

A sad note had entered his voice. Perhaps he was thinking of soldiers—past and present—who had never come home. She didn't want to feel sympathy for him—she would far rather not feel anything—but it swelled within her all the same.

She turned the coin over. On the reverse was a woman holding a scepter and a ladle, with the single word *Vesta*… the virgin goddess. Theodora didn't want to think about virginity, either. Hurriedly, she dropped the coin back in his palm. She retrieved her pencil and paper and returned to work on her sketch.

Garrick set the other chair on the opposite side of the brazier. He sat and warmed his hands. "I owe you an apology."

Could this get any more uncomfortable? She flapped a hand, wishing he would go away. "Quite unnecessary, I assure you."

"It *is* necessary," he said. "I was extremely unkind to you last night. As you so rightly put it, I have become a rude and unpleasant person. However, had I known I was speaking to you, I wouldn't have said what I did."

Her pencil stopped moving of its own accord.

"I would never speak so impolitely to you, much less accuse you of chasing me. I thought I was speaking to Miss Concord."

Oh.

"You wore a cloak with a hood, and you and she are much of a size."

True. Theodora bit her lip.

"She is by far the most persistent of the ladies, not only flirting incessantly, but stalking me in the corridors day and night."

A weight slipped off Theodora's shoulders. The cold grip of sorrow let go of her heart.

"She even hid in my bedchamber once, but my valet found her and shooed her away."

Theodora stared, unable to prevent an incredulous smile. "Not truly!"

"Yes, truly," he said. "I wanted to make it clear to her last night that if she compromised herself, she would suffer for it—not I."

Theodora let out a long breath. He didn't think horrid things about her. She needn't be angry or hurt. She began sketching again, and for a while neither of them spoke.

"I'm not usually rude and unpleasant," he said.

Now it was getting embarrassing again. "I beg your pardon. I shouldn't have said that."

"No, you were right. It was a home truth, coming as it did from such an old and valued friend. I realized immediately that I must mend my ways."

"I would never presume to suggest such a thing," she

said. "It's just that..." She stopped right there, since she had implied exactly that.

"It's not that I don't care. I think perhaps I care too deeply, but about other things than what matter to most of our class. I've lost my patience with folly and ignorance and indifference." He shrugged. "You've heard me expressing my opinions, whether or not people want to hear them. I'm not usually so tactless, but this dashed Christmas party got to me."

She'd noticed the new lines on his face, but she hadn't had the chance to truly study him until now. He didn't merely look older than before, but careworn. "What do you mean?"

"I didn't want to hold a party. I've been feeling unsociable and...rather grief-stricken, to tell the truth. I lost many comrades at Waterloo, and I'm still in a sort of mourning. I told my aunt so and said in no uncertain terms that I wasn't in the mood for marriage. She planned this party against my express wishes and didn't let me know until it was too late to cancel. All I could do, short of barring the doors against all comers, was to avoid my guests whenever possible and make it clear that I didn't intend to court anyone."

No wonder he'd been so cold and unfriendly. "That explains the lack of mistletoe, I suppose."

He nodded. "If you'd seen the appalling amount she'd had put up, you would understand why I lost my temper. I envisioned myself being dragged into corners willy-nilly by one rapacious female after another."

A giggle burst from Theodora. "Poor Garrick."

"I thought so," he said ruefully. "Unfortunately, the lack of mistletoe hasn't discouraged Miss Concord. I won't marry her regardless of what happens, but it would be better for all concerned if she didn't bring about her own ruin."

"Definitely," Theodora said. If Garrick were thought to have compromised Miss Concord, it would tarnish his honour as well as hers.

"If I can make it safely through the next five days," Garrick said, "life will return to normal."

"You need someone to keep guard," Theodora said. "A knight in shining armour to frighten the villainess away."

He chuckled. "Do you forgive me, Dora?"

"Of course I do." How sweet of him to use her childhood nickname.

"Good, because I've lost too many friends. I can't afford to lose you, too."

A shrill scream broke the wintry air.

They sprang to their feet. "What the devil was that?" Garrick demanded.

"Help! Save me!" cried a pathetic female voice. Garrick and Theodora exchanged glances.

"It sounds like Miss Concord." Theodora hurried toward the edge of the pit.

"What in God's name is she up to now?" Garrick said.

"It must be another attempt to trap you," Theodora said. "I'll see what's going on."

"While I do what, sneak off into the bushes? Not likely." At the edge of the pit, Garrick took Theodora by the waist and lifted her out. He inhaled her warm, feminine fragrance—and reluctantly set her aside. He leapt up beside her.

"As long as I'm here, she can't accuse you of compromising her," Theodora whispered, hurrying into the old refectory. "You're safe with me." An arrested expression stole over her face—one he remembered well from their childhood. It meant she was up to mischief.

"What?" Garrick said.

"I've just had the most brilliant notion. I'll tell you later."

Another scream cut the air. They emerged into the ruins of the old abbey. Miss Concord's bodice was ripped, showing the curve of one breast above her shift. Hands clasped to her cheeks, she cried, "Save me! Help!"

Garrick strode forward. "For God's sake, Miss Concord, stop screeching."

"Lord Westerly, how *could* you?" Her voice wobbled pathetically. "I am a virtuous woman." Her face puckered. Good Lord, was she about to feign tears?

"Whatever is the matter?" asked Theodora. "Why is your bodice torn?"

"It's—it's—" Her face fell ludicrously at the sight of Theodora. From the meadow came the thud of approaching footsteps. "It was a—a wasp," she blurted.

"A wasp at this season?" Garrick said, as Mrs. Concord and Aunt Esther hurried into the ruins. "That's the most ludicrous story I've ever heard."

"Oh, my dearest girl, whatever is wrong?" Mrs. Concord cried dramatically.

"Garrick, what have you been up to now?" Aunt Esther shouted, and then subsided as she noticed Theodora. Thank God, because a hysterical, bellowing Aunt Esther would alert the entire countryside. "What is going on out here?"

"Miss Concord had a fright," Theodora said, removing her cloak in a hurry. "She didn't say a *wasp,* Lord Westerly. She said a *louse* went down her bodice. Isn't that right, Miss Concord?"

Miss Concord glared at Theodora, but she accepted the cloak and clutched it around herself. "Yes, of course."

"Miss Southern, you must be frozen," Mrs. Concord said. "Lord Westerly, do the gentlemanly thing and give your greatcoat to my daughter so poor Miss Southern can have her cloak back."

Not bloody likely. "Much easier to give it to Miss Southern," Garrick said, wrapping it solicitously about Theodora's shoulders. "Come to think of it, what's Miss Concord doing out here without a cloak of her own?"

Miss Concord went red. Her bright cheeks clashed with her ginger hair. "It must have fallen off," she said in a sulky voice.

"Does it have a faulty clasp?" Theodora asked sweetly, looking small and cuddly in Garrick's greatcoat, which was too large for her in every way.

"We'll bring it if we see it," Garrick said. "Auntie, take Miss Concord and her mama back to the house."

The warm, masculine aroma of Garrick's greatcoat enveloped Theodora. It was all she could do not to close her eyes and breathe him in. Memories rushed into Theodora's mind—of an embrace beneath the mistletoe, of the thrill of his maleness, so close and warm and enticing, and of her very first kiss.

Lucille was entirely right. Theodora did indeed want Garrick in a carnal way. She'd been trying to ignore her improper feelings for him, but it had been a week now, and the attraction had grown stronger each day.

Well then, why shouldn't she have him? Unlike Miss Concord, she didn't want to force him into marriage. She knew he valued her only as a friend. She wasn't a romantic young girl anymore, but a mature, practical, lusty woman. Instead of looking for another prospective lover, why not throw off her shackles here and now—with Garrick! Their carnal relations would be only for their mutual enjoyment— no traps, no caps, no apron strings and no inconvenient emotions.

An enticing prospect, but how would she persuade him to oblige her?

"I'll sketch the hypocaust some other time," she said when they reached the pit again. "My arms are too short for your coat sleeves, and..." She eyed him, doing her best not to laugh out loud. "Oh, Garrick, wasn't that preposterous?"

His mouth twitched. "Thank you for rescuing me, oh, knight in shining armour." He cocked his head to one side, eyes dancing. "What was your brilliant idea?"

"Exactly that!" she said. "I'm going to be your knight. Well, perhaps not quite that. A sort of bodyguard, like a king might have."

"A bodyguard," Garrick repeated.

"Just for five days," she said. "The only way you'll be safe from Miss Concord is if you are never alone."

He raised his brows. "Never?"

"I know you're feeling unsociable and would prefer solitude," she babbled, "but I shan't bother you with conversation. I don't suppose a king chats much with the men who protect him, does he?"

"I haven't the faintest idea." Garrick stared as if she were insane.

She kept on trying anyway. "I'll guard you whenever you need me—day and night." She felt herself blush— how annoying.

His lips twitched again. He said nothing.

She mustn't allow herself to become disconcerted. She'd given him a hint; now she must allow him some time to think about it. "Well, then. It's perfect, isn't it? We've an excellent reason for spending time together. You're interested in antiquities and intend to write a scholarly treatise."

He laughed. "And make a presentation before some learned society, I suppose."

"Yes, the Society of Antiquaries," she said. "My father is a member. I shall provide illustrations for both the treatise and the presentation. That should keep us occupied for five days, don't you think?"

"Undoubtedly." He was frowning slightly, as if puzzling something out. Hopefully, he would come up with the correct answer.

She gathered her sketchbook and pencil, and he pocketed the coin and comb. He lifted her out of the pit again, and she had to stifle a tiny moan of delight. He came up beside her and offered her his arm. His mere proximity sent floods of pleasure through her. Her fingers tingled and itched. It was all she could do not to squeeze his arm. She wished she weren't obliged to wear his coat, because she couldn't get close enough. The mere thought of his arm brushing the side of her breast made her shiver with heat.

All too soon they were at the house. Garrick brought her to his library immediately. Bookshelves lined one wall, and opposite them a row of windows gave onto a lawn, with a prospect of trees and fields. "It faces south, so you'll get the best light all day long," Garrick said.

He had an old drawing table brought down from the attic, and while she sketched, he cleaned and polished the other items. He even had refreshments brought upstairs, to the annoyance of his aunt, who asked what he thought he was about, monopolizing Theodora when she was needed to organize the evening's entertainments.

"You'll have to organize them yourself, Aunt Esther," he said, blithely feeding her some nonsense about the Antiquarian Society.

"Come now, Garrick. You have more important things to do than talk to a bunch of old fogies about even older pieces of rubbish."

"Not in my estimation," Garrick said.

"Such as paying attention to our guests."

"*Your* guests," he said.

"I need Theodora. She always helps with the Christmas festivities."

"And so she has, until now. It's my turn to take advantage of her kind assistance."

"Theodora!" Lady Westerly bellowed. "Explain to Garrick that I *need* you."

"I already did, my lady," Theodora said, which wasn't a lie, as she had foreseen this conversation. "He is adamant that he needs me even more."

It wasn't merely a ruse; Garrick truly *did* need Theodora. It rained that afternoon, a chilly rain only a touch away from snow. He lit branches of candles to improve the light and tended a roaring fire in the grate—anything to keep her with him and content to stay so. With Theodora, he felt so... *Safe* wasn't the word for it. Comforted, perhaps.

True to her word, she didn't talk much, but concentrated on sketching his finds. At first he preferred the blessed silence, but it left his mind free to wander in the wrong direction. He managed to keep his eyes off Theodora's breasts, but it didn't stop him from dwelling on them with something perilously close to anticipation.

There's nothing to anticipate.

He glanced at her far too often, at the dusky ringlets falling over her brow and about her ears, at her hands as she sketched, at her lower lip as she bit it in concentration.

Did she realize what she had more or less offered to him? Surely not; she was an innocent. She would give herself only to her husband, and as she had stated so firmly the other night in the ruins, she would marry only for love.

He went to bed that night congratulating himself on two accomplishments: he had managed to feign cordiality the entire evening, and he had stifled all lascivious thoughts about Theodora.

In his dream, Theodora came to his bed, naked and brimming with mischief. He succumbed to her charms like a starving man. She beckoned him on, inviting him to do anything and everything he'd ever wanted with a woman. He indulged himself shamelessly, feasting on her, taking his time, and was poised to enter her when he woke.

Damnation. Thinking about Theodora this way was just plain wrong—but as with his nightmare, he had no control over his sleeping mind. In this case, he didn't want to— no point lying to himself about that. He threw off the covers to cool himself down. When he finally slept again, the nightmare woke him, stronger than ever.

In the morning, he woke weary but determined to at least control his waking mind. That didn't stop lascivious longings from nudging their way past his good intentions, with the result that he became surly and unpleasant again and stalked away to the library before he swore at one of the guests.

Theodora arrived soon afterward, frowning slightly. He hated that frown. He wanted her to smile at him. No, he didn't; her smiles were dangerous. Garrick ground his teeth and stared at the floor.

"Penny for your thoughts," Theodora said.

Confound it, had his ears gone red? He never blushed, but as a boy, that had been a sure sign of embarrassment. He raised his eyes, trying to keep his expression bland.

Her mouth had dropped open. She had the loveliest, most kissable pink lips....

Stop it.

Theodora averted her eyes, pretending to examine yesterday's sketch of the comb. Whatever he'd been thinking, he didn't want to tell her. To get past the awkward moment, she said, "You keep turning that brooch over and over in your hands. I wondered if you're remembering one of the soldier friends you lost." She risked a glance at him.

He nodded, letting out a long, shaky sigh, and she longed to run to him and fling her arms about him, but that would be improper.

Oh, to hell with propriety—or at least halfway to hell. She set down her pencil, plunked herself next to him on the sofa and put an arm about his shoulders. She squeezed. That was as far as she dared go. She withdrew her arm and folded her hands together.

"Tell me about it," she said. "Unless it's too painful, but…"

"It's because I promised him," Garrick said. "It wasn't my fault that I couldn't keep my promise, but that doesn't seem to have absolved me." He paused. "I'm not making sense, am I? I'd better start from the beginning."

She all but held her breath, hoping he wouldn't change his mind.

"Will Cooper was a common solder in the same regiment as I, and the best of good fellows. I asked him to work for me when the war was over. He had nothing to return to—he'd had a rough upbringing and took the king's shilling as a way to get fed regularly. A respectable job on the estate of a peer was beyond his wildest hopes." Garrick paused, turning the brooch in his hands. "He was killed at Waterloo."

"I'm so sorry." Theodora glanced up at his somber profile. "Which isn't your fault, but for some reason you feel that it is?"

"I've been having nightmares," Garrick said. "Worse since I came home. In the dream, I'm trying to save Will, but I can't get to him in time. It's not at all logical—I was running dispatches whilst he was in the thick of the fighting, so we were nowhere near one another—but my sleeping mind keeps bringing up the sight of Will dead on the battlefield, and although he doesn't move or speak, he seems to be accusing me."

"Poor Garrick."

"It's absurd, because Will wouldn't hold me responsible for his death." He ran his hands through his hair. "I've told myself so over and over, but almost every night I have the same dashed dream."

"No wonder you look so weary," Theodora said.

"I do?"

She nodded. "It's most worrisome."

"It is?"

"And meanwhile your aunt insists on painting you as a hero, which must make you feel even worse."

"It infuriates me," Garrick said. "It's all I can do not to

shout at her and drive all these idiotic people out of my house."

As if conjured by his words, Mrs. Concord appeared in the doorway. They'd had to leave the door open for propriety's sake, which meant any number of nosy people could make a nuisance of themselves.

Mrs. Concord simpered. "Lady Westerly is at her wit's end, dear Miss Southern. She cannot find the spillikins and asked me to fetch you."

Garrick gave a rough bark of laughter. "You're running errands for my aunt?" He rose slowly enough to verge on rudeness, his jaw tight. "I think not."

Mrs. Concord reddened. Hurriedly, Theodora said, "They're in the mahogany cabinet in the drawing room, bottom shelf."

"Lady Westerly asks that you come and find them," Mrs. Concord said.

Garrick ignored her, scraping at some nonexistent flaw on the brooch with his fingernail. "Miss Southern, why not sketch the fibula on a Roman soldier, cloak and all?"

Mrs. Concord stalked away. A second later, Miss Concord stomped past the doorway. She must have been lurking close by.

Theodora took the fibula and returned to her drawing table, determined never to relax her vigilance. Garrick's honour was in her hands.

So was his male member, in her dream that night. Garrick prowled into her bed, all lustful eyes and roaming hands. She lay hot and utterly naked to his gaze, and he toyed with her, licking and suckling. She guided him toward her entrance, eager and straining, but woke just a second too soon.

She slid down under the covers and went over the entire dream again in her head, bringing herself to completion with her hands. Even asparagus pudding couldn't drive such ecstatic remembrance away—so why even bother to try?

Garrick woke with another erection, harder than the previous night. No wonder, since he'd done everything he wished to Theodora in his dream—short of entering her.

Whatever sparring Val and Lucie were doing with dreams, he couldn't help but enjoy the unintended effects. Was Theodora having erotic dreams, too? She showed no sign of it the next day. As the afternoon drew to a close, she put the finishing touches on the drawing of the Roman soldier, stood up and stretched her arms over her head. From his chair across the room he watched, entranced.

"I thought about your dream, Garrick," she said.

For a second he was utterly suspended. Oh. She meant the nightmare. He'd had it again last night, but it had paled compared to the dream about Theodora. Maybe Val was right, and a woman was what Garrick needed.

This woman.

Theodora's eyes widened, and her cheeks flushed the most delicate pink. Perhaps they were both remembering other dreams, delightful ones of the night before. Who was the lover of her dreams?

God help him, he wanted to be that man.

"It's not Will who's accusing you in the dream—it's yourself," Theodora said at her most prosaic. "It's your own disappointment that you couldn't keep your word and lost a friend you cared about."

How typical of her to appreciate his friendship with a

common man and to accept his mourning for what it was. Gratitude and relief swept over him. "You're perfectly correct, but I don't know whether my dreaming mind will accept your conclusion."

"Your dreaming mind ought to find something more pleasant to dwell on." She turned hurriedly away to finger through the coins for another subject to draw. Was she blushing even more?

Intrigued beyond the dictates of common sense, he rose and prowled over to her.

"Oh, there you are, Miss Southern," said a coy voice from the doorway.

Mrs. Concord again. "Get out of here, damn you!" Garrick shouted. "Go away!"

He felt Theodora's astonished eyes on him, but anger thrust aside the chagrin. He stalked toward the obnoxious female. "Out! Now!"

"How dare you?" Mrs. Concord shrieked. "I have never been so insulted in my entire life!" She scurried away. He slammed the door shut behind her.

Theodora gaped from him to the closed door and back again.

"I beg your pardon," he said, shaking with the attempt to control himself. "I'll open it again. Give me a minute to recover."

She nodded, wide-eyed. He took a deep breath. He'd just ruined his chance with Dora—if he'd ever had one to begin with.

"Please forgive me," he said. How pitiful.

"There's nothing to forgive. That woman would try the patience of a saint."

"Yes, but that doesn't excuse my outburst."

She flapped a hand. "You are too hard on yourself, Garrick."

That was kind of her, but he had to regain his self-control. Somehow, he managed to get through the evening. He refused to apologize to Mrs. Concord, despite his aunt's pleas, but he didn't lose his temper again. He succeeded in feigning cordiality and retired thankfully to bed.

His nightmare returned full-force. He tossed and turned, tangling the sheets, alternately sweating and freezing, and woke late in a foul mood. He half expected Theodora to avoid him for fear of more outbursts, but she came to the library after breakfast and sketched as usual.

That afternoon, Miss Concord tried again.

Garrick woke from a nap on the sofa—and a very pleasant dream—to angry hisses. "How dare you?" That was Theodora. "I can't leave for two minutes to use the necessary without you pouncing on him. Get out!"

"I shan't!" retorted Miss Concord. "He doesn't belong to you."

"He doesn't belong to anyone," Theodora said. "He's sleeping, for heaven's sake. Stop ogling him."

Garrick suddenly realized that he had an erection. He was lying on his back, so it must be all too obvious under his breeches. If he were capable of blushing, this would be the moment to do it.

"I wonder if he's dreaming," Miss Concord said. "Everyone in this horrid house is having improper dreams. I heard Mama and Lady Westerly talking about it."

"If he is," Theodora said, "they're not about you. Go away."

Miss Concord huffed. "Why should I?" Garrick didn't

have to open his eyes to see her angry stance, hands on hips, narrowed eyes, versus Theodora's unflappable composure.

"Because he's asleep," Theodora said. "Because you are making a fool of yourself. Because he will never marry you. Do you need any more reasons?"

"Everyone says you're setting your cap at him, and he's too stupid to realize it," Miss Concord panted. "I won't let you steal him from me. He's mine!"

"Over my dead body," Theodora snarled. Miss Concord stomped away, her footsteps receding into the corridor.

Garrick grinned to himself. It seemed Theodora had a temper, too. Foolishly, that made his own lapses less unbearable. He yawned, sat up and swung his legs off the sofa. Their eyes met.

Theodora went very white. "It was only to be expected. They don't understand that we have been friends forever and will always remain so. The talk doesn't bother me in the least."

"It bothers me," he said, disappointed. He'd thought their mutual bursts of temper might bring them closer. "It tarnishes your reputation."

"Pooh! My reputation isn't important. I've set myself up as confirmed spinster who is more than a bit eccentric. Perhaps I should wear a cap. That should convince them."

"God, no! You're much too young and pretty to wear a cap," he said.

She blushed faintly. "It creates a certain impression, you see. I learned the importance of impressions after my betrothed died."

Futile jealousy rose within him. "Ah, yes. You were engaged at one time. My aunt mentioned it in one of her letters."

"Hubert was killed in a hunting accident," she said.

"After a few months of mourning, people began urging me to go about in society and find a replacement, but I didn't want to in the least. My engagement to Hubert taught me that I should marry only for love."

"Yes, I heard you say as much."

"I have made it plain to everyone, and since then people have mostly let me be. The cattiness now is because you're not courting one of the younger ladies. They have no real reason to believe I'm setting my cap at you."

What a pity, he thought.

He must have looked unconvinced, for she huffed. "For heaven's sake, Garrick, you can't be thinking about the time I asked you to marry me." She rolled her eyes. "I was immature, little more than a child, and terrified I would never see you again—that was all. I'm a grown woman now with plans of my own."

"You had the perfect opportunity to flirt with Lord Westerly and you threw it away!" Lucille sounded seriously peeved. "He was aroused. He had probably been having an erotic dream. He was primed and ready for bedding, and you did *nothing!*"

"Except make a complete idiot of myself," Theodora said. They were seated together before the fire that evening. Miss Wedgewood had performed on the harp, and another young lady, Miss Rogers, had sung a ballad. Lucille had brought out her tambour frame and was setting exquisite stitches in a pattern of wildflowers while Theodora embroidered a pair of slippers for her father. "'Over my dead body.' I can't believe I said that!"

Lucille muffled a snort. "You played the role of a knight

in shining armour to perfection—until you neglected to claim your prize."

"Because I was mortified." Theodora sighed. "And yes, I admit it—afraid."

Miss Concord took a seat at the piano. She ran her fingers over the keys and launched into a sequence of very loud chords. She glanced at Garrick with hungry eyes.

"The knight doesn't slay the dragon and then trot merrily away all by himself," Lucille said.

Miss Concord pounded away at the keyboard as if possessed. Perhaps she was—by jealous rage. What if she finally succeeded in sneaking into Garrick's bedchamber? Garrick might say he would let Miss Concord ruin herself, but Theodora feared that when it came down to it, he wouldn't be able to tolerate such a stain on his honour.

"Look at it logically," Lucille said. "When will you ever be in the same house as Lord Westerly again, night after night?"

"Never," Theodora said glumly. "If his aunt invites me, I shan't come."

"So this is your only chance to bed a man you find extremely attractive. What harm is there in a little *affaire?*"

"For one thing, I might get with child," Theodora retorted.

"There are ways of preventing that. I am sure Lord Westerly knows how to be careful. He will wish to share a night of pleasure with you only."

Pleasure. If her nightly dreams were anything like the reality… Longing quivered down Theodora's spine. If only…

"If you want him, you must do something about it," Lucille said. "It was clever of you to say you have plans of your own, but that is not enough."

"Even if I get up my courage," Theodora said, "he will refuse me, because he's a proper gentleman."

"A proper gentleman doesn't swear at his female guests, however provoking they may be," Lucille said. Mrs. Concord had made sure everyone knew about his rudeness.

"She deserved it!" Theodora retorted. She didn't blame him in the least; her own temper was wearing almost as thin. She'd snapped at Miss Concord, and she didn't know how she would bear another night of dreams that made her itch to crawl all over Garrick like a shameless wanton. She had never, ever had such dreams or longings before. It was as if some bizarre erotic magic had taken hold of her.

"I'm sure she did, but it shows that his propriety is a flimsy facade," Lucille said. "He's a man like any other."

"He won't bed a respectable spinster. He would feel obliged to marry me."

"Then you must convince him that you are not in the least respectable, and that your plans do not include him at all."

That evening after dinner, Garrick escaped the billiard room for a glance into the blue saloon, where Theodora sat on a sofa with Lucille. He felt compelled to check up on Theodora, and no matter how much he chided himself, the impulse couldn't be denied.

Plans? What plans? She'd refused to tell him when asked, but what could they be, except to return to the home of her parents, go to London for the Season, visit various relatives and so on, as always? None, but the way she'd thrown her independence in his face unnerved him.

Theodora and Lucille spent too much time with their heads together. Garrick tried to stifle his dismay at Theodora's friendship with such a woman. Madame Beaulieu played the part of a respectable widow reasonably well, considering the handicap—he recognized it as such—of being a succubus, but he didn't trust her to treat Theodora with the propriety an innocent lady deserved. She might influence her in unacceptable ways.

Later, over their brandy, Val said, "You've spent four whole days in Miss Southern's company, and you haven't even found an opportunity to kiss her? Christ, Westerly. Thirty-one years old and you've still got a stick up your arse."

"There were plenty of opportunities," Garrick said. "I chose not to take advantage of them."

Val shook his head disbelievingly. "Look at it this way. Inevitably, someone will awaken Miss Southern's sensual side. Why not you?"

"Because she's a respectable unmarried lady. It's simply not done."

"So you'll leave her to the wiles of…Maynard Buxton, who spends each night in a different bed? That's bloody unchivalrous, when she's doing her damnedest to protect you from the Concord chit."

"Theodora wouldn't give Buxton the time of day," Garrick said, revolted. That couldn't possibly be her plan!

"He's not a bad-looking fellow, and he's been dangling after her forever." Val sighed heavily. "Maybe Lucie and I should leave. The orgylike atmosphere might die down enough to save Miss Southern from Buxton."

"I don't want you to leave. You and Theodora are all that has made this party tolerable."

Val shook his head. "Whatever you like, but you're taking a devil of a risk with Miss Southern's chastity. If she gets desperate enough, she might give in to Buxton, and—"

"No," Garrick said. "She wouldn't."

"Unless, of course, you get to her first."

Garrick ground his teeth. "It would be wrong of me to—"

Val threw up his hands. "Stop thinking in terms of vice and virtue, wrong and right. She's a woman with the usual desires, and you're a man, ditto."

"It's not that simple, Val." One courted a woman, married her and *then* bedded her. It had been made entirely plain to Garrick in the past few days that he wished to wed Theodora, but *she* wanted to marry for love. Even if he could mend his temper, even if the nightmare went away for good, courting her would take time, and he was damned if he wanted to attempt it with all these people milling about.

"It is exactly that simple," Valiant said. "What's the matter with you, Westerly? There she is, ripe for the picking. Don't you want her? Can't you just *taste* her?"

Theodora dreamt of Garrick again. His large, hot hands made a playground of her naked body. He spread her legs and toyed with her privates, and she thrashed and moaned. His member entered her, thick and powerful, and at last she was his. She woke abruptly on an intense crest of pleasure....

It wasn't just lust, but an ecstasy of love for Garrick.

She still loved him. Oh, no! She threw the covers off and leapt out of bed. What a disaster. She didn't want to love him; what was the use of that, since he didn't love her?

So much for no inconvenient emotions.

But she couldn't let that change her plans. She'd had enough of dreams. She wanted the reality. She deserved it. If she could have him only once, so be it.

But it wouldn't happen on its own. She had to do something about it. She had to be bold.

She gave up on sleep. A cup of tea might help her think of a forceful action. She put on her wrapper and slippers and crept down the back stairs to the kitchen.

And there, before the kettle even boiled, she found the answer in full view on the walls.

Mistletoe.

Garrick went to bed in turmoil and woke abruptly, his heart hammering, from a dream where Will Cooper, still dead, told him to get out of the damned muck, sir, while Theodora hovered on the edge of the battlefield, poised to flee.

What if Val was right, and the atmosphere of the house would drive Theodora to desperation? Garrick didn't think she would lose her grip on common sense, but he'd witnessed the bizarre effects caused by incubi and succubi during the war. What if she was in bed with Buxton even now?

No, it wasn't possible. It wasn't even likely. He should know better than to let Val influence him, and he had better warn Theodora to beware of any advice that came from Lucille Beaulieu, but... Oh, damn.

The realization came over him, making him feel like a fool. He'd been suspicious about the presence of both an incubus and a succubus in his house, but he'd been too irritable to follow the suspicion to the obvious conclusion. Val's mission was to awaken Theodora's sensual side, but not by seducing her. Val was therefore trying to persuade Garrick—a decent man—to do it. He'd probably enlisted Lucille to egg Theodora on. To convince her that being a respectable spinster was a bore. They'd sent erotic dreams about to get both of their victims aroused.

He cursed again. The more he thought about it, the more it all made sense. Much as he would like to wring Val's neck, he had to take care of Theodora first. He was bloody well *obliged* to seduce her before some handsome, slippery fellow came along and ruined her or forced her into marriage for her money.

Fuming, he donned shirt, stockings and breeches, and slipped out into the passageway.

Uncharacteristic silence greeted him; he'd become used to random grunts and moans, and the occasional thudding against a wall. Perhaps by now they'd all worn themselves out and fallen asleep. A chill stole over him. What if he was too late?

Christ. He'd fought in numerous battles. He'd risked his life time and again. He'd even ridden perilous missions into France, and now he was fretting like a girl. Disgusted with himself, he went straight to Theodora's room and softly opened the door.

The bed curtains were open. The bed was empty. Dora wasn't there.

Theodora found a stepladder in the butler's pantry and some scissors and twine in the stillroom. She set the ladder against the kitchen wall and hiked her nightdress to climb it. Carefully, she tugged down one sprig of mistletoe from amongst the other greenery.

The servants would be up soon; she had to hurry. She crept quickly down the dark passages that led to the front of the house and soon entered Garrick's library. Now, where to put the mistletoe? She couldn't hang it over either her drawing board or Garrick's desk, because the ceilings were too high and there was nothing to attach it to. The curtain rods? Also too high, even if she stood on a chair. A soft sound made her whirl.

In the doorway, a dark figure loomed. She squeaked, her heart in her throat.

"It's only me." Garrick's eyes lit on the mistletoe. His lips twitched. "Is disobeying my orders part of your plans?"

"Er…"

He plucked the mistletoe from her hand. "It should be. I deserve to be disobeyed." He brandished it over their heads, then bent and swiftly kissed her.

A river of surprise coursed through her. She opened her mouth to say something, anything—and he kissed her again.

"Once again, I've been most remiss." He tossed the mistletoe onto the sofa and pulled her close. His lips brushed hers. "In my attempts to avoid kisses from the other women, I deprived myself of the opportunity to kiss you." He grinned. "And you of the opportunity to kiss me."

She put her arms around his neck and melted into him. *Oh, thank you. Oh, please.* She poured all her passion for him into returning his kiss. She ran her hands up into his hair, cupping his dear head between her hands, opening to his seeking lips and the sensual thrusts of his tongue.

She groaned and squirmed against him. He broke the kiss with a tiny laugh. His eyes gleamed in the candlelight. He went for her mouth again, while his hands roamed downward to rest on her hips and squeeze gently. Tremors ran through her, darts of golden delight shooting straight to her core.

He loosened his touch, his fingertips grazing her waist. "Do you know why this is happening?" he murmured.

Because I'm madly in love with you? No, unfortunately that wasn't it; he'd kissed her first. *Because some ancient goddess of love has granted my prayer?* "Er…"

"It's because of Lord Valiant and Lucille Beaulieu," he said. "I'd better explain before you get carried away."

"What if I want to get carried away?" She tightened her arms around him and rested her cheek against his broad chest. She breathed in his heady male aroma, so much easier to get at when he wore only a shirt. She imagined nuzzling him naked. Hot golden thrills rippled through her.

"Then I expect you shall, but I think you should be properly informed first. You may or may not have noticed the excessive amount of carnal activity at this party."

She raised her head. "How could I help but notice, what with all the vulgar sounds coming from the bedchambers. It, er…"

"Makes you think of a Roman orgy?" he said with a grin.

"Yes." Heat suffused her face. "Not that I know the first thing about orgies, but…" It would never do to confess that she had imagined such events. "What does that have to do with Lord Valiant and Lucille?"

"As spies, their expertise was in seduction."

"Oh." She blinked up at him, fascinated. "Lucille was a *spy?*"

"She hasn't told you yet? You seem to be such bosom bows that I thought she must have."

"Perhaps she thought I would sever our friendship, but of course I shan't. I like her very much." She pondered a moment. Lucille had most likely spied for France, but the war was over, and she could hardly fault a Frenchwoman for defending her own people. "I would never have thought of seduction as a weapon in war. How very courageous of Lucille."

"How so?"

Men seemed to lump women into two categories—the chaste and the unchaste. The chaste showed no interest in sensual matters, and the unchaste were willing to indulge in intimacy with any and every man. It was the most ridiculous notion. "For example, if I were a seductress and spy, and my mission was to seduce...oh, Maynard Buxton, I should have to drum up all my courage and determination to overcome my disgust."

He laughed softly. He pressed a kiss on her hair. "In any event, people like Valiant and Lucille invariably cause a certain amount of turmoil, arousing the desires of everyone around them. I suspect having the two of them in one house has intensified this effect."

"Hence the atmosphere," she said gruffly.

"Day and night," he said. "In those who have no other way of satisfying their desires, it causes erotic dreams."

"Is that so?" she said in a strangled voice.

"Indeed it is." His smile sent chills down her spine. His lips caressed hers. He licked the corner of her mouth, making her knees go weak. "In turn, those dreams increase one's desire to experience the reality."

She tightened her arms around his neck and said simply, "Yes."

"Which may not be a wise idea."

"I should have known," she muttered, stiffening. He was about to kiss her good-night and send her back to bed. To hell with him; she would find someone else. She pushed at him.

He didn't let her go, and his eyes were serious. "I'm merely offering a friendly warning, Dora. You're a respectable woman, and—"

"And you're an honourable man. I know, I know. I'm sick and tired of being respectable, and if you would kindly suspend your honour for a short while, I would appreciate it!"

"You're such a darling." His hand cupped her cheek and stroked the length of her jaw. His lips followed it, trailing kisses from her ear to her chin, then settled once again on her mouth. Desire shimmered through her breasts and belly. The sweet spot between her legs began to throb.

"You have no idea how much I would like to throw honour to the winds right now." His hand brushed her breast, exactly as in her dream. His lips roamed her forehead. He kissed one eyelid and then the other. "But I fear that you don't understand what you're letting yourself in for."

Oh, she understood well enough—pleasure followed by heartbreak. "Garrick, please," she whispered, closing her eyes the better to savour him. "I'm not a baby. I know what men and women do together."

"My delectable Dora." His hot breath tickled her ear. Silver thrills shuddered down her spine. "Let's make certain. Shall I tell you what I'll do?"

"Yes," she whispered, clinging to him now, eyes closed. "Tell me."

He nipped her earlobe, making her squirm. "I shall undress you little by little, until you are naked and wanton and shaking for my touch."

I'm already shaking. She ran her lips along the stubble on his jaw.

"I shall feast my eyes on your glorious breasts." His eyes

caressed her. "I shall suckle them one by one until they ache for more."

Her breasts swelled with anticipation. She pressed as close as possible, rubbing herself against his chest through the thin layers of her nightdress and his shirt, relishing their near-nakedness.

"Your nipples are already hard, just from thinking about it."

"Yes," she murmured, and his hands slid to her behind and pulled her close. His arousal pressed against her.

"I'm hard and swollen, too," he said. "And yes, I *was* dreaming on the sofa yesterday—of what I want to do to you."

She groaned, her knees weak, the blood heavy in her veins, the throbbing insistent in her core. He desired her. He *dreamed* of her.

His lips caressed hers. "Have you dreamt of me?"

"Yes." *Oh, yes—for years and years.*

"Our dreams will come true. I will touch and caress and lick until you writhe with pleasure. I will thrust inside you and stroke you with my cock and watch you shudder and twist and moan. I will—"

Footsteps sounded, along with the clatter of dustpans and buckets.

"Damn," he said. "The servants are already up." He let her go. "Think about it, Dora. Be sure you want to do this. I don't want you pushed into something by circumstances— or by advice from your friend Lucille, which you may regret later."

"I won't regret it," Theodora said, head high as she made for the door. "As I said before, I have plans of my own, and they don't include sitting about being respectable for the rest of my life."

She would never regret bedding him. As for the pain in her heart—she wouldn't regret that either, although it would never, ever go away.

Theodora fetched her tea from the kitchen and went back to bed, but she couldn't sleep. By giving her time to change her mind, Garrick had also given himself time to change *his*. She didn't trust him not to; she had to make sure he didn't. She spent an hour tossing, turning and thinking hard, and came to a conclusion. She rang for a maid to dress her and went down to breakfast. Now that she knew a little more of Lucille's history, she had no compunction whatsoever in enlisting her aid.

Lucille smiled and patted a seat next to her. Lord Valiant was slouched on her other side, sipping ale and looking as decadent as ever. The others were clustered at the far end of the table, avoiding Lord Valiant, as usual.

Lucille leaned close and said, "They are gossiping about you again."

Theodora added sugar to her tea. "Have they nothing better to think about?"

"They are convinced you have found an underhanded way to set your cap at Lord Westerly. They say no woman could possibly be interested in relics from Ancient Rome."

"Good," Theodora said. "That fits in perfectly with my plan."

Lucille's violet eyes twinkled. "Ah, you have devised a plan! Excellent."

"Yes, but I need your help." She whispered in Lucille's ear. "I think I have convinced him to bed me, but he wants me to think about it first. He wants me to be sure I will not regret it."

Lucille rolled her eyes. "*Mon Dieu,* what a very proper gentleman he is."

"I'm afraid he will decide that *he* will regret it."

Lucille tsked. "With most men, I should say that is unlikely, but Lord Westerly is a very hard nut to crack, as they say. What do you wish me to do?"

Theodora leaned close and whispered again.

"But of course," Lucille said. "You may count on me."

Garrick arrived wearing a faint frown, but he served himself eggs and bacon and took a seat next to Theodora. Lucille brought up the topic of the ruins at Pompeii, which she had visited as a friend of the previous excavator, Pietro la Vega.

"It was most fascinating," Lucille said. "Fortunately, Pietro was not shy about showing me some of the more improper finds." She lowered her voice to a stage whisper. "For instance, a brothel."

"Skeletons *in flagrante delicto,*" Lord Valiant said. "What better way to die?"

"Oh!" cried Theodora, doing her best to act as if she'd just had an idea. "What an excellent notion that is!"

"Dying *in flagrante delicto?*" Lucille said loudly. Conversation at the other end of the table came to a halt.

Theodora giggled—convincingly, she hoped. "No. Visiting Pompeii. And Rome and Segovia, and all the other places you mentioned. I've been thinking how much I should love to travel—it's so tedious here in England—and Italy is the perfect place to visit. It will be a real adventure!"

Lady Westerly stared. "My dear Theodora, you must be raving. Are you coming down with a fever?"

Lucille touched her hand to Theodora's forehead. "She feels cool to me."

"I'm not ill," Theodora said. "I'm *exhilarated*." She glanced briefly at Garrick and away again. She didn't like his frown, but she soldiered on anyway. "I'm grateful to Lord Westerly for letting me sketch all the relics he dug up. I never would have thought of it if not for him." She flashed a queasy smile at Garrick and returned immediately to Lucille. "Since you knew Pietro la Vega…" She feigned hesitancy. "Dearest Lucille, would you write me a letter of introduction to the excavators?"

"I should be delighted, *chérie*." Lucille glanced about. "Why is everyone staring at us?"

"I have no idea," Theodora lied.

"Such a plan is preposterous!" Lady Westerly said. "Your parents would never permit it."

"They have nothing to say in the matter." Theodora forced herself not to glance at Garrick again, but his disapproving presence felt like a cloud hovering next to her, ready to drench her with cold rain. Had she taken the wrong tack? It was too late to change that, but she wished it were Garrick who now looked at her with lustful intent, instead of Maynard Buxton.

"Come now, Theodora!" Lady Westerly cried. "This isn't like you at all."

It *was* like her. It was *exactly* like her, but she hadn't had the courage to say so until now. She clenched her fists under the table. "I have a fortune of my own, and I can afford to go anywhere I wish. I've always wanted to travel to the Continent, but the war made it impossible. I'll engage a couple of servants who are accustomed to foreign ways. I'm sure it will be great fun. I shall go to Segovia to see the aqueduct, and to Rome and Pompeii. Perhaps even to Greece!"

"Nonsense. Respectable women don't travel alone," Lady

Westerly said. Another lady tsked, and Mrs. Concord and her daughter looked both appalled and smug.

"Respectable women lead boring lives," Theodora said. "I intend to *enjoy* mine."

"You and Lucille have been planning this all along," Garrick said. He'd spent a tedious day with his male guests at the stables of a neighbour with a string of hunters for sale. There'd been no opportunity to confront Valiant until after dinner, so he'd bearded him in his bedchamber, where he'd gone to fetch a greatcoat. "You sent me to the ruins that night because you knew Theodora was there."

"Lucie wasn't involved in that. We were barely speaking at the time." He shrugged into his coat. "But yes, since then we've been working together."

"You've been herding us like sheep," Garrick said. "I suppose she had a mission to reawaken my interest in women, just as yours was to arouse Theodora."

Valiant grinned. "Ludicrous as it seems, yes."

"And Madame Beaulieu has given her advice as preposterous as what you've given me. Not only that, you colluded to send us both the sort of dreams that make abstinence well-nigh impossible."

Valiant smirked. "You and Miss Southern wouldn't have done a thing if left to your own devices."

"Yes, we would. It would merely have come about in a different way." He hoped. Would bedding her make her fall in love with him? Maybe temporarily, but that wasn't good enough. "Bedding the woman one marries should be a result of love, not a damned inconvenient itch that gets in the way of everything decent people hold dear."

He couldn't bed her and then send her off to the Continent alone. Nor could he send her off to the Continent to be bedded by someone else. He'd seen the gleam in Maynard Buxton's eyes. He didn't like the notion of following Theodora about like a lovesick puppy dog while she sought a true love to replace the one who had died, but what choice would he have?

"We had to fulfill our missions," Val said. "It's not our fault if people in power want you both wed—'for the good of England,' Lucie's spymistress said."

"Bollocks," Garrick said. "All you've done is push Theodora into taking a stand she would never have thought of on her own."

"That's not true," Val said. "She *did* think of it on her own. She asked Lucie to help her, but it was all Theodora's idea."

"And it was her idea to bed me, too, I suppose?"

"Of course. Lucie merely got her to admit it. Lucie wouldn't encourage another woman to bed a man she wasn't attracted to. She was forced into that all too often during the war."

"I suppose so." Garrick didn't doubt that Theodora found him attractive. She was a terrible actress, as she'd proven at breakfast, but her passionate kisses were all too real. But why in God's name would she publicly declare her intention of adopting a dashing style of life, if not to prove to him that she intended to abandon propriety—which made bedding her acceptable—but that she didn't love him? "You've forced us both into immediate action, which we may regret."

"Immediate action is good. Don't tell me you'd rather court her for months than wed her right now, because I won't believe you. Why should you regret it? You're perfect for one another."

Yes—if only he could make Theodora believe it.

* * *

Theodora spent the day submitting to a great deal of scolding from Lady Westerly. It helped get her mind off worrying about whether Garrick would change his mind. At last, the time for the wassail ritual arrived. Twelfth Night was bright and clear, a vast spread of stars over their heads, children from the village catcalling and laughing amongst the apple trees, playing at hide-and-seek while their mothers tried vainly to shush them. From the distance came the chant of the wassailers, who went from orchard to orchard to chase the evil spirits away from the trees. It was nearly midnight, and judging by their singing, they were all a little over-merry.

Everyone from Westerly House came out to watch. Garrick seemed to have got over his disapproval since breakfast, for he sought Theodora out with a smile in his eyes.

"This was my favorite celebration as a child." His voice was deep with reminiscence. "Running about with the village children, making as much noise as I wished…" He tucked her hand in his arm. "This is where I first kissed you. Remember?"

It was also the day she'd asked him to marry her and had been rejected.

"I haven't changed my mind," he said softly. "How about you?"

"Of course not." Perhaps this was his way of telling her that he was willing to bed her, but if she tried to coax him into marriage, his answer would be the same.

"Good," he said. "Here they are—the King and Queen of the Wassail. Come with me to greet them."

"Your aunt is the lady of the house," Theodora said. "She should go with you."

"I don't want her," Garrick said simply. "I want you."

Theodora's heart twisted. For one night and one night only, she was to be his lady. She must make the best of it. She must revel in it now and treasure it forever.

The king and queen—actually the local butcher and one of the barmaids from the Rose and Crown—danced forward, arrayed in outlandish costumes. Garrick bowed low to the wassail royals and Theodora curtsied. Garrick welcomed them to his orchard and escorted them to the oldest of the trees. Servants passed out cups of cider. Everyone joined in the song.

"Here's to thee, old apple tree, we all come to wassail thee!"

While everyone sang through the verses, the king and his attendants picked up the giggling queen. She raised the earthenware cup with sops dipped in cider and presented it to the tree, setting the sodden toast in the crook between two boughs and splashing cider wildly over the branches.

"Bushels full! Sacks full!" Everyone sang to encourage the trees to produce abundantly. Toasts were drunk, sops savoured, hands shaken, and then the clamour began. Everyone had something to drive away the evil spirits— drums, pots, pans—making a dreadful racket. Theodora had brought a gong from home. After a minute or two, Garrick, his gamekeeper and two other men raised their guns and shot a volley into the air. "Huzza, huzza, hip, hip, hurrah!"

The ritual done, everyone drank up, and the wassailers wended their way onward. Village women herded children toward home. The guests hurried back to the great house, Miss Concord with a distinct stomp to her gait. She disappeared into the darkness ahead of the rest.

"There's no one indoors to stop her from hiding in my bedchamber," Garrick said, as he and Theodora took up the rear. "Which means I shall come to yours." He kept her close beside him, his arm brushing her breast through her pelisse. Thrills shivered up and down Theodora's spine.

For a while he didn't speak. Then he said, "You're absolutely determined to travel to the Continent, are you?"

"Absolutely." Her voice wavered. "Do you object?"

"Not at all. It's an excellent notion." Must he sound so pleased? Why couldn't he argue with her, like a pigheaded, uncomprehending man was supposed to do? "There are so many fascinating places to go, sights to see…" His voice drifted into wistfulness. "I've never been to Rome, but I hope to go someday."

"You should." She wished he could come with her, but that would be far too improper even if he wanted to, which he obviously didn't. "Wouldn't you like to see Pompeii, too?"

"Indeed I would."

After that came more waiting in agonizing expectation whilst everyone drank more cider and finally went up to bed. Theodora took a bedroom candle and followed. She paced back and forth before the hearth in her chamber, her heart pattering, her palms sweaty in spite of the chill.

Garrick strode lightly down the dark corridor. He knew his way almost by touch. Either Miss Concord had given up or was hiding in his room; he didn't care which. The house was quieter than it had been lately—no creaking bedsteads, no thumping against walls, no cries and groans. People were too tipsy or too tired to indulge their carnal desires yet again.

Tonight was for him and Theodora—and a ghost. How could one compete with a dead man? Garrick had committed to satisfying Theodora's desires tonight, but would passion encourage her to relegate her dead fiancé to the past where he belonged? She must have loved him dearly to become so adamant about marrying only for love.

He reached her bedchamber and slipped silently inside.

A solitary candle lit the room, casting tall shadows, barely showing Theodora as she paced back and forth. She stopped, wringing her hands. Went to the window and parted the curtains, staring out. Turned again and saw him.

"You've changed your mind," Garrick said.

"No," she said. "No, I can't change my mind." Yet she didn't come to him, merely stood there, clasping and unclasping her hands.

"Of course you can." He went across to the hearth, stirred the banked coals and added some kindling. He plied the bellows.

"No! I want this badly, Garrick."

"You don't look like you want it." He added a couple of split logs to the fire, replaced the fireguard and lit a branch of candles. "There, now I can see you properly."

She paced again, back and forth, back and forth.

"Are you frightened?" he asked.

She whirled. "Of course not," she said scornfully. She returned to the window and parted the curtains again, resting her forehead on the cool window glass.

He moved slowly across the room to her, trying to gauge what was wrong. "Then what is it? It's all right if you don't want to."

Her voice shook. She hugged herself. "No, it's not!"

Garrick put his arms around her, holding her against

him. He kissed her soft, scented hair. "Dora, I am and always will be your friend."

She whimpered, but not in a good way. She didn't want to be his friend? Or being his friend wasn't enough for her? He hoped it wasn't enough.

"Dora, if it's because of your decision never to marry except for love, I understand." Oh, he certainly understood, but his gut ached with the pain of it. "Love, passion and marriage belong together. If you can't do this because you don't love me, it's all right."

"Oh, Garrick…" She straightened and turned within his arms. "I want this more than anything, and I want it with *you*."

"Then what's wrong? I won't hurt you, and I won't get you with child." She said nothing, so he went on. "There's no reason to be ashamed. Society's rules and standards are for our protection, so women won't have children without a husband to support them, and men won't have cuckoos in the nest."

"I understand all that!" she said indignantly.

He stroked her hair. He rocked her back and forth. "So between you and me there's no cause for shame or fear…. Isn't that right?"

"Yes, it's right." Her words were firm, her voice less so. "I don't think doing this with you is wrong. I *know* it's not. How can it be, when I—"

"When you…?"

She'd almost blurted that she loved him. "It doesn't matter."

"Maybe carnal activity isn't right for you," he said.

"Maybe you've simply been influenced by the presence of Lord Valiant and Madame Beaulieu. Maybe—"

"How dare you!" She clenched her fists. "Just because I'm a spinster, just because I'm hedged about by society's rules, doesn't mean I don't have any carnal desires."

"Perhaps not, but—"

She gritted her teeth. "I *am* wanton. I am...I am *brimful* of lusts and desires and cravings."

"Are you sure?" Was his dubious expression real or feigned?

Either way, it made her furious. "Yes, I'm *entirely* sure, damn you, and you're making me so angry I could...I could *kill* you!"

"I'd much rather you bedded me." He beckoned, the corner of his mouth curling up teasingly, and she went to him, still and always the girl who would come when he called. "Let's get on with undressing you. Or you could undress me, if you like."

"Both," she said, unbuttoning his waistcoat with determined fingers. She freed the ends of his cravat and attacked the knot. "Why do you men wear these ridiculous things?" she muttered. "Such as that piece of folly, the *Trône d'Amour.* It's a barrier to love!" At least she could still carry on a civilized conversation. "We women bare our necks and half our bosoms. Don't men *want* to be nuzzled and kissed?"

"This one does," Garrick said. "I never bother with starchy sorts of cravats like the *Trône,* which just goes to show you." She tossed the cravat to the floor and buried her nose in his throat, and he responded with a low, satisfied "Mmm."

She closed her eyes and breathed him in, the exquisite

male scent of him sending heat spiraling down to her toes. "You smell *delicious*."

His lips trailed from her temple to her ear. "As do you, my love." The endearment both thrilled and chilled her. She couldn't afford to think about that right now. She tugged his shirt out from his breeches and pulled it over his head.

"Oh, my." His muscled chest, with a smattering of dark hair. A trail of hair leading to his navel and below, to the bulge that caught and held her eyes.

"Do I meet with your approval?" His murmur shot an arrow of heat straight to her core. He laughed and stripped off her pelisse. He pulled her close and kissed her hard, then more gently, opening her to his teasing, exploring tongue, whilst his fingers began on the hooks and ties of her gown.

How could he so easily do two things at once? It was all she could manage to keep her hands coordinated. All she could do to control the tendency to make embarrassing little sounds. Gently still, he pulled the gown over her head and tossed it onto a chair.

She stood in her shift and stays, eyes closed but in control. He set about unlacing her, and she whimpered.

"That's my girl," he said. "Let it all out, my lovely wanton."

His nimble fingers finished with her stays and dropped them to the floor. She stepped out of them, and a draft travelled up under her shift, washing chilly over her privates. Oh, *God*. She was naked but for her stockings and shift. Desire caressed her in waves.

Now his fingers touched her bare skin, stroking her thighs, cupping her buttocks. He pulled the cheeks of her arse lightly apart, and she whimpered again. He skimmed lightly over her privates, and she moaned. He chuckled in her ear and slipped his fingers between her nether lips. She cried out, panting, and gripped his shoulders, throwing her head back.

"And we've barely begun." He brushed his hand across her nipple through the fabric of her shift, exactly as in her dream. Slowly, tantalizingly, he lifted her shift—past her hips, skimming her waist, over her bosom and away. For a long, long moment there was silence. Was something wrong? She opened her eyes.

He stared at her, such heat in his gaze that an answering heat rose within her, a blush of desire across her breasts and belly and thighs. "You're so beautiful, Dora."

"Oh, Garrick." Whatever happened, she would treasure this night forever.

He cupped one breast in his hand and bent, laving the nipple gently, then sucked it into his mouth.

She almost collapsed from heat. "Oh, no," she breathed. "No, I can't. It's too much."

"No, it's not," he growled. "You can take everything I have to give you. Undress me."

She gathered herself and went for his breeches. She was shaking again, but she managed the buttons. His cock sprang out, long and hard, its musky smell curling into her nostrils. "Touch me," he said.

She didn't need any encouragement; she'd longed for it. She'd done it in her dreams. She took his cock in her hand, marveling at its velvety softness, running her hands up and down and over the head of it, while he hissed and threw back his head, eyes closed—just as she had done when he touched her. His evident pleasure gave her courage. He wanted this, too. That made it right.

All at once he stopped her, shucked his breeches and

swept her off her feet, carrying her to the bed. He nestled under the covers with her and kissed her again, all the while caressing and probing and exploring. She clung to his broad back and quivered and shook and writhed, as he licked and suckled and drove her mad, exactly as he'd promised. He trailed his tongue down her belly and between her nether lips, and licked her sweet spot until she cried out.

"Garrick," she panted. "It's time." At last she would get what she had yearned for so many years ago. "I can't wait any longer. Make me *completely* yours."

"It will be my pleasure." He licked his way up her body and kissed her, the taste of her juices mingling with his. He kneed her legs apart and nudged her with his cock. She spread her legs, arching toward him. He ran the head of his cock up and down her privates, making her throb and throb. He centered it on her core and pushed. She opened for him bit by bit, each probing thrust welcoming him a little more.

He pushed hard, and all at once he was completely inside her. She squeezed, tightening herself around him as she'd done in her dreams.

"Oh, Dora," he said. "You're so tight and hot and perfect." He kissed her hard, and she twisted beneath him. He began to move, and she moved with him, their bodies thrusting and parting in unison. She stretched her arms wide in utter abandon, and he laid his arms on hers and took her hands. They were connected *everywhere*. She flew, lost to everything but pleasure that built and built and built, finally exploding in a shower of gold and silver throbs.

He pulled out of her at the last second, expending his seed on her belly. "Christ," he said, rolling off her and drawing her into his arms. "It took everything I had to pull out in time." His breath came out in a laugh. "I wanted to stay inside you forever."

She sighed. "I wanted that, too." She lay still, too still, in his embrace, and he sensed the tension building within her, minute by minute, when by rights she should drift off to sleep.

She struggled out of his arms and sat up. "Thank you, Garrick. I'll never forget this. I wish…"

"What do you wish, sweetheart?" He took hold of a lock of her hair and twisted it round his finger. She had the most lushly beautiful breasts he'd ever seen. If he didn't stop himself from staring at them, he would be hard again in seconds.

"That I didn't have to leave England." Her voice thickened. "But I don't have a choice."

"Of course you do." He gave in and lowered his mouth to one pebbled nipple. He blew on it, and she shivered. "Nobody's forcing you to go."

"*I'm* forcing me." She heaved a sigh. "I *should* be able to travel. Lucille says I can become a woman of the world. That I shouldn't let the restrictions and prejudices of society hold me back."

He pulled her back under the covers. "It doesn't matter what Lucille says. You have to do what's right for you." He kissed her and licked his way down to her breasts. He roamed her hills and valleys and grew hard again. "Doesn't this feel right?"

"Yes, but it's impossible, and you know it. Garrick, I'm so sick of being caged in by propriety. I want see the world. I want to go to Paris and Venice and Rome, but it will be so—so *lonely* there." She couldn't bear to look at him; from now on, she would have to forget him. She lowered her forehead to his chest.

"Why would you be lonely? I'll be with you."

At first, it didn't register. Slowly, she raised her head. "*You'll* be with me?"

"You can't rescue the fair hero, take him to bed and then abandon him," Garrick said. "You have to take me with you wherever you go."

"Don't be ridiculous." She pushed away again, shoving the coverlet off, flapping her hands at him. "You can't possibly come with me."

He propped his head on one hand, watching her. His other hand slithered across the sheet towards her. "Why not? I want to go to all the same places as you. I have a perfectly good steward to manage my estate and a man of business in London. I can go anywhere I please."

This was utterly absurd, and yet his voice, his face, were so serious, his eyes so intent.

"But you'll have to marry me first," he said.

"No!" She slapped his wandering hand away, and his heart stuttered with dismay. She *had* to marry him, ghostly fiancé or not. There simply was no choice.

"Don't you dare be all respectable and proper and—and start thinking you've compromised me, because you haven't," she said. "I did this of my own free will, with no apron strings attached."

His heart resumed its usual steady beat. "And I'm asking you to marry me of *my* own free will."

"No, you're being chivalrous. Well, I forbid it!"

"I'm not being chivalrous. I'm not the least bit inclined that way, as you should know by now."

"You don't want to marry." She shivered. Her teeth began to chatter. "Y-you said as much earlier."

"I didn't want to marry *yet,*" he said. "I didn't want to marry the ladies my aunt chose for me. I wanted to be alone with my sorrow." He pulled her close again and covered them both.

"Dora, you've brought me back to life. I was angry and unhappy, but I think that's passing at last. I'm so thankful you're here for me to love—and I do love you, with all my heart." He paused, willing her to feel the same. "I hope you can learn to love me."

He loved her? "Are you sure you're not being chivalrous?" Theodora demanded.

"Absolutely sure," he said, rolling on top of her. "I'm being utterly and completely selfish." Just to prove it, he kneed her legs apart and poised himself at her entrance.

She moaned softly. "Oh, Garrick. You really do want to marry me?"

He kissed her. "Indeed I do, more than I've ever wanted anything in my life."

She let out a long, trembling sigh and admitted it. "Of course I love you. How could I not?"

"Er, your erstwhile betrothed," he said. "My ghostly competition."

She gasped, half laughing. "He's no competition. I didn't love him. I didn't dislike him, but my family pushed me into that engagement. I was sad for him when he died, but very, very relieved for me."

"You're sure about that?" Garrick said. "You're not being chivalrous, either?"

She caught her breath, half sob, half laugh. "You're making fun of me again." She thought about telling him how much she loved him, how she'd daydreamed about him for years and years, when a ghastly thought came over her. "Oh, *no*."

"What is it, my love?" He pressed his lips to her hair.

"I'm a dreadful person, and I didn't realize it until now." She hung her head. "I thought I was protecting you, but that wasn't it at all." How could she have fooled herself so completely? All along, she'd wanted him for herself—forever. "I really *was* setting my cap at you, just as everyone said." She shuddered. "Chasing you."

"You naughty girl," he said. "Just the kind I like." He pushed slowly inside her.

"The kind a man doesn't want for a wife, remember?" Sometimes he made her so furious—such as now.

"If it's the right woman chasing him, he does," Garrick said, and began to move.

She gave up and gave in; at last she was wholly his. But no, she wouldn't tell him she'd been in love with him all along. He would never let her hear the last of that.

Afterward, Garrick pulled Theodora into his arms, nestling her on his shoulder. He considered telling her the truth—that she'd been tricked into chasing him, and he'd been forced into embracing life and happiness once more.

No, he wouldn't tell her. She might turn chivalrous again and reject his offer of marriage. The Offices of the Incubi and Succubi wouldn't accept failure; instead, they would persevere and make his life intolerable. He and Theodora were perfect for one another, and he didn't intend to go through this folly again.

After all, it couldn't end better. Val and Lucille would report their completed missions, and someplace in London, an extremely self-satisfied spymaster and spymistress would congratulate one another on the success of their matchmaking scheme. Garrick and Dora would marry and travel wherever their fancy took them.

One day, when they were long past questioning one another, he might, just might, let her know.

* * * * *

Snowbound with the Sheriff

LAURI ROBINSON

To Janet Turley King who so graciously loaned
me her son Chayston's name

Lauri Robinson's chosen genre is Western historical romance. When asked why, she says, 'Because I know I wasn't the only girl who wanted to grow up and marry Little Joe Cartwright.' With a degree in early childhood education, Lauri has spent decades working in the non-profit field and claims once-upon-a-time and happily-ever-after romance novels have always been a form of stress relief. When her husband suggested she write one, she took the challenge and she has loved every minute of the journey.

Lauri lives in rural Minnesota, where she and her husband spend every spare moment with their three grown sons and four grandchildren. She works part-time, volunteers for several organisations and is a die-hard Elvis and NASCAR fan. Her favourite getaway location is the woods of northern Minnesota on the land homesteaded by her great-grandfather.

Chapter One

Southern Montana
December 1886

Spring Valley's Main Street was only a few blocks long and from where he stood outside Svenson's Dry Goods, Chayston Williams could see a mile or more up the road where nothing but a sea of bright white snow left from last week's storm met his searching gaze.

Irritated, Chayston spun around and stomped back inside. Stationed next to the stove, he waited while Lars assisted a customer—ElleDee Scott and her brood of youngsters. When the woman and her children, all boys with black hair who looked just like their father, gathered up their packages, Chayston walked over and opened the windowed door.

"Thank you, Chayston," she said, "Merry Christmas."

He had nothing to be merry about—this year, Christmas was just another day to him—but he responded in kind before closing the door behind her.

"Wire said the stage left Cedar Grove this morning, right after the train arrived," Lars said with his deep brogue.

"I know." Chayston checked the watch clipped to his pants "Which means Riley should have been here an hour ago."

"No telling how bad the road is," Lars offered. "Stage hasn't come through since the storm."

Chayston glanced out the window at the sky again. The nuisance of all this sat like lead in his lungs. He had even less desire to haul the General's new bride all the way out to the ranch in the middle of the night than he did during the day. It was ludicrous—a man ordering a bride. But the General had, and he'd bade Chayston to see her to the ranch.

A Christmas bride, no less. That really gulled him.

"'Course, others have," Lars said. "The Johanssons were in town this morning."

"That's only five miles out." Chayston buttoned up his coat and checked the leather strap securing his holster to his thigh. "I'm going to ride out that way."

"If you're not back—"

"I'll be back," Chayston interrupted. The stage had to be somewhere between Spring Valley and Cedar Grove. The twenty miles through the pass was always slow going, and all this snow could make it treacherous.

That's all he needed—to deliver a body to the General instead of a wife.

In no time, he had his horse saddled and they headed out. Buster was more than happy to leave his stall after being cooped up most of the week and tossed his head as they took off up the street.

Chayston could relate. Had he known the amount of paperwork that went along with being a sheriff, he might not have taken the job. Then again, considering the way he'd been railroaded, he couldn't say no.

Just like last year, when he hadn't had a choice at all. He'd been on the verge of taking a bride, had even bought a ring to give her for Christmas, but it turned out his bride-to-be had been in love with another man. His best friend, Seth Johansson. He sure hadn't seen that coming. Becca hadn't hinted toward it either. But she and Shep were married now. With a baby due shortly.

The road was clear and the five miles to the Johansson place went by relatively swiftly. Chayston hadn't planned on stopping, but Seth saw him coming and ran out to meet him.

"Stage is late," he said.

"No telling how bad the pass is," Seth replied. "No traffic's come through since last week's storm."

Chayston nodded. He and Seth had gone to school together, along with Willis, Becca's older brother. It hadn't been until two years ago, when she started working for Lars, that Chayston noticed Becca had grown up.

"I'll saddle a horse and ride out with you," Seth offered.

"No, thanks," Chayston said, pointing to the thick, dark clouds rising up over the mountain peak. "The weather's going to get bad again. You best stay home."

Seth glanced toward the house, were Becca stood on the front porch. She waved, and Chayston, swallowing the bitterness that still let loose inside him at times, waved back. No one had ever known about the ring he'd purchased, and no one ever would.

Bidding farewell to Seth, he urged Buster into a trot.

The gelding was sure-footed and took to the mountain grade as easily as he'd traveled across the valley. Here, too, the trail was clear, but if snow had let loose it would be higher up, where the road made a long S-curve and the mountainside was the steepest. A couple of miles later, as Chayston rounded the first corner, shouts had him nudging Buster into a faster pace.

Following the road all the way around the curve, he slowed momentarily. Sure enough, a snowslide covered the road a short distance ahead. The stage was there, up to its axels, and Riley was pushing, while his shotgun rider, Coop, was tugging on the reins of the four harnessed horses.

Chayston had yet to pull Buster to a complete stop when a head popped out of the stage window. He couldn't see much except a thick red scarf.

"Yoo-hoo," a female voice shouted. She was waving a hand, too. "You, on the horse. We are in need of assistance."

Obviously.

"Would you mind?" she continued before he had a chance to let his thought loose.

He minded, all right. Minded a lot of things right now.

"Glad to see you, Chayston." Coop dropped the reins and rested both hands on his knees. "We've been at this for hours."

Chayston withheld the fact he'd already surmised as much and dismounted. The snow he trudged through to check the stage horses grew to knee deep. The animals were sound, though tired from trying to pull the rig.

"We're stuck," the woman said.

He let his gaze bypass her to land on Riley, who was sweating despite the temperature that was dropping by the minute.

"Picked up a boulder trying to roll through the snow. It's stuck in the spokes, up against the axel." Riley took off his hat and brushed back his mass of curly gray hair. "Tried to pound it out, but the snow's packed it tight." He nodded toward the snow-free wider section of road where Buster stood. "Gotta get through the snow before I try again. We're too close to the edge here."

The snow piled up against the mountain had forced the stage to travel near the far edge. Chayston noticed, too, the deep ruts behind Riley that disappeared when the road curved again around the hillside.

"Can you help us or not?" a demanding voice asked.

Chayston couldn't remember disliking someone on sight, but it was happening. This woman was making his stomach ferment like a barrel of apples turning into vinegar.

"He'll help, all right," Riley said. "This here is Sheriff Williams." Gesturing toward the window with a thumb, Riley said, "Chayston, meet Miss Violet Ritter from Cincinnati."

Chayston didn't bother glancing her way. He'd already known her name and where she was from.

The snow was thick and hard to plod through. As he passed the window, she asked, "Williams? Are you related to General Williams?"

"He sur—"

"How long have you been pushing this thing?" Chayston asked, interrupting Riley before he could say more.

"Over a mile," Riley answered. "I've been trying to hold up the back end. The front axels are turning, but the back one's locked tight."

Chayston's well-placed kick was a mistake. The snow between the spokes was rock hard and the action shot a sting from his toe to his knee. Riley had been driving the stage for years, and there was no doubt the man had already tried everything within his power to get it rolling again. "You've been holding up the back end?"

"Not much else we could do," Riley answered. "Tried shoveling, but that just gave way for more snow to fall." Lowering his rough and raspy voice, he added, "I didn't dare pound on the axel too hard. If the wheel broke this close to the edge, the stage could tumble right over the edge, taking your papa's new bride with it."

Violet slapped four fingers over her lips to stifle her gasp, but wasn't quite fast enough. The sheriff had turned around. His glare was so dark and cold her very toes shivered. Of course they—her toes—had been shivering all day. If she ever found who'd stolen her boots she'd see them tarred and feathered. Arrested, too.

The door of the stage flung open, almost striking her head still poking out the window. Startled, her shoulder collided with the window frame and then the curtain got caught on her scarf, blinding her. Somewhat frantic, she tugged the material away from her face only to find those menacing eyes glaring at her again, now from inside the stage.

Violet gulped. The General had known her stepfather, so she'd understood he'd be older, but not so much he'd have a son older than her.

"You'll need to get out, ma'am," the sheriff said.

Son or no son, the General was her one chance at happiness, and she wasn't going to give that up. "It's Miss. Miss Violet Ritter," she replied staunchly. "And, no, I don't need to get out."

"Yes, you do."

His tone held so much contempt the smile she forced upon her lips hurt.

"No. I. Don't."

"Yes. You. Do." He gestured toward the snow. "We gotta carry the stage, and need to get rid of as much dead weight as possible."

The stage rocked and the noise overhead said one of the other two men was unloading things off the top. Her things. Violet sat back and crossed her arms. "I am not dead weight."

"Right now, that's exactly what you are."

Mr. Riley's voice floated down from above. "She doesn't need to get out, Chayston."

"Yes, she does," the sheriff answered, never taking his eyes off her.

"No, I don't," she argued. "The driver said so."

Without a hint of warning, he grabbed her by both arms and dragged her off the seat. Violet tried to catch ahold of something, anything, and finally managed to snag the door frame. "Let go of , you beast!"

"Let go of the door," he demanded.

"No." Digging her fingernails into the wood, she held on with all her might.

It wasn't enough. With another completely uncalled-for wrench that pulled her right up against him, he hauled her out of the door. Fearing he might dump her into the snow, Violet grabbed his neck and wrapped her legs around his waist.

He grunted and twisted, trying to dislodge her, but she hooked her ankles and clasped her hands together.

"For Christ's sake, woman," he growled, "let go."

"No."

His hands were tugging at her thighs, which had her cheeks burning, but keeping all ten toes was worth a bit of embarrassment.

"She ain't got any shoes."

That was Mr. Riley, and thankfully his comment caused the sheriff to quit trying to pull her off him.

"No shoes?" he barked like a vicious dog. "Who the hell travels to Montana in December with no shoes?"

Good and flustered, Violet snapped her head back to glare at him. "I had shoes—boots—but someone stole them on the train. Outlaws, no doubt, the sort you should be out chasing instead of accosting women."

His eyes were brown, with tiny bits of gold, and glaring at her with enough loathing she should shrivel up like a raisin. Which was not about to happen. Her body, though, where it was plastered against his, was tingling in ways it shouldn't be.

He let out another very unflattering growl and then grasped her bottom as he spun around.

The shock of that had Violet unhooking her ankles and hands. "Put me down."

"Sure," he said, loosening his hold.

She grabbed his shoulders again. "No!" Her toes were already numb, and she truly feared losing them to frostbite. "Please don't drop me."

He made no comment, nor did he look at her, but his hold turned firm again as he trudged through the snow. A few seconds later he unceremoniously planted her on a horse. Sideways, so both of her legs hung over one side. Thankful for the separation, she grabbed the saddle horn and scooted back. He gave her a nasty look as he gathered the reins and tied them to a tree growing out of the rocks. They did that— trees—grew out of the mountainside. She'd been amazed by it during the long train ride. Other things had amazed her, too. Like waking up and finding her boots and money gone. Her bag was still under the seat as it had been when she'd fallen asleep. But her boots were gone, along with her small cache of funds, leaving her no choice but to board the waiting stage shoeless.

Twisting about in the saddle, Violet pulled up her legs, crossing them to tuck her cold toes beneath her thighs.

Chapter Two

There was a boulder stuck in the spokes, all right, and it took all three of them, Chayston, Riley and Coop, to get it out. Just as it had taken all three of them to get the stage out of the snow. The clouds he'd noticed earlier were now overhead and dropping flakes the size of silver dollars that were going to make the trip to Spring Valley miserable.

As if *she* hadn't already made him miserable enough. Having Miss Violet Ritter plastered to his chest had ignited sensations that had no right being awakened. Not here, not with her.

Chayston bent to pick up another bag, but before tossing it up to Coop on top of the stage, he glanced toward the woman sitting on Buster. She'd tucked her toes up beneath her, and he wondered how she'd stayed balanced in the saddle, perched like that. She had, though, for more than an hour.

No shoes. None. With all this luggage. Absurd. So was the way she sat there like an Indian chief wrapped in her red scarf and the buffalo-hide blanket Coop had provided her out of the stage.

Thoroughly disgusted, Chayston tossed up the last bag and then walked over to pluck her out of the saddle. This time he carried her with one arm behind her back and the other beneath her knees so she couldn't wrap her legs around him. A few steps later, and without a single word, he dumped her onto the floor of the stage and slammed the door.

"Let's go," he ordered. "This storm's only going to get worse."

As predicted, the weather got worse—edging toward a full-fledged blizzard—and a mile or more after they'd passed the Johansson place, Chayston wondered if he should have made everyone hold up there. Storm or not, staying there, with Seth and Becca, was not something he could do, therefore trekking onward to Spring Valley was the only choice. Hopefully they'd make it to town before the heart of the storm hit so he could see Miss Ritter settled in the hotel until he could deliver her to the General.

There, too, things didn't go as he planned. The hotel was owned by Gertrude Guldbrandson, who hated Chayston and wasn't in the mood to grant him any favors. "Surely you have a cot or even the couch in your parlor she can sleep on," Chayston argued without looking toward the adjacent room. Gertrude's daughter, Winifred ,was in there, waving at him. His refusal to court Winifred had put him permanently on Gertrude's bad side, but even if he was ever—ever— stupid enough to consider marriage again, it wouldn't be to Winifred. She was about as pleasant to be around as her mother.

"Absolutely, not," Gertrude replied to his suggestion. "I'm

full up. Every room taken." Planting both hands on her mile-wide hips, the woman continued, "And don't bother asking Ruth Sutton to take her in, either. No one's happy about the General's foolish behavior."

Chayston kept the contempt surging inside from showing on his face. He wasn't impressed his father had ordered a bride, either, but the all-out scorn Gertrude was showering upon Violet was truly uncalled for.

Spinning about, he grabbed Violet by the arm. Coop and Riley hovered at the door, waiting to know where to deposit her luggage so they could get the horses to shelter and find a place to bed down themselves. "Haul her stuff to the sheriff's office," he ordered gruffly.

Once the men exited, he hoisted Violet into his arms again and walked out, Gertrude slamming the door so hard her Christmas wreath hit his back before it landed on the porch.

Violet cringed in his arms. "The sheriff's office? Do you expect me to spend the night in a—a jail?"

"Yes."

"Well, that won't do," she said.

The storm was still picking up momentum. Seeing much of anything was difficult and grew impossible when the wind caught her scarf, flapping it over his face. "Unless you want to start trekking through the snow to the ranch on your own, you don't have a choice because I'm damn sick of carrying you."

She pulled the scarf off his face and grabbed ahold of his neck. "You're a beast."

"Yes, I am," he stated, faltering slightly while searching for the bottom step of the hotel's porch. "Remember that."

Thankfully that shut her up and he trudged forward.

The floor of the sheriff's office felt as cold beneath her stocking feet as if he'd set her down outside in the snow. Violet didn't dare move, though. The place was as black as a hole. A lantern was soon lit and she got her first look around while Chayston told Mr. Riley and Mr. Coop to set her luggage down by the door and go see to the horses. She bid both men goodbye and thanked them for all of their efforts while huddling deeper into her wool coat, wishing she'd taken the buffalo-hide blanket from the stage.

She wasn't a stranger to winter weather—Ohio was known for its snowfalls, but the magnitude of this storm worried her. Or maybe it was the coldness she'd felt at the hotel still freezing her blood. She'd thought by leaving Ohio she'd be escaping spiteful women, but evidently that wasn't to be. Ever since their parents had married—her mother and Eleanor's father—her stepsister had hated her, but Eleanor's wrath was put to shame by Gertrude Guldbrandson's.

If only her boots hadn't been stolen. Then she could have...What? She had nowhere else to go. And a promise was a promise.

Chayston was building a fire in the stove across the room, and with her body craving the heat his had given off—right through his heavy coat every time he'd picked her up— Violet examined the room more closely. Spying a door, she moved a few steps to open it, the light from the lantern on the desk highlighted the area enough for her to make out two cells complete with iron bars. She quickly closed the door.

"Leave it open," he said. "Or you'll be frozen by morning."

She did open the door again, but spun around. "I'm not..." Pausing to search where he could have disappeared to, she noticed another open door and spoke louder, "Not sleeping in a jail cell."

He didn't comment, but light appeared in the other room. She rounded the desk to peer in. It was living quarters of sorts, complete with a kitchen stove, table and chairs, cupboards and a rather comfortable-looking bed. He was busy building another fire in the large cookstove. She took note of other things, too, like the tub sitting upside down in the far corner, and the sink, complete with a water pump. It had been a week since she'd had a bath.

Although she assumed the answer, she asked anyway, "Whose bed is that?"

"Mine," he answered without glancing up.

"Well," she said, moving farther into the room, inspecting things thoroughly, particularly how clean and neat everything appeared, "a gentleman would give a lady his bed while he slept in one of the cells."

"Who said I'm a gentleman?"

"No one, but—"

"I'm not."

"Not what?"

He shut the stove door and turned to face her as he unfolded his legs and rose to once again become a good head taller than her. "A gentleman, nor am I going to give you my bed."

This man was infuriating in so many ways. Tall and broad shouldered, his size was a bit intimidating, but it was his looks that had consumed her mind while traveling the last trek of her journey to Spring Valley. It had led her to wonder if his father looked like him. Not that it would matter, she'd promised her stepfather she'd marry General Williams, and she would.

In fact, she was looking forward to it. Her mother's marriage to her stepfather had been arranged by a family member and they'd come to love one another deeply. She'd witnessed it, and knew it was a real possibility for her, too. Her optimism had gulled Eleanor to no end, making Violet even more determined to make this marriage work and prove Eleanor wrong once and for all.

Chayston hadn't taken off his coat, and was pulling his gloves back on. "It'll warm up in here fast enough," he said. "Make sure to add wood to both stoves."

"Where are you going?"

A determined stride carried him across the room. "Out."

"There's a blizzard out there," she reminded him.

"Yes, there is," he said. "Which makes it even more important I check that everyone's accounted for."

Violet held the other protests that surfaced. She certainly didn't want him thinking she was concerned for his safety, because she wasn't. Furthermore, anyone foolish enough to go back out in that weather wouldn't listen to common sense. She waited until the outer door closed and then re-entered the office area. Grabbing the chair from behind the desk, she rushed toward the stove. There, she opened the door and sat down to hold both feet in front of the flames. They stung at first, chilled to the bone, but soon started to warm.

The heat was wonderful and she could have sat there for hours but didn't. After adding more wood to this stove and the one in the living area, she carted both of her bags into the living space. She then pushed, shoved and tugged all three of her trunks in there as well. Gentleman or not, Chayston would be the one to sleep in the cell.

By then, delightful heat filled the rooms and she removed

her coat and scarf, hanging them on hooks she made available by transferring what must be Chayston's clothes to other hooks. Warmed by the fire beneath it, the coffee-pot on the cookstove started emitting a scent that sent her stomach growling. Finding a good supply of foodstuff, she made a fresh pot of coffee and assembled a pan of bacon and beans, as well as a batch of biscuits. Used to being busy, she set a pan of water to heat and found a broom. The entire area, including the office and the cells, was surprisingly clean, leaving Violet to wonder if Chayston lived by himself. There were no signs of a woman, but there was a shelf with several fancy teacups and a picture of a very pretty woman near the bed.

After sweeping and mopping up the water left behind from the snow that had melted off of Chayston's boots and her luggage, there was little else to do, other than set the table. When that was done, she poured herself a cup of coffee and carried it with her, taking tiny sips as she explored the office. Wanted posters and newspapers were stacked on a shelf in the corner. She glanced through them, wondering more about the sheriff than anything else. Like where had he gone? When would he be back, and how did he get that little scar on his chin?

Eventually, cooking drew her back into the other room. She'd just transferred the biscuits onto a plate when the front door opened. Violet wasn't sure why her heart skipped a beat, other than she'd been thinking about her future, of having a meal on the table when her husband came home. It's what she'd always wanted—a family where everyone loved one another. Up until now that had been impossible. Eleanor had seen to that. Violet had tried, as she'd promised her mother she would from the moment they'd moved into John's house, but Eleanor had never ceased reminding her that they weren't sisters—that John wasn't Violet's father—right up until the moment she'd boarded the train for Montana.

The sound of stomping boots jostled her and she moved to carry the plate to the table, glancing through the open doorway in the process. Chayston was knocking the snow from his pant legs, and she couldn't help but speculate about his father again and hope just a bit that the General was perhaps as handsome as his son. A tiny bit of excitement danced inside her at the thought of sending Eleanor a letter about her new, overly handsome husband. That would be spiteful, but spite was something Eleanor knew well.

Violet went back to the stove to retrieve the pot of bacon and beans. Chayston entered the room, and frowned deeply as he glanced from the table to her then to the table again as he moved toward the hooks where her coat hung. After moving a few other things, he hung up his coat and hat, and her heart fluttered again. His hair was dark brown, cut short and parted on the side. Once again, writing Eleanor came to mind, but this time a small portion of her optimism plummeted. Her stepsister would write back and point out her new husband was probably too old to want more children.

Without a word, Violet filled a cup of coffee for the sheriff and then sat down, placing both hands in her lap while waiting for him to take the opposite chair.

Chayston's nerves were in high gear, ticking beneath his skin as if he was o waiting for robbers to strike. That had only happened once, and they'd captured all three, but he'd never forget the sensation. Keeping his eyes averted, he moved to the sink and washed his hands, slowly. He hadn't expected this. A meal on the table that smelled so good he was practically drooling.

Violet Ritter, without her red scarf and encompassing gray coat, was something of a surprise, too. He'd known she was tiny from carrying her, but he hadn't notice how unique her eyes were—pale blue like the sky early in the morning. He hadn't noticed her hair, either. It was as yellow as dandelions and though it was pinned up, several corkscrews hung around her face and ears. The women of Spring Valley were going to be in an uproar when they spied her, and his father would be the target of their disdain. For years, every widow in town had their sights set on the General, and being overthrown by someone this pretty, and young enough to be his daughter, was sure to set tongues wagging.

Chayston had been in their sights, too, mainly for their daughters. Up until Becca, he'd laughed them off, and after Becca, the thought of marriage left him disgusted.

He flipped the towel over the hook next to the sink and made his way to the table. Despite the wonderful scents filling the air, his stomach had soured. Why did he have to be the sheriff right now? The ruckus following Miss Violet Ritter was going to be worse than what those robbers had caused.

Chapter Three

Chayston spent most of the meal trying not to look at Violet. It hadn't worked very well. His eyes were drawn to her, and a little voice in his head was conjuring up things the men in town might say about her. Like how she was the prettiest thing they'd ever seen and how lucky the General was.

After taking a long swig of coffee—which he almost choked on—he said, "Thank you. That was very good."

Her smile was tiny and the shine of her cheeks appeared bashful. "I'm glad you liked it."

"I did," he answered honestly. "And I didn't expect it."

She frowned and tilted her head to one side slightly. "Expect it?"

"Yes, expect it." He took another swallow of coffee. "You didn't need to cook."

With a little shrug, she said, "I've been cooking for as long as I can remember." After patting her lips with her napkin, she added, "My mother taught me. For the last three years, since she died, I've been in charge of preparing all the meals."

"For who?"

"My stepfather and stepsister, and for the past four months since her marriage, my stepsister's husband."

"In Ohio?" he asked, already knowing her answer. Other than her name and where she was from, the General hadn't said much, just to bring her to the ranch posthaste.

"Yes," she said. "Ohio." Straightening her already stiff-back posture, she added, "I'm sorry I didn't have time to make something for dessert."

"I'm used to faring for myself, so I don't have desserts very often." Chayston met her gaze again. "Not like the General. But he has a cook."

"He does?"

Why he wanted her to know that wasn't clear, yet he said, "Yes, a fine one."

She nodded, never looking his way. After a few quiet seconds had ticked by, she asked, "Who is the woman in the picture?"

Busy contemplating how his father might have found her, it was a moment before her question registered. "What picture?"

"The one on the shelf with the teacups."

He glanced across the room. "That would be Roy's wife," he said. "How'd you and the General start writing?"

"We didn't write," she said. "Who's Roy?"

"The sheriff," he answered. "Did you send telegrams to each other?"

She frowned and shook her head. "No, the General and my stepfather wrote to each other. I thought you were the sheriff."

"Who's your father?"

The tiniest little laugh sounded as she set her chin in

her palm and gazed across the table. "Can we stick to one subject?"

More curious than he should be, Chayston answered, "Sure. Who's your father?"

She let out a small sigh, but answered, "John Lassiter."

Recognition surprised him. "Lieutenant John Lassiter?"

Her eyes took on a shimmering brightness and a full smile found her lips. "Yes. Did you know him? He and the General were stationed together."

"They were, and yes, I knew him. Before the General left the army for ranching, we all lived at the fort. The General and John were close friends." Chayston had to grin, remembering how John had given him a knife one year for Christmas—back when he looked forward to the holiday. "How is John?"

Her smile faded, so did the gleam in her eye. "He died two—no three weeks ago."

Remorse washed over Chayston. Unable to come up with anything better, he said, "I'm sorry."

She sniffled and rubbed at her nose. "I am too."

At a loss, Chayston picked up his coffee and swallowed the last—now very cold—mouthful.

"So," she said, "how can both you and Roy be the sheriff?"

"I'm just filling in for Roy Galveston. He captured a couple of bandits, robbers who'd hit a few trains and banks, last fall, and took them down to Texas where they were wanted for their crimes. He'll be back by the end of January." Chayston hoped that was still the plan. He'd had enough of being a lawman and was ready to get back to ranching. The General had insisted he wouldn't be needed at the ranch during the slower winter months and could fill in while Roy went south, and the town council agreed, which was usual. No one ever defied the General. His mother said he'd be like that, too, someday. She'd been right, at least when it came to the stubborn and bullheaded traits.

A shiver rippled his spine, like a goose walking over his grave—another of his mother's sayings—and Chayston let his gaze settle on Violet, who was looking at him just as seriously.

Then, pushing away from the table, he rose.

She jumped to her feet too. "Could we make a deal?"

Another shiver almost paralyzed him. "What sort of deal?"

"I'll clean up." She gestured toward the table and then the stove. "And cook all the meals until the weather lets up enough for me to travel to the General's ranch, if you let me sleep in here instead of in a jail cell."

He'd already figured he'd be the one sleeping in the cell, even before learning she was John Lassiter's daughter, but there was worry in her eyes and for some inexplicable reason, he wanted to tease it away. "You'll make desserts?"

Watching the smile form on her lips was like watching a sunrise.

"Yes," she said. "I'll make desserts."

Chayston tried to swallow the thickness forming in his throat but couldn't. He should go back out in the snow, find someplace else for her to stay. She was far too pretty, too... feminine to stay here with him. Alone.

Having already carried her plate to the sink, she turned and—still smiling, still looking pretty and feminine and sweet—said, "I do have one other small request."

He gulped. "What's that?"

"The use of your bathtub," she said. "It's been over a week, and I—"

Spinning around did not stop the vision of her sitting in water up to her chin from leaping into his head. "I'll see you in the morning, then," Chayston said firmly, closing the door separating the office from the living quarters with a solid thud. Living at the ranch would be hard, but tonight, being snowed in with a death-defying blizzard stopping any chances of leaving, was going to be hell.

He struggled for a breath of air, but his body was recalling how she'd plastered those sweet little curves of hers against him. Things had spiked then and were now throbbing. Painfully.

Honeysuckle and spring. That's what she smelled like, and it was damn near impossible not to envision her all warm and slick, stepping out of the bathwater.

Disgusted by his thoughts, Chayston crossed the room to add a log to the stove, only to be thwarted again. Violet had stoked the fire there as well, and he wondered how she'd found the time to accomplish everything she had in the short time he'd been gone. The wind was so strong he'd barely made it up and down the boardwalks on both sides of Main Street. Everything had been locked up tight; folks had hunkered down to wait out a storm that could last several days.

Days.

Aw, hell.

Lifting the lamp off the desk, Chayston made his way into the narrow room holding two cells. Even with the stove going, the area was cold. Nothing like the living quarters. 'Course, it never seemed quite as welcoming as it had tonight, all toasty warm and smelling of fresh-baked biscuits.

John Lassiter's daughter—if that didn't beat all. An eerie sensation tickled his spine, and Chayston turned back around. That couldn't be. He crossed the room and waited until she bid entrance before he pushed the door open. "How old are you?"

At the sink, she continued washing dishes, looking his way over one shoulder. "Nineteen. Why?"

"I remember John talking about his daughter, but—" He stopped. John had claimed his daughter was close to Chayston's age. He'd been about ten then, twenty-five now.

"That would be my stepsister, Eleanor. John's first wife, Eleanor's mother, died shortly after he returned to Ohio. A few years later, when I was eight, he and my mother married."

"Eleanor. That does sound familiar." And made more sense.

"Did you ever meet her?" she asked.

"No."

She grinned, but it was more of a grimace, and turned back to the dishes.

"What's that look for?" he asked.

"What look?"

"The one that makes me glad I've never met Eleanor," he replied.

Her laugh was musical, and although he knew he shouldn't, he crossed the room.

"I'm right, aren't I?" he asked.

"Eleanor is Eleanor," she answered.

"The two of you don't always see eye to eye?"

With a groan, she answered, "The two of us have never seen eye to eye." She glanced at the towel he picked up. "I can do this. You don't need to help."

"I normally do it," he said. "And the cooking. It comes with the job."

"One you don't like," she said.

"How would you know that?"

She bowed her head slightly. "The same way you figured out how I feel about Eleanor, I suspect."

He let that settle for a moment, or tried to. Trouble was, his mind had moved on. Thoughts of kissing her now danced like fireflies in his head. He'd bet his last coin her lips were softer than flower petals and sweeter than maple syrup. Cutting off that thought, he answered, "I suspect so. It's not a bad job, though, as far as jobs go."

Lifting one finely shaped brow, she nodded. "And Eleanor's not a bad person. She just didn't like sharing her father, and I can't really blame her for that."

"Are you trying to convince me or yourself?"

"You tell me first." When he frowned, she added, "Were you trying to convince me it's not a bad job, as far as jobs go?"

He dried the last cup, but rather than putting it in the cupboard, he filled it with coffee. It was a little like playing with fire, being this close to her, and that was rather enticing. "A little of both, I guess," he said after taking a drink. "I miss ranching. One of those things you don't know how much you like it until it's gone."

"I know exactly what you mean." She turned around and leaned her backside against the counter. "I don't remember my father, he died when I was little, but we lived with my grandmother then, and I remember her. We were a family."

He sensed melancholy and asked, "Were?"

She nodded. "Gran became ill. My father and John were

cousins, and Gran arranged for my mother and John to marry so we wouldn't be alone after she died."

"And now your mother and John are both dead, too."

She nodded again. "Yes, they are." Letting out a sigh, she said, "John was ill for the last year, but I still wasn't ready to lose him."

"We never are," he said honestly. "Never really ready for most things life throws at us."

"Isn't that the truth," Violet said, blinking at the tears the conversation had caused.

"Are you all right?"

She nodded, but then, unable to stop herself, shook her head. However, the next moment, when his arms pulled her close, sadness was not what overcame her.

Chapter Four

Violet, heart racing, sprang free from Chayston's arms. Fighting for every breath, she spun around. *Tramp. Jezebel.* Eleanor's screeches invaded her mind. It wasn't true— she'd never encouraged Eleanor's husband in any way—but her stepsister had insisted she had. And Eleanor hadn't stopped there, she'd spread rumors throughout town, and men had come calling, hoping to sample what Violet supposedly gave away freely.

Gaining control of her breathing, Violet lifted her chin, but a lump had formed in her throat. The sensations Chayston ignited inside her were the exact opposite of the ones she'd experienced when other men had touched her. Such feelings should only come about with a husband.

"I'd like to take a bath now," she said without turning to face him. "Please leave."

"I'll get the tub for you," he said. "Don't bother trying to dump it. Not with the wind blowing like it is."

She moved to the sink, to pump water into a kettle, and when the door to the office closed, a flock of butterflies let loose in her stomach at the thought of his being just in the other room.

It wasn't proper, taking a bath with a man so close. Staying with one wasn't, either, but what choice did she have? *Not* to think about him. That was a choice she had. She would soon be marrying his father and John had promised her the General was a gentleman. One that would treat her well, and grow to love her. Her stepfather had loved her, just as she'd loved him. He'd known, too, how hard she'd tried to please Eleanor, and he'd stood up for her, against Eleanor's lies and assaults, and the men who'd come calling. Not once in all the years since she and her mother had gone to live with John had he let her down, and Violet wouldn't let him down, either.

Especially not this time.

By the time several kettles of water had been heated, she'd regained control, and soon lowered herself into the warm bath to soothe away the last of her frustration and soak sore muscles left from the many days of sitting on coal dust–covered train benches and hard stagecoach seats. She washed her hair, too, and when her head started bobbing, she regretted the fact she had to climb out of the water. The idea of sleeping in a nightgown rather than the same clothes she'd worn for the better part of a week had her toweling dry and tugging on her nightdress in record time. Knowing a man was on the other side of the door may also have had something to do with her swiftness.

Chayston was still on her mind. How his touch had turned her feverish and left her yearning for more. Even if she'd had a mind to blame that on Eleanor, she couldn't. One isn't called a Jezebel without knowing what it means. She had friends, married ones, who explained things. Marriage didn't scare her, nor the act of love. She wanted it. To be special to one person. A husband. Not one like Albert, though, Eleanor's husband. He was the reason she'd readily agreed to marry the General. She hadn't felt safe around him, not even in her own house, and she had known it would get worse after John died.

Heaving out a sigh, Violet crossed the room and knelt to open her second trunk. She'd gathered her night things out of the first one before her bath, but this was the one she'd packed her mother's comb and mirror in.

She'd barely hoisted the lid when her gaze landed on the contents of the trunk. Stunned, she didn't react fast enough. The heavy lid caught three of her fingers as it slammed shut. Screeching at the pain, she tried to unhook the latch, but it wouldn't release.

"Are you all right in there?"

"No," she answered Chayston's question through gritted teeth. The intense pain of her fingers had her eyes watering. "Please help me. The latch is stuck."

Seconds later the lid lifted, freeing her fingers. Rocking back on her heels, she clutched the throbbing fingers with her other hand.

"Let me see."

"No, they'll be fine in a minute," she argued, completely doubting her words. In truth, she was afraid to look. The ends could very well be missing from three of her fingers.

"Let me see, Violet."

His tone was firm but coaxing. She gave in, but looked the other way as he peeled her hands apart and gently uncurled her throbbing fingers. The warmth of his touch caught her off guard, too, when it sent some sort of invisible fire up her arm.

"Ouch," he said softly. "That had to hurt."

The pain momentarily disappeared. "Ouch?"

He grinned.

She pulled her hand out of his. "Yes, it hurt. It still does."

"You still have all four fingers." He stood and crossed the room.

"Thank you for noticing," she said, shaking her head at how he made light of the situation. Her fingers were all intact, and though still stinging, she moved them gingerly.

Chayston returned with a wet cloth and took her hand again. "Here, this will help take away the sting."

The cool dampness did help, and Violet held it on her fingers with her other hand. "Thank you."

"What happened?"

"I opened the trunk to get my comb, and—" She shook her head, still not believing what she'd seen.

"And?"

Violet shifted slightly, to peer around him. He twisted and lifted the trunk lid. Sure enough, there sat her boots. The sight made her gasp again, just as it had the first time.

The gaze in his brown eyes became reminiscent of when they'd first met. "I thought you said you didn't have any shoes."

"I didn't."

"Then whose are these?" he asked accusingly.

"Mine," she answered.

He pushed the lid all the way open, where it couldn't fall shut again, and stood. "What kind of game are you playing here?"

"What kind of game?" she repeated, mainly for her own clarification.

"Yes, game," he said. "Did you want everyone to feel sorry for you by pretending you'd been robbed?"

Indignation flared from the pit of her stomach. "I wasn't pretending. I had been robbed."

"Are you even John's stepdaughter?"

"Yes." She leaped to her feet. "I don't know how my boots got in there, but they were taken from me on the train, along with my money."

He shot her a nasty glare before picking up one of her boots. Digging his hand in the top, he pulled out a roll of bills. "This money?"

Shock spiraled inside her so hard she nearly lost her balance. "How'd that get there?"

"I'd guess by the same person who put the boots there." The bits of gold in his eyes glowed like flames. "You."

"Me?"

"Who else?" He dropped the money in the boot and the boot into the trunk. "You made me carry you all over this town—"

"I didn't make you do anything." Furious, she continued, "Do you really think I wanted you to carry me?"

"Like I was going to make you walk through two feet of snow in socks?"

"That would have been fine by me."

"It would have been fine by me, too," he said, storming toward the door. "Except you had your arms locked around my neck."

Flustered by an unusual fit of anger, Violet pulled the rag from her hand and threw it at him. It hit the back of his head and hung there for a moment before dropping to his shoulder and then the floor.

He turned slowly. "Why, you little—"

"Me?" she interrupted, stomping toward him. "You're a brute. The furthest thing I've ever seen from a gentleman."

His eyes narrowed as her steps brought them closer. "I told you I'm not a gentleman."

"I believe that now."

"Good." He grabbed one of her shoulders and spun around, propelling her toward the open doorway. "Enjoy your jail cell."

Violet flattened her bare toes onto the floor. "I am *not* sleeping in a jail cell."

"Oh, yes, you are."

His swiftness startled her all over again. With little more than a single fluid movement, he'd hoisted her into his arms again and started marching toward the doorway. Violet stuck her legs out and leaned her head back, stiffening her entire body, so no matter which way he turned, she wouldn't fit through the door frame.

"Damn you," he growled, jostling her about.

Fearing she was about to hit the floor, she grabbed his neck but kept her head back, her body stiff, which caused particular body parts to leap to life as if she'd never imagined they could. The peak of her left breast brushed the bottom of his chin, and the result sent a flash of fire shooting through her.

He made a deep growling sound and withdrew the arm beneath her knees, causing her legs to drop toward the floor. His other arm, still around her waist, pulled her up against him. Her breasts flattened against his chest and the thinness of her gown had every inch of her body feeling the intense heat of his.

A brief bout of good sense told her to push away, but a feral heat coiling in the pit of her very being was far stronger. His other hand grasped her head, and when his lips landed on hers, hard and demanding, she met them. Just as forceful, just as challenging.

The entire room started to spin, and she grabbed the sides of his face, just to keep upright. It was as if she'd waited for this very moment in time to come to life. Nothing inside her was quiet. Everything was flushed and rushing, and excited.

Rather dazzled by it all, she offered no protest when the tip of his tongue teased the seam of her lips. Instead, she parted them.

A sweet, riveting shiver raced all the way to her toes and back up again as his tongue swept inside her mouth. She clutched him tighter, holding on for all she was worth as her nipples tightened, stinging as they turned hard and sensitive.

All sorts of wild, new and stirring vibrations swarmed her body. Yearnings and desires that had her feverish all over again.

Chayston had never known such perfection. Her curves fit against him like a glove and the taste of her was enough to make him lose his mind. Which is exactly what must have happened. He'd lost his mind.

Grasping her chin, he tried to break away from the kiss, but she stretched onto her toes.

Torn between all that was right and wrong, he growled and pushed harder, tearing his lips off hers. Gasping, she looked up at him with those sky-blue eyes that could make a man lose more than just his mind.

"If you weren't my father's soon-to-be bride," he snapped, "I'd show you just how much of a gentleman I'm not." He headed for the door then, before he did something he'd really regret.

Chapter Five

Cursing himself up one side and down the other hadn't done any good, and the blizzard still howling outside offered no immediate relief to his present circumstance. Chayston's entire being was rigid and parts of him felt downright raw. He'd barely slept a wink last night, and the muffled sounds coming from the other room said Violet hadn't either.

How the hell had he let that kiss happen? Seeing her in nothing but her thin nightgown had shot his desire to an entirely new level, but her haughty little attitude—that had cut him to the quick. Those long golden curls, wet and hanging down her back, her sky-blue eyes sparking like miniature flames, and her breasts...The gown hadn't hid them from view, not nearly enough, and when that little nub touched his chin, a dozen rough riders wouldn't have been able to stop him from reacting to the hot jolt of desire that had overtaken him.

He squeezed his temples. She was the General's bride-to-be. His father had always been adamant that women were to be revered, cherished and protected. Chayston felt that way, too, which is why he never let on what had happened with Becca.

This wasn't about Becca ,though, it was about Violet, and that was worse.

He hadn't just kissed Violet. He'd wanted her. Still did. But she wasn't his to want. She was engaged. Engaged. To his father.

Chayston glanced around the office. It would be a month or more before Roy returned, and he had some serious decisions to make before then. Returning to the ranch was no longer an option, not with Violet as a stepmother.

The sound of the door opening behind the desk he sat at had his already-tight muscles straining, and once again he lifted his gaze to the outer door, wishing for the millionth time the blizzard had blown itself out. As it was, he couldn't even step off the boardwalk. Winters were serious matters in Montana, and everyone who'd lived through one held them in high regard. When weather like this hit, no one moved. Many a life had been snuffed short by foolish behavior during a snowstorm. Blizzards even took precedence at the ranch. A rope would have been strung from the bunkhouse to the barn, to see to those animals, but the herds would be on their own until the weather cleared.

"There's coffee done, if you'd like some, and I made gravy to go with last night's biscuits."

Another wave of regret washed over him at how timid and hesitant she sounded.

"I'm fine," he said.

"All right," she answered. "It's on the stove if you change your mind."

Like that was an option. Chayston pushed away from the desk, but only went as far as the corner, where he picked up a pile of wanted posters.

A while later, after he'd read every sheet—but couldn't have named even one of the profiled outlaws if pressed—a presence had him looking up.

Violet set down a cup and a plate. "It's getting cold."

"Thank you," he said, trying to sound as normal as possible.

The relief in her eyes sent his heart tumbling into his stomach. He ate, and afterward carried the empty dishes into the other room.

"Just leave them there, on the table," she said. "I'll wash them when I'm finished."

He'd heard her rustling about but had pretended not to. Just as he'd pretended not to notice how fetching she looked in the purple dress she was wearing. He should set the dishes down and leave but couldn't bring himself to do it. "What are you making now?" he asked, gesturing to the bowl she held in one arm while stirring with the other hand.

"I thought I'd make you some Christmas cookies," she said.

He spun around to face away from her. Last year made him hate Christmas. This year it would be forced upon him…complete with Christmas cookies.

Hours later, after shuffling the papers around his desk numerous times, beating the dust out of the mattress, sweeping the jail cells and doing anything else he could find to do, he walked into the living quarters. The smell of baking permeated every room and he couldn't ignore it any longer. The table was covered with little gingerbread people, all decorated up with raisins and icing. He loved gingerbread and raisins. Damn it.

"Help yourself," she said, near the stove again.

A bowl of soup had been left on his desk while he'd been beating out the mattresses earlier, but this smelled even better.

"I only used a little bit of the ham for the soup," she said. "I'm baking the rest of it with carrots and potatoes for supper."

Was she purposely trying to drive him crazy? Cooking. Baking. Looking downright adorable. He snatched up a cookie, and then took two more before going back into the office.

He'd barely sat down when she appeared in the doorway. "I truly don't know how my boots got in my trunk."

"I know," he admitted. She was too genuine, too sincere to be deceitful, leaving him to wonder what had actually happened.

"You do?"

He held up a cookie. "You don't seem like the conniving type. Baking cookies and all."

There was a hint of disbelief in her eyes, as well as a touch of mirth. "I hope you like them."

He bit the head off one, chewed and swallowed. "They'll do." They would have to be about the best cookies he'd ever eaten, wouldn't they.

Biting her lip as if hiding a grin, she retreated to the kitchen.

Finishing the cookie, he rose and followed her. He was the sheriff and should investigate such things. "So," he asked from the doorway, "who do you think hid them? Your boots and money?"

Her face grew serious and sad. "I don't know. If it wasn't impossible, I'd suspect Eleanor."

"Your stepsister?" he asked, munching on another cookie. "Why?"

"Because she's spiteful." Her expression turned distressing and her cheeks flushed slightly. "She thought I was enamored of her husband."

"And you weren't?" he prodded.

"No."

She was stacking the cookies on a plate, and glanced up at him, somewhat wary. Chayston held his tongue, letting her come up with her own conclusion if she should say more or not.

"He was the reason my stepfather wrote to your father," she said.

Chayston crossed the room and filled a cup with coffee. Her hair, though a portion was pinned back, hung down her back in a cascade of spirals almost to her waist. He could only imagine it had been the opposite—that the brother-in-law was enamored of her. He couldn't really blame the guy.

"Eleanor never liked my mother or me. John said he wanted to know I'd be taken care of after he died, and asked if I'd do him a favor."

"What was the favor?"

"Leave Ohio," she said quietly.

Chayston pieced together several things in his mind. "And marry the General?"

She nodded. "Why do you call him the General instead of Father?"

"From growing up at the fort," Chayston answered. "Everyone, even my mother, called him the General. Both my sister and I called him that more often than Father."

Her eyes grew wide. "You have a sister?"

He shook his head. "Did… She and my mother died while we still lived at the fort. Rheumatic fever." That was part of what made not returning to the ranch difficult. Though still young enough now to run the place, someday his father wouldn't be, and, as his son, it would be Chayston's duty—and right—to take over. "My father's a good man. Fair and honest. He'll take good care of you."

Her cheeks were once again crimson.

"I just hope you and I can come to an agreement on something," he finished while he still could. No matter how attracted he was to her, he wouldn't do what Seth had done to him.

"What's that?"

"That what happened last night is forgotten, never mentioned."

Even her neck turned red, yet she nodded. "I think that would be best."

"Yes, it would," he regretfully agreed, "for everyone's sake."

Chapter Six

It was another full day before the storm let up, and Violet found herself sitting in a wagon outfitted with sleigh runners and being pulled by two huge draft horses with jingle bells attached to their harnesses and sprigs of greenery tied in their manes. If not for the heaviness in her chest, she might have enjoyed how festive the stable owner had made the horses.

Though thankful she and Chayston had formed an agreement, it hadn't taken away her memory of the kiss. They'd been civil to each other the past two days, but that somehow made her yearnings stronger, and the stain of it all had her about to jump right out of her skin. Maybe she was a jezebel. If so, marrying the General would help, wouldn't it?

She had no idea, and that frightened her. She couldn't let John down. Could not. Not after all he'd done for her. And she still wanted a family. A husband.

Eleanor had hated her and her mother for encroaching on John's attention, and she couldn't help but fear how Chayston would eventually look upon her once she married his father. Why was everything so complicated? All she wanted was people who accepted her love. They didn't even have to love her in return. Eleanor sure hadn't, yet Violet still thought of her as family—and always would.

She doubted, though, that she'd be able to think of Chayston as her stepson. That was almost absurd. She'd never be able to forget him though.

How could she? She'd be married to his father.

"There it is," Chayston said.

Violet let her gaze wander toward several black dots amongst the snow in a valley below them. "Your father's ranch?"

"Yes," he said, "my father's ranch. The Big Basin."

The almost-despondent tone in his voice had her rubbing both arms as a shiver raced through her system. The eerie sensations that shiver began grew stronger a short time later as they glided into the ranch, where men emerged from every building.

Even without the fact he stood on the front porch of the huge house, Violet would have known her soon-to-be husband was the General. The man was simply an older version of Chayston.

At one time she'd hoped that. Now she wondered if it would make her marriage that much more difficult.

He descended the steps and made his way to the wagon by a shoveled path, even before the horses came to a complete stop. "Violet," he said with a voice that was as close to Chayston's as one could get. "You're even lovelier than John insisted." He reached up and encompassed her waist with two huge hands and lifted her right out of the wagon, not so unlike his son in that manner, too. Glancing over her head as he set her feet on the ground, he said, "I thought you'd wait until the roads were clear, son."

His tone wasn't gruff, but Chayston's was when he replied, "I figured I better get her here as soon as possible."

The General grinned as he lowered his gaze to her again. "I'm glad you're here," he said. "Welcome to the Big Basin."

Her tongue was thick, yet feeling inclined to speak, Violet willed her voice not to crack. "Thank you, General Williams."

"Call me Ralston," he said. "Or just General, like everyone else." Wrapping an arm around her shoulders, he turned her toward the house. "Come inside."

Violet wanted to turn around to see where Chayston was, but feared that wouldn't help her nerves at all. Instead, she walked beside the General, squeaking out answers as he asked about her journey. When he questioned how her hotel accommodations in Spring Valley had been, a fresh wave of the jitters assaulted her. "The hotel was full, sir."

"Full?" he asked, opening the front door and ushering her inside.

"Yes, sir,"

"Where did you stay?"

The room before her spun slightly and Violet closed her eyes. She feared her answer might upset him, and *that* she didn't want. Not because of herself, but of Chayston. Coming between the two of them made her wish she'd never left Ohio.

"She stayed at the sheriff's office."

Violet flinched at Chayston's answer. The General, though, merely cast a friendly smile toward her before gesturing across the room.

"This is Anita," he said, introducing the older woman

standing near a swooping staircase. "She's my housekeeper, cook and the wife of my foreman. You follow her upstairs, and she'll help you get settled."

Violet had no chance to respond before he started speaking again. "Chayston, see her things are hauled upstairs and meet me in my office."

Chayston had known that was coming, and even welcomed it. Having already instructed men to carry her luggage, he turned and followed his father down the hall and into his office.

"The hotel in Spring Valley is never full." The General moved straight to his desk, where he dropped his hat.

Chayston closed the door and removed his gloves but didn't bother unbuttoning; he wouldn't be staying that long. "I know, but Gertrude Guldbrandson wasn't about to let Violet stay there. Seems your decision has the women in town a bit flustered." Anticipating what his father would ask next, Chayston added, "Gertrude insisted I not try Ruth Sutton, either."

"Nosey old bats." The General cracked a grin as he crossed the room to gaze out the window. "So you took her to the jail."

"I couldn't leave her standing in the middle of the street." Chayston ignored the jolt that shot through him. Violet hadn't stood in the street. She'd been in his arms. The exact spot he wouldn't mind finding her again. No matter how hard he tried, his desire for her grew and grew. The last two days had him coiled tighter than a new spring, and just as bouncy.

His father glanced his way. "I'm thinking a Christmas Day wedding. How's that sound to you?"

Shitty. Chayston bucked up in order to ask, "Do you think

two weeks is enough time to get to know someone well enough to marry them?"

His father laughed. "I knew I'd marry your mother in the blink of an eye." He leaned one hand against the window frame. "I was leading a troop through Charleston when I saw her sitting on a porch swing and stopped the march right there to ride my horse across her front lawn."

Chayston had heard the story before, but chose not to interrupt, hoping memories might change his father's mind.

"There were five of them, women close to Violet's age, on that porch, and your mother shoved the rest aside to tell me to get out of her flower bed. She was so damn adorable, all flustered and snippety. I told her I'd move, but that I'd be back and she best be ready for a wedding when I returned." With a smile that said he was remembering things fondly, the General continued, "Two months later we were married, and I took her North, and when the war ended, I brought her out here, where the Mason-Dixon line didn't exist."

The invisible land marker that had mattered to some had never come between his parents despite the number of times his father claimed he was from the North and Chayston's mother the South. What did matter to Chayston was the invisible line that would forever keep him and Violet apart. It had created a battle inside him and left him on the losing side. "Well, if you like snippety, you'll like Violet."

The General chuckled. "She got on your nerves, did she?"

"I'd rather have been snowed in with a rabid dog."

The General nodded then asked, "Any word when Roy's returning? It's been lonesome out here without you."

"No," Chayston said. "I'm assuming it's still the first of

February or so." Though his gut clenched, he added, "You won't be lonesome anymore. Not with Violet here."

"She tell you who her father is?"

"Was," Chayston corrected. "He died."

After a respectful head bow, the General continued, "You remember John, don't you?"

"Yes," Chayston admitted. Unable not to voice it, he said, "Don't you think she's a bit young for you?"

His father's expression grew serious. "John Lassiter saved your life when you were a baby. During an Indian uprising, a brave thought it would be acoup to steal my son. John rescued you and had you back at the fort before I returned from the battle. From that moment on, your mother thought the sun rose and set on John's head, and I considered him the best friend I'd ever have."

Chayston hadn't known that, but had known a strong bond existed between his parents and John.

Opening a desk drawer, his father pulled out several letters and laid them on the desk. "John wrote to me a couple of months ago. Told me he was dying, and that he'd found a husband for his daughter, Eleanor, which in his own words, hadn't been easy. He wasn't worried about her, though, not like he was Violet. She, he said, was tender and loving, and he feared what might happen to her once he was gone. It seemed Eleanor's husband had eyes for Violet. John wanted her out of Ohio, and I told him to send her here. From his letters I understood it wasn't just the husband, it was Eleanor's hatred John feared. I told him to go in peace, that Violet would be welcomed at the Big Basin and protected from anyone who might try to harm her for the rest of her life."

Having already assumed it was something along those

lines, Chayston said, "I still don't see why you agreed to marry her."

"Read the letters," his father said.

"No, thanks," Chayston said, tugging on his gloves and heading for the door.

Chapter Seven

It had been over a week since Violet had stood at her bedroom window and watched Chayston drive away. Although she hadn't seen him since, she thought about him nonstop. Couldn't help it. Besides resembling his son in looks and actions, the General talked about Chayston a lot. The stories were endless, some funny and sweet, and others full of the mischievousness she believed still lived inside Chayston. Her stepfather was included in some of the storytelling, including how John had rescued Chayston as an infant.

That particular story allowed her to understand why the General had agreed to marry her—as repayment. One child's rescue for another. In a way, it made her more beholden to fulfill her promise to John.

Like everyone else, she referred to him as the General, and had discovered Ralston Williams was a remarkable man. Generous and kind. A man she could easily love.

But not in the way a wife should love her husband, and that frightened her.

A knock sounded on her door and she turned from the

window, where she'd watched wagons pulling in for the holiday celebration the General had planned. "Come in."

The General's tender smile made her heart hurt. "The house is filling up," he said. "Are you ready?"

Holding in her stomach, she pressed a hand to the butterflies.

"There's nothing to be afraid of, sweetheart," he said, folding an arm around her shoulders.

"I'm just nervous, I guess," she said.

"Of what?"

Seeing your son. She'd been caught between a father and his child once before and feared being there again. Biting her lip, she shrugged.

He chuckled and gave her shoulders a solid squeeze. "You'll soon be Mrs. Williams, the matriarch of this entire valley."

"Those are awfully big shoes," she said, "and I have small feet."

His laugh was heartier this time, and as they moved down the hallway, he said, "That was a nasty trick your stepsister played on you."

"One of many over the years," she said. A letter, along with a surprising sum of cash, had been delivered to the ranch. It had been from the railroad, explaining how Eleanor had paid each porter to pass a note onto the very last one, who was promised a fair sum if he'd steal Violet's luggage, shoes and money so she'd arrive in Spring Valley a forlorn burden to her new husband. The man said he'd been tempted, but once he'd taken her boots and money, couldn't go through with the ruse and placed them in her luggage at the last moment. The letter had also expressed thanks to Sheriff Williams for his investigation.

The General insisted Chayston had wanted to prove her innocence, but Violet wasn't so sure about that.

Voices wafted up the stairs and she clutched the banister.

"It's just a few people," the General said, "to celebrate the festive season."

No, it wasn't. It was the entire countryside coming to meet his bride-to-be—and they'd probably all be back next week for the wedding.

"By the way, Violet, the house looks wonderful. You did an outstanding job decorating it. I'm quite proud to show it off, and you."

The house was beautiful, and she had worked hard, strategically placing bows and containers of pinecones and stringing garland. She wanted to please the General, truly did, yet, swallowing against the dread threatening to overcome her, Violet had a great desire to run back to her room.

"Here we go," he said, coaxing her onto the staircase. "One step at a time."

A short time later, Violet admitted things weren't as scary as she'd imagined. The General had a way of commanding people and though everyone held very curious glances, no one asked probing questions.

She found the ability to relax a bit, and the courage to smile, until the door opened once again. Her heart clawed its way into her throat, where it blocked her entire airway.

Still at her side, the General patted her back, which was enough to get her breathing again. But when he proudly announced, "There's my son," her lungs locked tight again.

That's when it hit her. The true reason she was so distraught. She was in love with the son—wanted him as her husband, not his father. But Chayston's cold glare slicing her in two said he liked her about as much as Eleanor did.

Having thought of little else except her the past week, Chayston couldn't pull his eyes off Violet. She was more beautiful than he remembered, and the desire leaping to life forced him to admit he had to get it over with—the reason he'd come. As painful as it was, he turned to his father. "Could I see you alone?"

Without a hint of surprise, his father agreed, "Certainly, son." He then bowed to Violet and whispered something.

Every muscle went stiff as Chayston watched her nod and offer him a feeble smile. His father then motioned for Anita, who gestured for Violet to join her near the stairs.

Chayston led the way to his father's office, and closed the door firmly behind them. "Roy will be back by mid-January," he said.

"Good," his father answered, taking a seat behind his desk. "It'll be good for things to get back to normal."

Nothing would ever be normal again. He was giving up what he wanted most. "I've accepted a position as deputy sheriff in Cedar Grove."

The General leaned back. "Oh?"

Chayston crossed the room to gaze out the window. "Yes, I've decided not to return to the Big Basin."

"What about Violet?"

Chayston refrained from answering. Seeing her again had him questioning his decision. He'd fallen in love with his father's bride. Deeper and harder than he'd ever imagined possible. In a matter of mere days. But there was no way for them to be together. Ever. Though he could fight his father, he wouldn't. Violet deserved the family she wanted, and the General would see she got it and the happiness she sought.

"I promised her father she'd live at the ranch," the General said. "If you'd read the letters, you'd know John felt the only way Eleanor would allow Violet to leave was for everyone to *believe* Violet would be marrying a much older man."

Chayston's heart flipped, and he frowned, not sure why. "I told him I had to meet her before I'd completely agree."

"Agree to marry her?" Chayston asked.

"No, before I'd agree to our children marrying."

Chayston whirled around. "Your children?"

His father nodded. "You and Violet."

Stunned, although it was what he wanted more than anything, Chayston couldn't quite believe it could be this easy.

"I wouldn't have considered it," his father said, turning to watch him pace, "but ever since that Becca girl married Seth instead of you—"

"You knew about that?"

"Of course I knew. I'm your father." He folded his arms. "No one else does though."

Becca and Seth had become the least of Chayston's worries. He'd never gotten around to courting Becca properly because he hadn't loved her, not like he did Violet. His heart rate increased significantly, but a splattering of caution held him from rushing for the door. "What does Violet think of that?"

"She doesn't know," his father said. "But she's been mooning at the window ever since you drove away." With a shrug, the General added, "Of course, if you don't want to marry her, I'll find someone suitable, or maybe marry her myself."

"Like hell you will," Chayston said.

Laughter echoed in his wake as he tore out of the room. "She'll be upstairs in her room, son. The one right next to yours."

That's where Chayston found her, jumping off the bed

with a startled expression when he threw open the door. She said his name, but that was all the time he gave her before grasping her upper arms and pulling her into an embrace that included a deep, rather chaotic and frantic kiss.

She responded instantly, clinging to him, kissing him with as much desperation as he felt. Being separated from her the past week had been miserable, and though he wanted nothing more than to go on kissing, he stopped.

Gasping, she covered her mouth with one hand as she stumbled backward when he released his hold.

"Oh, no," she muttered, turning beet red.

"Oh, no, you don't." He reached back and closed the door with a solid thud before approaching her with slow steps. "Don't be turning all shy and timid on me now, Violet Ritter."

Her hands flew to her hips as her mouth opened and closed. She seemed to collect her senses then because she stomped forward. "Shy and timid? Is that what you think I am? Well, I'm not," she insisted. "Appalled is what I am. How dare you—"

"Will you marry me?" he asked, getting straight to the point. This time around, he wasn't wasting time.

Her mouth opened and closed again before she asked, "What?"

"It's a simple question," he said, smiling. "Will you marry me? Yes or no?"

Light rose in her eyes like a sunrise coming over the mountain, and her lips twitched as if they didn't know if they could smile or not.

It was the question he'd imagined never being able to ask her, and in the moment it took her smile to fully form, he felt utterly vulnerable, as if stripped down to nothing. Much as he'd felt the last week.

"Yes." Tears trickled down her cheeks as she nodded. "Oh, Chayston, yes, yes."

He lifted her off the floor by her waist, pulling her into his arms again, and kissed her until neither of them could breathe, and then he kissed her some more.

It was only when he knew for certain what would happen if he didn't stop that Chayston forced himself to back off. Taking her hand, he led her to the doorway.

"Where are we going?" she asked.

"To announce our engagement."

"Oh, goodness," she muttered, "what is this town going to think of me?" Grabbing the doorway as she had the frame of the stage the first time they'd met, she brought them both to a complete stop. "What is your father going to think?"

"My father," Chayston said, "despite being sadistic, is the smartest man I know."

He kissed the point where her brows were knit together. "He invited you out here to marry me, not him."

"He did?"

"Yes, he did." Chayston kissed her again. "Someday, perhaps when we learn we're expecting our first child, you and I will have the opportunity to return his favor."

She tilted her head sideways. "By naming a child after him?"

Running both hands over her slender, perfect waist, he answered, "Maybe, but first we'll play a dirty, downright nasty trick on him. I just can't think what it will be right now."

When she frowned again, he laughed. "You best get used to it, that's what we do in this family."

"Play tricks on each other?"

"Sometimes," he said. "But mostly we love one another." Growing serious, he whispered, "I love you, Violet."

"I love you, too, Chayston. I truly do."

Chapter Eight

Waiting to become Mrs. Chayston Williams was torturing Violet. Some nights, as she lay in bed, she pinched herself to make sure she wasn't back in Ohio, dreaming all this. The wedding she'd once feared approaching was now a charmed event. Chayston visited every night, and the kisses they shared had her anticipating their wedding night with such eagerness she could barely stand the wait.

The ranch house was once again filled with guests she'd watched roll in, but this time, when a knock sounded on the door, she excitedly bid entrance.

"Ready?" the General asked.

Fluffing the long veil Anita had cascaded over her head a few moments before, Violet nodded. "Yes, I am."

"You look beautiful," he said, holding out an elbow.

"Thank you," she said. "And thank you for, well, everything."

"I couldn't be more proud—"

The way he sniffed had her glancing up. Though tough on the outside, the General was all mush on the inside. A lot like his son. She squeezed his elbow tighter and when he nodded, they strolled along the hall and down the sweeping staircase to where her handsome groom awaited.

The ceremony was held at noon on Christmas Day, next to a perfectly decorated pine in the front parlor, and though her eyes were filled with mist, Violet reveled in the love shining in Chayston's as they repeated their vows to one another. She'd always enjoyed Christmas, but now would cherish it completely, knowing it really was a time of miracles.

Later that day, after a meal was served, her new father-in-law caught everyone's attention when he announced, "I'd now like to present my gift to the wedding couple."

Violet turned to Chayston, who grinned adorably, but shrugged.

"As you all know," the General said, "before Roy left town he deputized Chayston as acting sheriff and me as deputy sheriff. As of today, I'm moving to town to fulfill that role, giving my son and his new wife the next couple of weeks alone here at the ranch." He turned to them and grinned. "Just know I'll be back."

The crowd laughed, and in the General's commanding way, he soon had everyone making their departures, including his. As soon as the door closed for the final time, Chayston swung around and hoisted her into his arms.

She grasped his neck and returned his kiss, but when he started walking, she protested. "Put me down."

"Why?" he asked and then loosened his hold slightly. "Afraid I'll drop you?"

"No," she said, laughing. "There's no reason to carry me."

"I carried you before," he said, walking toward the stairway.

"Only because I didn't have any boots." She flayed her feet so he could see beneath her hem. "I have shoes on, see?"

"Oh, where is that porter when I need him?"

Having been caught up in her happiness, Violet had forgotten about her stolen boots. "Did you investigate that because you thought I was lying?"

"No. I wanted to prove your innocence." He kissed the tip of her nose. "Someday we'll have to visit Ohio, just so I can personally thank Eleanor for the scheme that put you in my arms the very first time."

The love she felt for him was so strong, there was no longer room for resentment in her heart, but, Violet had to admit she felt sorry for her stepsister. "Eleanor thinks the only way to have love is to hoard it. I hope someday she's learns that if you give it freely, it comes back tenfold."

Chayston looked at her, deeply, profoundly. "You," he said reverently, "are so…perfect."

"No, I'm not."

He'd climbed the stairs and walked down the hall, and now stood outside his bedroom door. "Fine, you're not. Now, turn the knob, you're getting heavy."

"And you're a brute," she teased in return, while opening the door. "No gentleman would say that to a woman."

"I know." He dropped her onto the bed playfully. She was still bouncing when he landed beside her. "I told you I'm not a gentleman."

Violet wrapped her arms around his neck. "I know, but I love you anyway."

"Good," he said, nibbling on her chin. "Because a gentleman would leave the room, let you get undressed and ready for bed." His hands ran down her arm and then over and up her stomach, coming to a stop on her left breast. "But I'm going to undress you myself."

"Promise?"

"I promise."

His voice was low and husky, his breath hot against the quivering skin of her neck. The line of kisses he trailed along her neck was infinitely tender, and his caresses, how he explored her torso, created an intense excitement. With each kiss, each gentle pass of his hands, her need increased, and when his lips finally glided over hers, Violet met them passionately.

There was no shyness, no fear where Chayston was concerned, and she embraced the freedom his love released inside her. Arched into his caresses, she let her hands roam where they may over him, and when he softly suggested they undress, she beat him off the bed. He laughed and, sitting on the edge of the mattress, turned her around to unfasten the long row of buttons running down her back.

"Can't you hurry?" she asked, trying to tug the gown off her shoulders.

"Maybe if you'd hold still," he replied.

The dress finally gave way and as she pulled it off her arms, letting it fall to the floor, he kissed the very bottom of her back. Her stomach muscles tightened and an intense heat flared deeper. His hands made their way around to her front and slid along the line where her stomach met her legs. Everything inside melted and she leaned back as he stood, resting against his solid frame.

His hand roamed upward, fondling her swollen breasts and teasing her hard, overly sensitive nipples.

"Is this a form of torture?" she asked after a long moan rumbled around in her throat.

"No, it's a form of pleasure," he answered, kissing the side of her neck.

"Then don't stop," she whispered. "Don't ever stop."

He didn't, even after they were both completely bare and stretched out on the bed. She'd been as adventurous as him, discovering pure pleasure by touching him, exploring parts she'd only allowed herself to be curious about. She hadn't yet touched him there, where she was most interested in, but when one of his hands went between her legs, she reached down to grasp him. It was as if they were each trespassing, but a welcome trespass, that had them grinning at one another.

So caught up in the wonders of it all, Violet didn't question the changes in her body. Every stroke had her wanting more. Holding nothing back, she followed instincts that had a savage yet earthly promise spiraling up from her very spirit.

Her breathing was uneven, catching in her throat and chest. When Chayston shifted, rising above her, she grasped his neck, pulling his mouth to hers for a wild, uncontrollable kiss that had their tongues swirling with one another.

When she needed air, she dropped her head deep in the pillow and shuddered with delight as his lips found one of her breasts, kissing it much as he had her mouth.

He continued, moving to the other one, and Violet wondered how much more she could take. Her center was throbbing and wet and a massive yearning burned inside her. "Please, Chayston," she begged. "I can't take much more."

"Sure you can, darling," he said. "Lots more."

As he spoke, he guided himself forward, making her hold her breath as the end of him probed her opening. His entrance was slow, meticulous, and Violet curled her toes at the anticipation racing over her. Her hips rose up to meet him, and though he tried to pull back, she wrapped her legs around his.

A quick flash of pain caused her to hiss.

"Aw, sweetie," he whispered, "I'm sorry, we needed to go slow the first time."

The pain had already dissipated and Violet lifted her hips again, this time relishing the way his length glided inside her. "Why?"

"So it wouldn't hurt," he whispered, pulling out yet again.

Unable to even comprehend pain at this precise moment, Violet released a pleasure-filled moan. "That does not hurt."

The pace of their coming together assembled a plethora of sensations into a massive culmination so great Violet couldn't imagine what might happen next. Until it happened—a burst of freedom so encompassing she felt as if she was falling from some nonexistent cloud in the heavens.

Chayston moved faster. She held on to his shoulders, meeting each of his thrusts with a final burst of energy. He let out a growling groan, and she glorified in imagining he'd hit the same high she had.

Violet relished the way her entire being filled with something so astounding she knew it could be nothing but undying love as they held on to one another for several long and wonderful moments.

She smiled, fully understanding she wasn't a jezebel, just a woman in love.

Their separation, the way Chayston slowly pulled out and rolled off her was as sweet as everything else had been. So was the way he slid an arm under her neck and pulled her close.

"I love you."

"I know," she said, letting out another sigh of contentment. "And it's quite marvelous, isn't it?"

He laughed and kissed her forehead. "Yes, it is." Tilting

her head up with his other hand, he kissed her lips. "As a child, I loved Christmas," he said. "One year, your stepfather gave me a knife. I still have it."

She smiled. "He did?"

"Yes," he whispered, "but nothing will ever top this year. He gave me a bride for Christmas."

* * * * *

Summoned for Seduction

JOANNE ROCK

To Dean—Merry Christmas!

While working on her master's degree in English literature, **Joanne Rock** took a break to write a romance novel and quickly realised a good book requires as much time as a master's programme itself. She became obsessed with writing the best romance possible and, sixty-some novels later, she hopes readers have enjoyed all the 'almost there' attempts. Today, Joanne is a frequent workshop speaker and writing instructor at regional and national writer conferences. She credits much of her success to the generosity of her fellow writers, who are always willing to share insights on the process. More important, she credits her readers with their kind notes and warm encouragement over the years for her joy in the writing journey.

Chapter One

Scottish Highlands
Winter 1072

He was gaining on her.

Resisting the urge to peer over her shoulder, Helene MacKail quickened her pace toward Domhnaill Keep's massive great hall where Twelfth Night festivities awaited guests hailing from all over the Highlands. If only she could reach the throngs of revelers before Léod mac Ruadhán caught her, she might slide into a seat beside her mother and avoid conversation with the brooding Scots laird.

The man sought more than her hand in marriage. He required her lands, her wealth and her body. And he wished to dominate them all absolutely.

"Lady Helene." The deep tone of his voice would surely carry over a war-torn battlefield at the height of mayhem. It reverberated now down the long, narrow corridor of an old tower with ease.

If she pretended not to hear him, she would offend the

most influential clan leader in all of Scotland. Word of it
would surely reach her father's ears. But to speak to the warrior here—alone in a remote part of the drafty old keep—
made her heart race unsteadily. Léod mac Ruadhán had
been known to turn on his own knights, keeping his men in
a heightened state of readiness fueled by fear so they might
fight for him at naught but a moment's notice.

She'd heard enough tales of his cruelty. And not just toward his own men. She also knew that his insatiable ap-
petites had sent his last wife running to the furthermost
outreaches of the Highlands until she perished from the inhospitable winter. Unfortunately, Helene's father had been
more concerned with Mac Ruadhán's ability to protect the
people of the clan MacKail than with his unsavory reputation with women.

Perhaps—knowing she could end up wed to the brute in
the spring—she would do well not to earn even darker lev-
els of animosity than his last bride.

For that reason, she slowed her step on the cool stone
floor.

"My lord." She faced him in the darkened corridor lit
only by two sickly tapers sputtering at either end of the
long expanse.

Was it possible he loomed even larger and more threatening than she recalled from previous meetings? He stood
far closer than she'd realized when she'd been hurrying to
increase the distance between them. The leather of his boots
was heavy, yet his step had been surprisingly light. Agile.
Stealthy, even. She could envision him prowling about the
Highland forests at night, personally gutting any man or
beast who dared to threaten his stock of fat sheep or his
stables of coveted horseflesh.

It helped that his hair, black as a raven's wing, would blend with the shadows. A strong jaw and prominent cheekbones made him appear as though he were carved in granite, an illusion upheld by the impossible breadth of his shoulders. A gray wool cloak drapeed him now, the fabric held by a heavy silver brooch at one shoulder, though most swept down his back like the folded wing of a great predatory bird.

Or perhaps she merely thought as much since she felt as nervous as a mouse about to be carried off in the grip of steely talons.

"I see you are in some haste to dine." He offered her his arm.

To escort her? Or to squeeze the breath from her with one careless touch?

Memories of the more graphic tales she'd heard came to mind. A maid in her father's hall had confided that the laird's dead wife had rattled the rafters with her screams on their wedding night. One of the laird's grooms had bragged to all her father's men-at-arms that his lord's... endowments... were the stuff of legend, as disproportionately large as the rest of him.

Helene had nightmares for many days hence.

"My lady?" Léod's voice pierced her inappropriate thoughts. "Will you join me to sup?"

Her cheeks flushed with warmth as an expression of annoyance sent his dark brows swooping downward. A frown curled his lower lip. Her breath caught in her throat at the thought of what he might do to women who displeased him.

She hadn't heard that he would eat them for dessert, but that did not mean she couldn't be the first.

"I am sorry." Flustered, frightened and angry that her father would give her to such a man, Helene executed a ridiculous little curtsey that would better befit a kitchen maid or a wine server. "I have forgotten my knife in my chamber."

Hoisting a handful of her skirt in one hand, she turned on her heel and sprinted away from him, her eating knife actually jostling her hip where it dangled from the chain at her waist. In a few moons' time, she would not have the legal right to run from this man. But for now, she would follow her good sense and put as much distance between them as possible.

Behind her, she could have sworn she heard him snarl like the ravenous beast he was reputed to be. And, skidding back into her chamber, she promised herself that no matter the cost, she would find a way to avoid a betrothal to the monstrous laird. Even if it meant openly appealing to another man in attendance at the holiday festivities. She could compromise herself, or at least create whispers of her unworthiness to wed, if she were to dally in dark corners with another man.

She had until Twelfth Night before her father packed her up and sent her back to the isolated mountains Léod called home. Less than a fortnight to make sure Léod mac Ruadhán viewed her as the last woman on earth he would choose for his bride.

It would be the last time Helene MacKail walked away from him.

Léod promised himself as much as the Highland beauty hid from him in her chamber. He needed to solidify a marriage contract before he returned home. He'd been away for too long after the debacle with his first wife, allowing his dark reputation to grow since it had the benefit of protecting his lands and people even more than his formidable skills with a sword.

But word had reached him that the reputation had begun to attract unsavory characters to his Highland keep—the kind of men who killed for sport and relished the notion of rule by brute force. The time had come to end the gossip and nothing would quiet the storm of suspicion as efficiently as a new wife. While he'd hoped to wed the only heir to the profitable MacKail lands, he would not force himself on an unwilling bride, especially after what had happened with Margaret.

Still, that did not mean he would stand by idly while the gently bred Helene snubbed him by skittering off into corners to hide from him. He'd treated her with deference.

Well, if not deference exactly, he certainly hadn't bared his teeth at her. He'd taken her riding one morn, and one of her lady companions had fainted when he'd brought down a boar. Later, he'd followed her onto the ramparts one day to speak to her privately, not realizing until she'd turned frighteningly pale that she assumed her life was in danger. Had she assumed he would toss her over the wall? He'd attempted to reassure her, but his soothing remarks had soured a bit when he'd thrown in a biting reminder that he'd never risk her life before he'd secured her dowry. But curse the Fates, he'd been in a foul mood by then.

He did not appreciate her looks of wide-eyed horror. Today's scrambling exit to escape with the bold lie of the eating knife was the last straw. As long as he celebrated the holiday at Domhnaill Keep when it overflowed with visitors from all over the Highlands, he would use the time to seek another wife to fatten his coffers and fill his bed.

But first, he would open Helene's eyes to what she missed

in running from him. Indeed, he would take great pleasure in such a diversion. It was the holiday season after all. Enticing a delectable maid to forget her reservations would be a gift beyond measure.

He just needed to find a way to seek her out alone. Preferably under cover of night so he could whisper to her in the darkness. That way, she would not know she spoke to the fearsome Highland lord who had unwittingly caused the death of his first wife. Helene would think she merely conversed with another suitor, a circumstance which she might greet with eagerness given her obvious aversion to him.

Nay, she would not run from him again. Tonight, he would ensure she came *to* him instead. Once he had her—alone and unprotected—he would soothe his wounded pride with the taste of her lips. Her first flush of passion.

Only then, when she panted sweetly beneath him would he consider today's slight assuaged. It was a fitting retribution. Considering his reputation for slaying his brides, stealing a feel of Lady Helene's sweet treasures was hardly a high price for the hardhearted maid to pay.

Chapter Two

A woman could starve to death for the sake of her pride.

Helene paced in her chamber later that evening while the rest of the keep danced and played games for the Twelfth Night festivities. Every now and then, when she dared to move the tapestry away from the room's lone window, she could hear the sweet strings of the *clàrsach* harp drifting on the icy breeze of a coming snowstorm. She could also smell the roasted fowl and boar meat that made her mouth water and her belly angry that she had been too much of a coward to walk to the great hall with Léod.

A knock at her door distracted her from her disgruntled musings.

"Yes?" She tucked the tapestry back over the casement and hurried to her chamber door, hopeful her mother had brought her a trencher left over from the meal.

Her father had sent a servant to check on her earlier when she'd not appeared at the table, but Helene had sent a message back saying she did not feel well. She walked a fine line with Léod when she made excuses not to speak with

him or spend time with him. Helene feared returning to the
great hall after her abrupt leave-taking tonight in the event
he—or her father—would upbraid her for her behavior.

They did not understand what it was like to lose their
freedom—possibly their life—to a mad Highland laird.

Wrenching open the door to the tower hallway beyond,
Helene found no one. Yet a tray sat at her feet, carefully arranged with three sugared figs and a small parchment scroll.

Curious.

She strained her eyes in the flickering shadows cast by
the weak tapers on the far ends of the corridor and failed
to find any hint of who had left the small pewter tray or the
treats within. Bending to retrieve the gift, she gobbled a fig
and moved deeper into her chamber to unroll the parchment.
Someone had cut the piece to size and it lacked a wax seal.
She simply needed to press the curling edges apart to read
the missive within.

> *I missed seeing you at sup. There is a full tray keep-
> ing warm in the mead house if you would like a meal.
> I only want to speak with you before you are wed and
> I have lost the chance forever. If you fear for your
> safety, bring one of the hounds from the hall.*

No signature followed.

Helene dropped the parchment and tugged open the doorway to look out into the corridor once more, but the hall
remained as silent as ever save the far-off sounds of the
clàrsach. The sweet wail of the instrument echoed the swirl
of unnamed emotions in her breast. Bereft at the thought of
disappointing her father and—more so—her mother, who
did not deserve a disobedient maid for a daughter. Indignant

at the thought of being betrothed to a murderous lord who demanded utter submission from his people. But more than anything else, she felt the quick race of daring in her blood to defy them all. With a dirk in her garter and a hound at her side, why should she not venture to the mead house for a meal provided by an admiring stranger? Lady Cristiana of Domhnaill had not invited ruffians to her Twelfth Night festivities save one Léod mac Ruadhán. So who would dare accost Helene on the lands of their wealthy and generous hostess?

Helene slid a dagger into the band about her hose and fluffed the train of her gown to ensure it remained hidden. She peered into a small looking glass to find her cheeks flushed with high color and her eyes bright with hopeful-ness. Ah, she had forgotten the rush of blood through the veins at the thought of a stolen kiss by a handsome man. There had been a time she had looked forward to betrothal and the kind of union that brought other women pleasure. But that had been before she'd learned what awaited her in the marriage bed was not the bliss

Tossing a woolen cloak about her shoulders for the short walk beyond the main keep, Helene scurried out the door of her chamber and down the drafty halls, careful to remain in the shadows even though all of the guests appeared to be within the great hall. The sounds of laughter and music grew louder as she reached the main floor, then quieted again when she hastened toward an exit out into the court-yard. She peered about for a likely hound to accompany her—the scroll's suggestion had been a good one—but the cagey beasts must all have found refuge in the great hall where bones would be plentiful after the feast.

Undaunted, Helene shoved open a wooden door guarded

by two of Domhnaill's men-at-arms. Engaged in a dice game, neither man spoke to her since both appeared as deep in their cups as any holiday reveler. She drew her hood farther over her head and braved a gently falling snow to cross the smooth stones near the entrance to the keep. Bonfires dotted the landscape as other men-at-arms kept their vigils and celebrated the season at the same time. The scent of burning pine and oak mingled, both sweet and pungent, in the crisp, cold air. Her heart eased at the sight of so many sentries about. Despite the lack of a hound to protect her, she would be safe.

Besides, if anything seemed amiss, she would simply take the tray and depart. She was starving, after all.

Arriving at the mead house, she could smell the fragrant honey and clover in the air from the brewing vessels within. The Domhnaill clan made the best mead in all of Scotland and the hope of receiving the sought-after libation brought guests from far and wide for Lady Cristiana's winter revel. Now, Helene stepped inside the darkened structure lit only by an untended blaze at the back of the room where a cauldron hung low over banked heat. The dull glow of hot ashes and a few short blue flames was not enough to reveal much of her surroundings and Helen kept the outer door open to the moonlight for a moment while her eyes adjusted.

"You came." A soft masculine whisper drifted over her though the voice emanated from a place far off.

The sound felt unearthly and very real at the same time, sending a shiver along her spine.

"Who's here?" she demanded, tensing. She was grateful to be standing so close to the door in case she needed to run.

"The bearer of your dinner," was the reply. The voice seemed calm and steady, as if the man behind it reclined in a distant chair and made no move toward her. "I left it by the fire so it would stay warm."

Was it her hunger, or could she suddenly smell roast duck and a rich glaze? Her grip on the door loosened, her gaze sweeping over the room's dark corners in the hope of finding her mysterious host.

"I would prefer to eat here in case I do not like your company, sir." Although, truth be told, she rather liked his voice. Warmth and confidence lurked in his tone. A vital man rather than a boy.

"Then you shall remain hungry, for you must retrieve it yourself from the middle of the room. For my part, I have promised myself I will not move from my perch unless you wish it. I think you'll feel safest if you know where I am at all times."

"Perch?" Her gaze moved upward. "Do you hang from the rafters then?"

She opened the door wider to admit an extra sliver of moonlight and a blast of wintry cold pelted her cheek with crystalline flakes of snow.

"I am not of a mind to be seen yet," he barked in that oddly commanding whisper. The brew house's round shape must help the sound to carry and surround her. "I pray you, be at ease and shut out the cold. I sit on a bag of milled grains and will not stir unless you wish it. You have my word."

"If I asked you to come out into the light, would you do so?" She could not begin to imagine who had invited her here. Who sought her company and promised to remain at her command.

The scroll he'd given her suggested he wanted to speak to her before her marriage, hinting at an interest of the most intimate kind. Another shiver lit up her spine as she waited for a stirring.

"That I will not do." The brew house remained silent save for his voice. "At least not yet."

Another chilly gust blew through the door, sealing her gown to her legs. Unwilling to suffer the cold any longer, she allowed the door to close, blanketing them in the dark. Alone.

"Why?" she asked, lifting her skirts slightly and slipping out of her shoes so she might steal silently across the floor toward where the tray of food awaited her.

"Haven't you ever wished to be known for the person you are within and not the person the world assumes you to be?"

His question gave her pause.

She thought of Leod and the assumptions the world made about him. But since he did nothing to stop the gossip about his relentless grip on his lands and his power, he surely had no desire for the world to believe anything different about his character. So who could the mystery man be?

Was he a castle steward or man-at-arms? She had not thought a man of lowly rank might approach her. Hurrying toward the blue flames glowing under the cauldron, she could make out the platter of food balanced on a low table that held a huge spoon and a few tools for the fire. As she retrieved the pewter tray, she looked around the room again to where she'd pinpointed the voice in the back, but if anything, being closer to the building's only light source made it more difficult to see.

"Everyone wishes for that sometimes." She steadied a flagon of wine and retreated with the tray. Carefully, she moved toward the door and then spied the shape of a work bench against one wall. She took a seat at the high stool and helped herself to a hearty bite of bread, wishing she could see him.

How could she tell if he was the right sort of man to risk compromising herself with?

"Does Mac Ruadhán know anything about the woman you are within?" The soft question echoed all around her, a trick of his melodic voice and the round walls, perhaps.

He'd made it clear he knew of her impending betrothal even in the missive he'd sent earlier. But hearing him say Léod's name now made her think he was indeed a Scots lord, for there was not a shred of deference in his tone when he spoke of a man who incited envy and awe in even his peers.

"I do not think he is overly concerned with knowing people. He seems content to amass wealth and inspire fear." Confiding her thoughts to this stranger in the dark should be awkward and yet she felt oddly safe as she savored the food he'd brought her and shared worries that her own parents had refused to let her voice.

She poured a cup of wine from the flagon and brought it to her lips before realizing the libation was not wine at all but the famed Domhnaill mead. The rich brew of honey and clover pleased her tongue and warmed her blood, infusing her whole body with a tingling contentment.

"What would you choose to share with your betrothed, if he could know one thing about you?"

That voice! It resonated along her ears like a caress. She almost recognized it. Or maybe the sound of it simply felt more familiar now that she'd grown accustomed to him sitting in the dark, just beyond her vision.

"I would not share even a shred of myself with a man who frightens females for sport." She speared at her meal with her eating knife, remembering how she'd run from him earlier. "He might be handsome, but his aspect is fierce. He is too impatient to listen to a woman speak."

Her companion said nothing for a long moment as she mopped the remnants of her meal with her leftover bread.

"You've avoided the question," he observed finally.

A laugh slipped free and she poured more mead, wondering about the man in the shadows. Was he handsome as well? Already, she found his disposition pleasing. His voice compelling. And his desire to seek her out, all the while respecting her honor by remaining on the other side of the chamber, had stirred a warmth inside her that had naught to do with the mead.

"I suppose I've been so consumed with the injustice of marrying a brute that I have not given much thought to what a union could be like." Should be like. "I would think a husband and wife should be able to speak freely."

"The way we are now?" His voice deepened and she could almost imagine he'd come closer.

Had he? Her heartbeat thrummed insistently.

"I suppose." She listened hard for any hint of sound, but she could hear naught but her pulse pounding in her ears and the occasional crackle of the hot ashes keeping the mead cauldron simmering. She thought she might understand what a slow simmer felt like. "Yes, actually. Just like this."

"What else would you wish for in your marriage, Helene?"

The way he said her name… Recognition teased at the corners of her mind.

"Do I know you?" she asked suddenly, rising from the stool to turn toward him.

She could guess where he sat now. Could even tell herself she spied an outline that could be a man.

"By reputation, perhaps. The same way any of us know each other when we come out of our far-flung homes but once every few years for entertainments such as this."

Venturing forward, she took a few steps toward him, giving the cauldron at the center of the room a wide berth since being too close to that lone source of light skewed her vision.

"What would *you* seek in marriage, sir?" She could not say why she felt so certain he would not leap out at her and deflower her on the floor of the mead house, but she knew he would do no such thing.

He wanted something from her and she began to think she wanted something—very much—from him as well. This man, this night, represented all she needed to dissuade Léod from marrying her.

"A woman willing to speak her mind." His voice wrapped around her like velvet, cloaking her in softness. "A woman who will come to me of her own will."

"The way I am now?" She did not know where she found such boldness. But she wanted, nay needed, to know that her mystery stranger found her desirable.

By the saints, she wanted to be with a man and not a monster.

"Aye." His voice went rough in a way that thrilled her.

Her skin heated beneath her gown and she realized she still wore her cloak. Reaching for the fastening at the throat, she unclasped the brooch and prepared to let it fall.

"Wait," he commanded, halting her in her place when she could not be more than some ten paces from him.

Although she must have mistaken his form for the outline of something else against the wall for the shape was too big to be a man.

"What is it?" She gripped the cloak and hood in her hand, peering behind her as if a ghost had followed in her tracks.

"I have enjoyed this and I am not prepared to let it end by revealing myself too soon."

Still he withheld himself? Helene tried not to feel affronted. She backed up a step.

"Perhaps I should leave—"

"I would like to kiss you, Lady Helene."

The pronouncement flashed through her like a lightning bolt, sparking heat all the way to her toes.

"It would be difficult to not reveal yourself if that is the case," she observed breathlessly. Hungrily.

Her eyes probed the shadows, desperate for a glimpse of him, for some hint of his identity.

"Nay," his voice whispered, soothing her and exciting her at once. "Not if I blindfold you."

Léod kept as still as his body would allow in the confined space with a provocatively curious maid venturing ever nearer.

She wanted to be kissed.

He'd heard it in the catch of her voice when he'd proposed as much. But the blindfold? That had been a risky proposition. Would she run from him once more? He cursed his lack of patience. But her ease with him here in the darkness had intrigued him. If he was honest, he'd been equally surprised by his own ease with her. He could not recall the last time a woman had that sort of effect on him. His encounters with worldly widows or other eager bedmates had been focused solely on physical pleasure. These stolen moments with Helene had been more than that. While he'd thought physical pleasure and a bit of revenge was his objective tonight, he found himself drawn to the hints of boldness in her that he'd never expected.

He found himself unwilling to let their time together end. Yet how could he resume his pursuit of a woman who would betray him—or at least betray his intentions toward her—by meeting privately with another man? He should not want her. Still, he understood her fear of him all too well

"Blindfold?" She had not run.

Neither had she come closer.

He could see her white fist clenched tight at her throat, clinging to the cloak and hood she'd been about to drop. Of course, he had a better view of her since he'd positioned himself beneath a high window, ensuring any moonlight filtered down and away from him.

The chamber was vast, built for housing fires, cauldrons and stacks of barrels, not lovers' games. But there was a cushioned bench nearby where he could seduce a kiss from her.

"Like Hoodman's Blind." He cited the children's game to make the notion sound less—sensual. But perhaps as a virgin untouched, the other uses for hoods and blindfolds would never occur to her innocent mind. "I would remain anonymous to you a bit longer yet we could sit closer together."

He strove to keep his voice relaxed, careful to hide his response to her as she stood poised like a woodland creature, unaware of the huntsman's danger. At this moment, more than anything, he wanted her to close the distance between them of her own volition.

"I will share my mead with you," he continued, tempting her shamelessly with the prized commodity. "I discovered a barrel back here that tastes less of honey and more of cinnamon."

And a fine brew it was, but the only taste he wanted upon his lips now was Helene.

"Will you swear on your honor as a Highland lord to allow me to leave whenever I wish?"

His lips curved in a rare grin.

"A clever bargain and one which I make with ease. I swear by my God that I will not touch you unless you wish it, and that you may leave at any time. If I break this vow, I pray my sword arm turns as errant as my tongue." He wondered what Helene would think if she knew it was the only oath he'd ever pledged to another living soul.

Ever since his father died in Léod's youth, he had forged his own path in the world, winning respect by the sword and not by words. But he was learning fast that his old ways would not work with Helene.

Would she believe any vow he repeated if she knew his true identity? A part of him mourned the fact that she would never know the truth. If anything, her discovery of his identity now would make her despise Léod mac Ruadhán more than she already did.

"Very well." With a curt nod, she relinquished her grip on the cloak but kept her hood in her hand. "I may require assistance."

Lifting the heavy swath of velvet, she was about to settle it over her head.

"Nay." He tugged a length of silk off his waist and thrust it in her direction. "Take this instead."

He had almost leaned into a moonbeam that arced down to pierce the brew house floor between them. But in the end, only the cream-colored silk caught the light. Helene reached for the strip of cloth with gently trembling hands.

"It is warm with your scent. Thank you." She stepped nearer to accept it, directly in the path of that pale moon glow.

She stared at him, unseeing, blue eyes wide with open curiosity that he burned to satisfy. Her skin turned alabaster in the blue-tinged moonbeam, as snowy white as the ground outside. Rivers of long dark curls streamed over her shoulders now that she'd removed her hood, with stray waves catching on the elaborate embroidery and tiny gemstones sewn into the bodice. The slashed sleeves revealed a light-colored muslin tunic beneath the heavy velvet kirtle. She smelled like roses and cinnamon, a fragrance he'd noted about her person even before tonight so he knew it wasn't just the mead that accounted for the hint of spice in an otherwise floral scent.

Blinking at him in the silent space that separated them, she withdrew the silk slowly from his fingers, dragging the fabric in a long, slow slide along the back of his hand.

"Perhaps you will help me." She guided the material to her eyes and then turned to present him with her back. "Would you care to tie it?"

She could turn on him at the last and catch him in the act. Léod wondered if that was her plan. But no. She'd made him swear an oath. He did not think she would play with him thus.

So, sliding off the sack of grain, he stepped lightly toward her. She was delicately made and half his size. No wonder he had frightened her off between his reputation and his height that towered over her. If he bent to kiss her head, she would fit neatly below his chin. For now, he settled for taking the strips of cloth that lay against her hair and tying the silk into a firm knot.

"How is that?" he asked, speaking softly into her ear from behind. If he leaned any closer, her hair would catch on the rough beginnings of a beard along his cheek.

"Fine. Good. I mean—" she babbled awkwardly, her heart racing so fast he could see the swift pulse at her neck as he took the liberty of peering down her bodice as far as the fabric would allow.

He could not see much more than her collarbone, but the slope and sway of her frame fascinated him, making it difficult for him to keep his hands to himself.

"Are you sure?" He lingered there, hating the thought of leaning away. He'd wanted to get close to her ever since arriving at Domhnaill a sennight ago, but she'd been running from him every time he neared.

"Nay." Her fingers moved restlessly up to the blindfold, smoothing along its length. "Rather, the blind is comfortable enough. But I find myself curious about something else."

His breath burned a path down his lungs. His body tightened immeasurably, every inch of him in readiness for whatever Helene might want.

"Tell me," he insisted, past the point of any elegance in his words.

"You promised not to touch me unless I willed it."

It was the last thing he cared to think about.

"Aye," he managed to answer, yanking his head up before his nose sank into the fragrant dark waves of her hair.

"Well, I will it."

He could not say how many heartbeats passed before his brain deciphered her words. Could she be offering him what he wanted most? Or was that merely a trick of a hungry body that wanted to lay her back on the grain sack and rent her rich gown from neck to hem so that he might view every lovely curve and nuance?

"You—" his voice growled out a hoarse note that he hastened to clear "-wish for me to touch you?"

He prayed with sudden fervency that he had not misunderstood.

"Please, my lord. I would like that more than anything."

Chapter Three

Was it bravery or utter foolishness to invite the caress of a stranger?

As Helene trembled behind her blindfold, tense and longing, she could not care one way or the other. For the mystery lord offered her a chance to compromise herself in a way that would deter Léod mac Ruadhán for good. And he tempted her on an intimate level she never would have suspected.

Brave or foolish, she trusted that this stranger would not break his word to her. She only hoped she could trust *herself* to walk away from this encounter without giving far more to him than she intended.

"Nothing could give me more pleasure." He spoke into her ear, his breath warm and honey-scented against her skin through the veil of her hair.

She waited for him to turn her, kiss her, take her fully into his arms. He did none of those things. Keeping her back to him, he reached around her shoulder to caress her cheek, his fingers trailing a slow path down from her temple to cradle her chin. He hovered close to her back, his scent a spice she did not recognize and the musk of vital strength. She had the vague impression of size, but he could not possibly be as large and looming as Léod. Her mystery stranger was a man of gentleness, she could tell by his restraint and his promise to her.

That belief made her tip her head toward his touch, seeking more of his warmth against her cheek. Her mouth.

As if reading her thoughts, his thumb found her lips. He outlined the full softness with a calculated touch until she sighed with startled pleasure that he could come in contact with so little of her and still incite a cascade of sweetness throughout her whole body. Even her toes curled at the small circles he traced upon her mouth. She swayed back toward him until her shoulders found steadiness upon his chest. She tipped her head backward and found he was built like a warrior, all muscle and sinew. Yet every inch of him radiated warmth, as if his body welcomed hers as much as she yearned for his.

"Do you remember what I want from you, Helene?" he asked, his voice more a rumble from his chest into her back than a sound she heard.

"I can think of little else," she admitted, rolling her head from side to side, blinded by darkness but more aware than ever of her other senses. Her cheek brushed the laces of his tunic beneath a linen hauberk. She recognized the fine silk as the same kind she wore about her eyes. "You claimed to want a kiss, but you have not yet taken it."

He was quiet for a moment and she wondered if he thought her too bold by half. Perhaps no respectable lord would claim a maid who behaved with such wantonness.

She stilled, thinking it was not too late to seek her chamber. Pretend this night never happened.

"I would prefer a kiss freely given," he admitted finally. "That way, neither of us will look back and think I took advantage of a blindfolded maid."

A bold warrior who would take such care with her heart and her body? The notion was a revelation. And provided her with a power she had never guessed she could possess.

Easing away from him, she turned so that she faced him. If she lifted her blindfold now, who would she see? Her heart pounded hard, but not out of fear. Even as she felt his gaze upon her, devouring her with his eyes, she did not want this moment to end. She liked learning about her mystery lord slowly, without the watchful stares of a hall full of family and clansmen as witnesses.

"I am willing, but untutored," she confessed, the scents of honey and cinnamon filling her nose until she felt drunk on the fragrance of mead if not the taste. "I may need guidance."

Licking her lips, she stretched up on her toes, seeking contact. The low growl he made in his throat rolled through her like a possessive caress, an assurance he wanted her with a hunger that bordered on primal.

By the time his mouth met hers, she flattened herself to him, her whole body seeking his. He gathered her tightly to him, his broad palms spanning her back and drawing her nearer, nearer until her spine curved into him.

Sensation simmered just beneath her skin, her blood stirring hotly at the feel of all that hard male heat against her needy flesh. But although his hold on her remained tight, his kiss was unutterably soft, his lips gliding lightly over hers with a teasing caress she had not imagined. It was delectable. Heavenly. And not nearly enough.

On instinct alone, her lips parted. That small accommodation rewarded her a thousand times over as his tongue stroked hers in a way that sent an echoing pleasure to her womb. Her hips answered as surely as her tongue, both pressing closer in a dance gone suddenly wild.

"Please," she murmured against his mouth, unsure what she wanted and certain he could provide it. She gripped his shoulders, needing him to steady her.

But perhaps he thought she signaled that he stop for he pulled away sharply.

"What is it?" she whispered, alert to some confusing change in the air.

He stood so still. So rigid. Had someone entered the brew house?

"Helene." He did not speak to her as a mystery stranger but with the cold reserve of a Highland laird in the great hall.

It was that note of wintry restraint that confused her. He sounded familiar in a way that made her stomach knot. Dread cooled her blood even before her brain caught up with what her instincts told her. Something had gone very wrong indeed.

Without warning, he reached for her blindfold and shoved the silk up, away from her eyes.

Revealing the mystery stranger clutched in her arms.

Léod mac Ruadhán. The monster who chased his wife from his home, leaving her to die in the inhospitable north. The very beast who sought a second bride to fill the place left by the first.

She realized she still gripped his hauberk in her fingers, an action she'd taken in the throes of a passion she hardly recognized in the cold air between them now. She relinquished it—him—as if burned.

He had tricked her. Called her out into the winter night alone to shame her and then revealed himself as her tormentor.

A weight closed on her chest like a tightening fist. She could not have formed words if she tried, but then all rational thought had fled from her head anyway. She could only feel a dark betrayal where unwise passion had been a moment before.

"I'm sorry," he muttered, releasing the blindfold like a child's forgotten plaything.

It sagged down her ear, a lopsided circlet of silk and foolishness.

But before she could think to accuse him with righteous indignation or maidenly outrage, the powerful Highland laird spun on his heel and stomped out of the brew house into the night.

The morning had not come fast enough for Léod. He would leave Domhnaill at once, but he needed some hint of daylight for the journey. Now, with a hint of dawn breaking on the horizon, he could finally dispense with all pretense of civility and depart the holiday festivities at the lavish keep. He'd never been one for merry-making anyhow. His life had been all about hard work and sacrifice. Making war and serving his king to enrich his own coffers. He'd never seen this trip to Domhnaill as anything more than a chance to find a wealthy bride to bring him more land and alliances.

Now, he had.

Because Lady Helene MacKail was not the sort of woman he could forget easily. He'd thought to trifle with her enough to make her see the error of her ways in refusing him, then choose another bride who would be more biddable and less frightened of him. He certainly had not planned to lie to Helene, play sensual games with her in darkened corners, and then marry her as well. No doubt she would hate him now more than ever.

But something had gone amiss in his carefully laid plans for her last night. She'd trusted him in a way that pleased and surprised him. He'd seen a glimpse of how he might break through her hardhearted opinion of him, and he could imagine a sizzling future with such a temptress in his bed. Yet, even as that occurred to him, he'd known that he could not sabotage her trust completely by continuing the pretense of being someone else. He didn't want her to fall for a mysterious stranger in a dusty brew house.

He wanted Helene to fall for him and no other, even himself in disguise.

Now, he gave the reins of his best mount to a groom outside the courtyard and approached the keep to retrieve his bride. He'd awoken her father from his slumber to confess a portion of his transgressions with the girl and demand her hand at once. Although the MacKail lord had protested the haste, they had finally agreed to a handfasting now and a formal exchange of church vows in the spring. All that remained was to obtain his wife.

The woman who first appeared in the hall was not Helene but their hostess, Lady Cristiana of Domhnaill. A frown creased the lovely features of the keep's famed mead-maker, her auburn hair only half contained in saffron-colored veils as she hastened toward him.

"My lord," she greeted him, granting him a deferential nod before placing a tender hand upon his arm. "Must you leave us so soon? All of the keep's winter revels have been leading up to our Twelfth Night festivities."

The lady managed to run the keep effectively as her father aged and relied heavily upon her. Yet, despite her head for politics and lands, she continued to be an attentive chatelaine. She would have made a fine wife for a man seeking lands and wealth, yet she did not call to him in a primal way as Helene had from the first. Léod knew now he would have no other for a bride.

"It is with regret I leave your fair company." Lifting her hand, he bowed over it briefly. "I am in haste to introduce my new wife to her future home."

At that moment, he felt Helene's presence in the corridor outside the great hall. She made no sound, but he sensed her nearness with a fever in his blood. Turning toward the stairs from the gallery, he found her at her father's side, her eyes dry but rimmed with red as if tears had been there recently. Her mother hovered in the background, her face pale as she touched a steadying hand to Helene's shoulder.

Memories of his first wife's vehement protests darkened his vision for a moment, the past tainting the present with ugly reminders that he'd already been found unworthy as a husband. He ground his teeth together to lock down his impatience.

"Good day, Lady Helene. Are you ready to depart?"

He looked to her father so he did not have to see her unwillingness. The MacKail lord gave a terse nod and nudged his daughter toward Léod with a hand at the back of her waist. Despite her frosty mood and her clear resentment, Léod could not help a hint of triumph at having her by his side. Later, he would figure out how to win back her passions. For now, he simply wanted to claim her.

"I would hear the vows declared now," Helene's father insisted. "Perhaps Lady Cristiana would be kind enough to act as a witness."

If the MacKail laird had been worried that Léod would not honor the marriage contract, then a witness proved wise. But Léod had no intention of withdrawing his suit. Helene would remain his from this day forward. He looked to her delicate form cloaked in travelling clothes and wondered how far he would have to travel to find some place to be with her privately. How long would it take to win back enough trust to have her come to him willingly again?

He remembered the taste of her kiss so vividly that his body responded immediately to her presence as he drew her into the circle of his arm. When their hostess nodded her agreement to serve as a witness, Léod spoke the simple lines to bind them together forever.

"I vow to take Helene MacKail as my legal wife...."

Helene had listened to the pledge in silence. She must have repeated her promise at some point, because before she knew it, her father and Lady Cristiana were hugging her, wishing her well and sending her out into the snowy dawn with the dark deceiver who was now her mate for life.

Any hope of a cart or her own horse was dashed when she spied the lone huge stallion in the courtyard. The beast pranced and snorted around the young groom who held him, as unfit for human company as the laird Mac Ruadhán himself.

She stood still as Léod swung up on the great animal's back. Her composure was more difficult to maintain when he bent down to pluck her off the ground, dragging her body across his as if his lap were a suitable saddle for her.

Her cheeks heated at the nearness as he kicked the horse into motion and guided them out of the courtyard and across the drawbridge to the open fields around the keep. She sat so close to Léod that she could catch his scent. Memories from the night before—when she'd thought him a more tender soul—came back in a rush. The silk of his tunic laces and the muted spice of his scent brought on a bolt of pleasure no matter how staunchly her mind refused to acknowledge such wayward feelings.

"Where are my things?" she asked, if only to avoid thinking about the way his chest felt against her shoulder where he had tucked her close. She attempted to peer backward over his shoulder, but his form was so broad and the snow swirled in the horse's wake so that she could not discern much. "My father said he would send my clothes and the dowry items."

"They will take longer to pack." As they darted around a low patch of brush, Léod readjusted his hold on her hip. His palm strayed low, grazing the curve of her rump and causing another flare of heat to sizzle over her skin. "A caravan will follow tomorrow once your father can assemble your belongings."

With his fingers curled around her hip, she could almost forget he had tricked her into marriage. Had deceived her just for the fun of seeing her humbled.

"I see." Her anger bubbled up to the surface again, blocking out the heat his touch still inspired. "And was this the same way your first marriage began? By force and deception?"

He peered down at her with an expression more forbidding than she'd ever seen. She swallowed hard and almost wished she could retract the question. But if she remained fearful of this warrior's ways, she would never find any peace in her marriage. If he planned to banish her, she would at least make her displeasure known first.

She would not run from Léod again.

"Margaret was not well from the first." His voice held a harsh note, but the words were quieter than their earlier exchanges. In fact spoken as they were, close to her ear, the sound called her back to their intimacies in the brew house. "Yet her father wanted an alliance with me, and did not care that his daughter considered me the devil on earth."

She could hear the bitterness, yes. But she also heard him confiding something in her, a secret perhaps, that reminded her of all they'd shared the night before. Hadn't they each expressed a desire to speak plainly and to be known for their true selves?

"I'm sure she had her reasons to think as much," she accused, though the words lacked force. Cocooned against Léod's chest as the horse tore through the snow-covered woods, Helene could not help but remember the way he'd held her the night before. She had wanted those touches to be real. To mean something.

Instead, they had all been an elaborate means to an end for him. A way to show her that she was at his mercy.

"Nay." Léod's response brooked no argument, his hand tucking her cloak under her thigh where the wind had freed a small section. "She had been fiercely protected by her parents all her life because she'd been born too fragile for this world. I think they believed she would be all right once she was wed, but they chose a man who embodied all of her girlish nightmares of a bloodthirsty warrior."

Helene could see where a sheltered woman might balk at this man's aspect. But she wondered at Léod's description of the maid as "too fragile." Helene had known a peasant girl whom she would have described as such—a sweet little thing who seemed to have been born with a babe's simple mind. Had this woman been afflicted with that same gentle madness?

It was the first time she'd considered the marriage from Léod's perspective, making her wonder why she'd never thought to do so before. Had she been too prejudiced against him because of his reputation?

"Rumor says she screamed herself hoarse that very first night," Helene prompted. Not to goad him. Simply to learn the truth.

"Aye." The set to his jaw and the dark glower in his brown eyes confirmed he was not happy to be reminded of it. "And I did naught but appease the needs of a church union on our wedding night—with an audience of a priest and her father no less. Still she behaved as though I would breathe flames and devour her whole."

Helene shifted awkwardly against him as the great stallion jumped a small ravine. Her hips jounced in his lap, sliding between his thighs until she had to hoist herself back up on top of his legs again. The whole business made her skin flush hot and she could not meet his gaze.

Ever since last night, her flesh seemed highly sensitive everywhere. Léod had woven some kind of sensual spell around her, making her captive to a man who had been a lie.

"So you sent her as far from your keep as possible, leaving her to waste away to nothing." Helene hoped if she concentrated on what he'd done, on the kind of man he really was, she could dismiss these awkward feelings for him—the heat, the ache, the needs that were too earthy to name.

Her desires had gotten all tangled up and it was his fault

for making her feel so itchy and responsive to every subtle movement of his powerful body.

"Nay." Again he denied the rumors the whole of the Highlands had repeated for many moons. "She begged help from travelers who visited my keep, convincing them I abused her person, then demanded passage to one of her father's far-flung holdings. I could not find her for weeks and by the time I did, she was sick beyond help. I brought her home to her mother, hoping they could save her, but her parents had grown weary of caring for her and demanded I fulfill my responsibilities."

The cold fury in his voice made Helene lift her gaze. And though she fully expected to see that anger reflected in his expression, instead she saw a naked pain that would have been impossible to misinterpret.

"You could not save her," she realized, understanding that he regretted that much at least.

His jaw flexed again, the muscle working ruthlessly as he mastered his expression into the impassive mask she'd seen so many times.

"No one could have. It is a unique pain to watch the anguish of someone who willed herself to die."

They were the last words Léod spoke for many leagues. And because Helene was not sure how she felt about his version of events in his marriage, she remained quiet for the rest of their journey. For miles and miles of snowy trails and evergreens heavy with white, they travelled in silence save for the rhythmic beating of the horse's hooves and the rush of the beast's harsh breathing.

As darkness loomed and still no words passed between them, she wondered where they would stop to seek shelter for the night. She had heard the Mac Ruadhán lands were situated high in the mountains. They could not possibly reach their destination in one day. Her former home, however, was only a day's ride. There were times when she'd checked the position of the sun and felt sure they were going in that direction. But as the sky grew more fully dark, she soon lost her bearings.

It was not until the stallion crossed an ancient Roman stone bridge over a little brook that she realized they were indeed right next to her home.

"My lord." She straightened on his lap, her hair clinging to his hauberk and her cheek imprinted with the design of the embroidered fabric after hours cradled there. "We seem to be close to my father's keep."

"I know." He steered the horse up a sharp hill as darkness settled fast on them. "He invited us to pass this night here so you would feel safe."

Her heart eased after the fears of the day and the tears of the night before when she'd learned she would have no choice but to wed the man who'd tricked her. At the time, the union seemed impossible, but with the new possibilities tickling her brain about his last marriage, and his willingness to spend the night in the home of her birth, she wondered if she misjudged Léod in more ways than one.

Could there be more hope for her union than she'd thought possible?

As the horse climbed the high, walled passage that led to her father's keep, Helene felt her heart ease by degrees. She waved to the gatehouse guard as she called out a greeting to a man-at-arms she knew well. The scent of a burning Yule log drifted on the breeze, the Twelfth Night festivities celebrated even though the lord and lady were absent. Though her parents were still at Domhnaill, Helene would be able to sleep in her own chamber. The thought soothed her somewhat.

Until she remembered she wouldn't be sleeping alone.

The wide pallet she'd never shared with another would become her marriage bed.

Chapter Four

Léod could have toured the lands that would one day belong to his sons. The MacKail holdings were vast and with his marriage to Helene, he would gain some now and the rest would go to their children. So he had every reason to care deeply about the property. But instead of meeting with the steward or interrogating the chamberlain, Léod strode to Helene's chamber as soon as he could reasonably free himself from a late Twelfth Night meal in the great hall. Helene had pleaded to take a more simple meal in her rooms despite the holiday, and he'd been inclined to allow it after the long day on the road. He'd eaten in haste with a handful of MacKail's closest advisers.

Now, he rapped on the chamber door that a maid had pointed out to him. Helene was within.

He could not wait another second to have her.

From somewhere inside, he heard a soft response. Unsure what she said or what kind of reception he would receive, he entered.

And found utter darkness.

"Helene?" He wondered now if a maid had answered him when he called into the chamber. They would freeze tonight if someone did not lay a fire in the hearth. What kind of keep celebrated Twelfth Night with no blaze in the bedchamber?

"I am not of a mind to be seen yet," came the reply in a voice that he almost did not recognize. The words, however, were immediately familiar. He'd spoken them himself the night before.

"Where are you?" He strained to see. Did she lie in wait for him with a dagger in hand?

Or did she have something far more interesting in mind than revenge? His pulse sped up at the possibility.

"Does it matter?" The cheeky response seemed to emanate from the far side of the chamber.

As his eyes adjusted, he could see now that there was a bit of firelight in a nearby solar, the dull glow flickering softly and casting a swath of illumination along one wall of the chamber. He could discern the shape of a pallet. A high arrow slit, the narrow opening wide enough for an archer to fire in defense of the keep. A washstand and a clothes chest stood nearby. But so far, no Helene.

"It matters a great deal." His chest constricted at the thought of how much he wanted her. "I am here to know the person you are within and not who the world assumes you to be."

In the soft silence that followed he caught her scent. The sound of her breathing. His sharpened gaze narrowed to a bench beneath the arrow slit and he spied her in the chamber's darkest corner.

"Truly?" She sat utterly still, her delicate form wrapped in a heavy wool blanket from the pallet. Her long, dark hair was unbound and damp from the bath. The scent of her soap permeated the chamber, mingling with the fragrant pine boughs that must be burning in the solar hearth next door.

"Aye." He closed the distance between them, trying to read her mood. Did she feel forlorn and alone? Or was this conversation in the dark her way of establishing a new peace between them? "I meant what I said last night. I want you to come to me of your own free will. After what happened with Margaret, I cannot have another marriage where my wife fears me."

"You tricked me." She spoke her mind freely, just the way he'd told her he wanted a wife to.

She clutched the blanket to her tighter than she'd held the cloak and hood the previous night. Strange that she resisted him more as his wife than she had as his lover.

And just what did she wear beneath that armful of heavy wool? His mouth went dry at the possibilities that came to mind.

"I thought you judged me unfairly. I wanted to prove that you were wrong about me and that I could make you want me. But I tempted myself a hundred times more than what I did to you. Things turned too hot too fast and I couldn't walk away."

"But you did." She rose to her feet and took a step closer. "In the middle of my first kiss, you stopped as if it was no matter to you."

His heart hammered his chest. His teeth were clenched so tight they'd be ground down to nothing by the morrow. With an effort, he wrenched his jaws apart enough to speak.

"You mattered." He didn't touch her even though she was close enough for him to reach her. Once he laid a hand upon her, he would not stop until he'd wrenched every last shred of clothing from her body. "That moment between us meant too much to take that kiss without telling you the truth. It was bad enough I let things go on as long as they did. But I couldn't let you give me kisses like that without you knowing who you bestowed them upon."

Her wide blue eyes searched his in the darkness, her features more distinct as they stood a hand's length apart and his eyes had fully adjusted to the room. The scent of her floral and spice soap hung in the air from her bath, so distinct he could imagine what her skin would taste like underneath that blanket.

"If I had known it was you when I kissed you that way—would you have stopped me?" Her breathing was fast. Shallow.

Her lips parted.

"Why don't you see for yourself what I would do?" He lifted a hand to her cheek, gliding a thumb down her creamy skin the way he had once before. The way he wanted to a million more times in this life.

Slowing the caress at her mouth, he stroked along the plump softness of her lower lip and prayed for enough restraint to let her come to him.

Helene had wanted answers from her husband tonight and she found them now. In his eyes. In his answers. But the biggest question remained. Would he fulfill all the half-formed fantasies that he'd inspired the night before?

Would he appease the hunger she hadn't known existed inside her?

She did not want to be frightened of Léod any longer. She wanted to find her mysterious stranger within the man she'd wed. But the search required this leap of faith in the form of a kiss. And Twelfth Night, her wedding night, seemed the time to do so.

Arching up onto her toes, she clung tight to the blanket about her shoulders and pressed her lips to his. Gently at first. Then, as her mouth remembered his, the kiss deepened. It grew fiery. Hot.

She groaned at the feel of it, her lips parting for a more thorough taste. It was as if none of the last day had taken place. She was right back in the brew house with her heart and her body on fire. Except now, she had the promise of a bed nearby and the thrill of knowing she could drop her blanket as soon as the moment struck her as right.

"Helene." He growled her name against her lips, his arms going around her back to press her tight.

Heat expanded inside her like a flame at the whim of the bellows, leaping with new fuel.

He wanted her. There could be no doubt now. And she was going to love every moment of his wanting her.

"Léod." She tested the name upon her tongue, knowing that he wanted to hear it. Recognizing his desire to be seen for more than his strength and fierceness. "Tonight we cannot walk away."

"I took vows to ensure it." He lifted her in his arms so that their bodies aligned hip to hip. Chest to breast.

His manhood strained against her stomach, his braies doing little to restrain the hard length of him. A shiver trembled over her skin and she undulated against him. The motion felt so good she did it again, her hips rolling in a way that felt sinfully delicious.

She dropped her blanket without thought, the heavy wool stirring the rushes at their feet and wafting the soft scent of dried roses as it fell.

Léod's head snapped back, his dark eyes fixing on her as keenly as if she were bathed in noonday sun.

"You're—" he shook his head, his voice cracking on a dry note "—so much more than I deserve."

Her heart swelled at the words and she rained kisses on his face. Her breasts tightened at the contact with his chest, the crests beading at the abrasion of his skin on hers. He swept her legs out from under her and took her down to the pallet in a gentle tackle.

The sheets were unbearably soft beneath her when she wanted to feel Léod's hard heat everywhere at once. His mouth trailed kisses down her neck to her breasts and she arched high off the bed to feel that tantalizing slide of his tongue and mouth over the soft swells. First one, then the other, teasing the taut flesh without taking the tight peaks until finally, she threaded her fingers through his hair and guided him right *there*.

He suckled and drew on her, his teeth nipping lightly and raking gently while her hips twitched restlessly under his. She worked on the laces of his tunic, and hauled the fabric of it out from his braies, but she wasn't sure she contributed much else to her wedding night. Léod knew precisely what to do to please her, his every touch firing her higher. Hotter.

She spanned as much of his flesh as she could with her fingers, savoring the feel of his bare skin. The muscle that had frightened her now fascinated her and she could not stop her busy hands from absorbing the feel of him as he stretched out over her. When he finally nudged her thighs apart with his knee, she was more ready than she would have ever imagined. He was a skilled, thoughtful lover. Her mystery stranger. And he was all hers.

Forever.

The notion was as heady as any caress, the realization that she would have this to explore and enjoy for the rest of her days. By the time he touched the secret place between her legs she was as dewy as a flower in springtime, her body ready for him. When he stroked the slick folds, sensation rocked her so hard she had to hold onto him or she might have flown apart. The tremors continued and continued, his skilled fingers helping her to ride out the delicious contractions.

By the time they were done, he was naked and poised above her. The thick length of him fit between her thighs, coaxed by the dampness there. She had heard it would hurt the first time. Knew he was an uncommonly large man. But after all he had done to ready her and all the ways he had proven the stories about his last marriage were false, she did not fear what was to come.

"It will be easier for you if it goes quickly. All at once." The whisper in her ear was like an anchor in a storm, keeping her steady in unfamiliar waters. She had half fallen in love with that voice before she'd known who it belonged to.

It only made sense now that it was his voice that gave her the courage to nod. To lift her hips so he could take her.

At first, the contact felt delicious. He started slow and sweet, giving her time to adjust. And then, when she was relaxed and loose-limbed, he pushed deep inside.

Pain ripped through all those sweet feelings and she cried out with the hurt. She would have moved back and away, but he held her tight. Utterly still.

"I'm sorry." His fingers pressed into her back, his voice rough and tender at the same time. "I swear to you, it's never going to hurt again after this."

She nodded, hurting too much to believe him. But as he

held her there and the moments ticked by with their heart-beats, she could feel the pain recede in increments. Soon, she realized that he continued to hold her in a death grip and it occurred to her that he'd been even more fearful of hurting her than she'd been of being hurt.

"It has passed," she assured him finally, edging enough space to breathe against his neck. "I will be fine."

"You're certain?" His lower body remained perfectly im-mobile, though he edged back from her with his chest. "I do not want to move too suddenly and make it worse."

"Nay." She shook her head, liking the way his body looked over hers, the powerful muscle under his ruthless control.

He would never hurt her. Not intentionally.

The truth could not have been more obvious to her in the way he remained solicitous of her feelings. Her powerful Highland laird was no brute at all. In marrying the strongest man in all of Scotland, she had gained the fiercest protec-tor imaginable. And her heart swelled with soft sentiment for him, her feelings undeniably tender.

"Are you certain?" he asked again in a way that would have sent her running for her chamber just days ago, never knowing his glower was his way of showing concern.

Caring.

A slow smile tugged at her lips and kept on pulling, a happiness that couldn't be contained filling her heart and soul and surely as her husband filled her body.

"Absolutely positive." She kissed his neck, tasting the clean saltiness of his skin. "I want nothing more than for you to claim me as your wife."

Her words seemed to free him, his long limbs easing until he unclenched his tight hold. Slowly, he tested the fit of their bodies together, withdrawing slightly and then pressing deep. His hips began a slow, rhythmic dance that made her forget everything else but this moment and this connection.

The heat built in her all over again, the sensations tightening more and more until she felt that same wild release. Pleasure flowed through her like a river, washing her in sweet bliss she'd never envisioned in the marriage bed.

"I love you, Léod mac Ruadhán."

Chapter Five

The most fearsome knight in Scotland had been vanquished by a woman.

Not in battle, obviously. But as Léod lay spent beside his new wife at dawn, he acknowledged Helene would forever hold sway over his heart.

He had been speechless in the face of her declaration of love at first, overwhelmed by the moment and the woman. Now, while the sun's early rays crept through the arrow slit and bled around the edges of the tapestry that covered it, he found his heart full of tender emotions for her in return. Still, she was new to the intimacies they had shared and he was not sure she understood the way they could tangle with a person's feelings.

She'd awoken him once during the night to make love to her, but he'd introduced her to another sort of pleasure instead, allowing any maidenly soreness more time to heal. Yet an hour ago, when she'd attempted to return that decadent pleasure he'd taught her in kind, he'd been powerless to decline. He'd taken her then, and his body had never been so sated.

"During the night, you spoke of love." He turned on her in the warmth of the thick pallet they shared, broaching the subject that had played through his head so many times in the long hours before dawn.

"I remember." She smiled, and then, perhaps catching his more serious expression, she sobered. "I thought you wanted me to come to you freely?"

Propping her head on her elbow, her blue eyes fixed on him. The long, dark waves of her hair covered her naked body like a siren's wherever the blankets did not touch her. So beautiful, outside and in.

"I do. Always."

"Then I assumed I could express myself freely as well." She shrugged, one creamy shoulder lifting casually, the movement bringing the swell of a perfect breast into view for one heart-stopping moment. "When I felt such feelings for you, I thought you would want to know."

"That is passion," he clarified, understanding how the two could be confused. Still, a part of him mourned the loss of a declaration that had brought him a surprising amount of deep-seated joy. Yet he would endeavor to make Helene experience that feeling so many times she would soon love him for real. Forever. "Sometimes the heat of the moment inspires a depth of feeling that can be mistaken for love."

She straightened in bed, taking the covers with her.

"Would you become the fearsome laird who would seek to know better than a mere maid again?" Her eyes flashed with annoyance. Anger, even.

"What do you mean?" Warily, he lifted himself higher on the pallet to handle whatever new bump in the road had arisen in his marriage so suddenly.

"I mean that I know whereof I speak and you must allow me to say it." Releasing the blanket she'd held up to her breasts, she gripped his shoulders with tender hands. "I know love, Léod. I feel it for you because of how you wooed me in spite of all my fears. If not for your game in the darkness, I might never have seen you for the man you are. And now that I have, I admire him." She caressed his cheek. "You."

He could have drowned in that blue-eyed gaze. She was so sincere. So passionate.

"Thank you." He pulled her into his lap and yanked the covers up high to keep her warm. His body stirred immediately despite all they'd shared the night before. He would never get his fill of her. "For loving me and for telling me what you feel. I am long accustomed to deciding what is best for everyone around me, so if I am inclined to lead, it is only force of habit."

Her posture softened, her body easing against his more fully. A smile curved her lips.

"Sometimes, I have enjoyed your vast experience." Her hip wiggled meaningfully against his hardening shaft.

But no matter the need for her that rose again, he wanted to address an even more pressing concern.

"I have not understood that kind of deep caring in the past." He'd achieved his goals in life alone, a bastard raised to power on the strength of his arm and his blade. "But with you, I am beginning to see."

Helene wrapped her arms around him, drawing him down to the bed to cover her beautiful body.

"You will not see it, my lord. You will feel it." She placed a kiss upon his chest above his heart. "Right here."

His heart pounded so loudly she must have heard the reply. She rubbed her cheek over that same place.

Speechless for a moment, he could only praise God and all his saints for sending him such a blessing. Twelfth Night had rewarded him richly.

"I have all the response I need already," Helene assured him, her hands wandering over his body as if they had all the time in the world. And indeed, they did.

"But you shall have the words too, my wife." He raised her up to kiss her mouth, understanding the vows they'd spoken the night before. "For my heart is yours, now and forever."

* * * * *

MILLS & BOON®

Power, passion and irresistible temptation!

The Modern™ series lets you step into a world of sophistication and glamour, where sinfully seductive heroes await you in luxurious international locations. Visit the Mills & Boon website today and type **Mod15** in at the checkout to receive

15% OFF

your next Modern purchase.

Visit **www.millsandboon.co.uk/mod15**

MILLS & BOON®

Why shop at millsandboon.co.uk?

Each year, thousands of romance readers find their
perfect read at millsandboon.co.uk. That's because
we're passionate about bringing you the very best
romantic fiction. Here are some of the advantages
of shopping at www.millsandboon.co.uk:

* **Get new books first**—you'll be able to buy your
  favourite books one month before they hit
  the shops

* **Get exclusive discounts**—you'll also be able to buy
  our specially created monthly collections, with up
  to 50% off the RRP

* **Find your favourite authors**—latest news,
  interviews and new releases for all your favourite
  authors and series on our website, plus ideas for
  what to try next

* **Join in**—once you've bought your favourite books,
  don't forget to register with us to rate, review and
  join in the discussions

Visit **www.millsandboon.co.uk**
for all this and more today!

MILLS_WEB